Secrets
of the
Cottage
by the
Sea

Rebecca Alexander

Secrets
of the
Cottage
by the
Sea

bookouture

Published by Bookouture in 2022

An imprint of Storyfire Ltd.
Carmelite House
50 Victoria Embankment
London EC4Y 0DZ

www.bookouture.com

ISBN: 978-1-80314-627-0
eBook ISBN: 978-1-80314-626-3

To the kind, mysterious and charming people of Appledore.

PROLOGUE

Patience Ellis has little life in her now, lying on the old sofa surrounded by her books and papers. A mouse scurries across the lounge floor and under the sideboard. The cat doesn't stir from his place on the arm of the settee, close to her head.

Her final breath drifts out, the last of her stories lost to the icy air. The cat stands, looks at the body of his owner, and makes his way to the broken corner of the window. From the sill he can access the overgrown front garden, the first sunlight touching his grey fur, his misted breath mingling with the last of hers.

The front door of Kittiwake Cottage is never locked. It sticks when it's damp, so Maggi shoulders it open. She walks into the living room. There is a different quality in the air, a thick silence. Patience looks as if she is sleeping. Her eyes are just a little open, her mouth sagging into a slight smile.

'Oh, my,' Maggi breathes. 'Patience, my lovely.'

A tiny sound. The mouse freezes between a stack of *National Geographic* magazines and a heap of paperbacks. Maggi presses her hand to her chest. 'I'd better call someone,' she says to the mouse, the words hanging like smoke.

Glancing around the room, she sees one of her late husband's paintings over the mantelpiece. It is a depiction of the island's quay at dusk, the houses leaning against each other like old drunks. She drinks in the saturation of colours in the sea and sky. She can't leave it, even though the cottage and contents will belong to someone else now. Maggi imagines a house clearance company making a bonfire of Patience's belongings, bringing in builders to create a holiday cottage.

She lifts the painting down. It's heavy in her hands as she walks through the door, through the garden, tears scalding her face.

'Goodbye, my darling.'

———

The last will and testament of Patience Martha Ellis, made this day, 13 November 2003. I, Patience Martha Ellis, presently of Kittiwake Cottage, Long Lane, Morwen Island, hereby revoke all former testamentary dispositions made by me and declare this to be my last will. I direct my executor to distribute the residue of my estate as follows.

All of the residue of my estate is left to Elowen Claire Roberts of 41 Delamere Road, London, England, for their own use absolutely, subject to the provision below

I wish the aforesaid Elowen Roberts of London to live in my house for one full year before she inherits Kittiwake Cottage. Otherwise, my estate is to be divided among the descendants of my siblings equally...

1

PRESENT DAY, 11 MARCH

Elowen Roberts clung to the side of the boat, staring into the muddy water. The driver tied it up to a ladder, bolted to the stone of the quay, which stretched up several metres. She swallowed a few times, trying not to throw up again as the open boat lurched against the wall. Behind her, the water stretched away towards a small beach, covered with the hunched shapes of birds, backs against the wind.

'What are they?' she asked.

'What? Oh, those.' The driver smiled. 'We call them northern penguins.' The boat grounded as a wave lifted, then dropped. 'Just in time,' he said. 'Tide's going out fast. On you go.'

Ellie grabbed her bag, pushed her blonde hair out of her eyes and staggered to her feet. The driver of the boat hadn't said a word to her on the journey except 'Oh, aye', when the harbourmaster on St Brannock's Island had suggested he give Ellie a lift to Morwen Island. Now he held the craft steady as Ellie looked up – and up – at the rusted ironwork, brown with dangling seaweed.

Ellie's mouth went dry. She struggled to hold the heavy bag

with her left hand while grasping a rung with her right, before realising she couldn't climb fifteen feet of ladder with one hand. She rearranged the long strap across her body, hoping it wouldn't strangle her, and started the ascent. Moving one limb at a time, the wet metal sharp in her hands, she concentrated on the stone in front of her. *Don't look down, don't look down.*

She crawled on hands and knees over the top, onto wet stones that made up a sort of roadway between the grey sea and a line of houses. She clambered to her feet, brushed her wet jeans down and turned to watch the older man spring off the top of the ladder.

'Well, then,' the man said, turning to leave.

'Wait!' The word came out with some force. 'I mean, I don't know the island at all. Do you know where this is?' Ellie rummaged in her pocket for the creased letter from the solicitor, which came with a key that looked like it belonged to an old shed. 'Kittiwake Cottage, Long Lane, Morwen Island,' she read out.

The man stared at her. 'If I were you, I'd get a room at the pub first. You'll need somewhere warm and a hot meal. It's going to be bitter tonight.'

She looked at the row of old houses facing the sea. They were an odd mix of two and three storeys, narrow and leaning together, and they were painted the faded pastels of sugared almonds. At one end was a large building with a board outside reading 'Island Queen' and the flaking sign had a painting of a ship. A few shops interspersed the row of houses, but they all looked closed.

'I think I need to go straight to the house,' Ellie said, shifting the weight of the bag, feeling the bulk of the sweater Leo had packed for her. 'I'll be fine for one night.'

The man stared at her for several seconds, making Ellie feel uncomfortable, before he spoke.

'Fair enough. Go up any of the roads off the quay. They all

lead to Long Lane. Then turn left. It's one of those detached cottages along the hill. There's a sign by the door.'

Ellie followed his pointed finger. The colourful houses of the town stretched up in several narrow lanes, ending at fields. A few grey roofs were scattered along the green edges. Behind them was a hillside of hedged squares, a few sheep moving beneath the clouded and darkening sky. The man turned and walked off without a word, but Ellie got the sense he was amused.

She started along the quay and up a narrow path called Warren Lane. There was no room for a car, she thought; the little houses almost felt like they were leaning towards each other at the top. She slipped on the cobbled surface before she got her balance. It was much steeper than she had expected, and no one else was out this late on a March afternoon. Cold air was trickling down her neck inside her coat and she almost stopped to put her jumper on. *It'll be warmer when I get in.* She pulled the key from her jeans pocket.

The road at the top was just tyre tracks in grass poking up through gravel. She turned left, glimpsing a slate roof in the hedge ahead. She hurried towards it and pushed open a gate in the stone wall.

The cottage was beautiful. It had low white walls, a gleaming slate roof and a few pots of plants gathered around the door. For a moment she felt a glow of relief. Walking closer, she realised she had the wrong cottage. *Tideswell.* There weren't any lights on, so it was probably a holiday let. The next house was equally pretty, but painted cream with white window frames. *Oystercatchers.* She adjusted her bag, which was digging into her shoulder, and looked back down at the quay.

This was nothing like her street in London. The patchwork of slate roofs led the eye down to the grey sea. Late sun was creeping out in patches, highlighting the island opposite, called St Petroc's, and an area of choppy sea between, which the boatman had called the Sound. Spots of white surged on the water, which was a shade darker than the grey sky. It seemed a thousand miles from home.

Beyond the cream cottage was something that looked like an outhouse, with tattered roofing felt and roof supports rising out of a mound of ivy. It wasn't until she found a gap in the wall and a path between the skeletons of weeds that she could see the sign. *Kittiwake Cottage.*

It had once been painted green, and the faded walls had collected a film of algae and moss over the cracked render. A bay window had been painted red, but now silvery wood showed through the cracks. One small pane was broken and there was an open portico with a bowed roof, inside which was a stack of spider-webbed logs, two sets of welly boots and a door. The lock took the key but wouldn't turn and she came back to it several times, bruising her fingers, but she was locked out. She decided to force the door since pride stopped her going down to the pub before she'd even seen the house. Her own property, if she abided by the terms of Patience's will.

She took a deep breath, turned the knob and forced the door.

It came open with a screech and she realised it hadn't been locked, just stuck. Inside was a dark hall leading straight up steep stairs, which looked unsafe for the old lady who had lived here. Wedges of daylight came through two doors to the side. She walked in, the floor creaking, and the house seemed even colder than it was outside. The air was still, the only noises the movement of sagging boards under her feet, and the metal-on-metal squeal of the hinges as she pushed the door into the first room.

It looked chaotic at first, but she could make out stacks of books and magazines in some order around the edge of a living room. A faded red sofa sat in front of the bay window, and another sofa, with a checked pattern, faced it. There was a rug on the floor covering the centre of the room under an old coffee table, which was covered with papers and a stained mug. The only other furniture was a bookcase and a sideboard, also covered with boxes and photographs, along the back wall.

There was neither a television nor a radiator, but there was a tiled fireplace with a few burnt bits of wood in it. She looked for the light switch. It was made of some sort of brown plastic, and the light didn't come on, nor did the tall lamp in the corner. *They must have turned the electricity off.* She found an old box with a meter under the stairs, but nothing happened when she switched it to 'on'. *Great. No lights, no heating.*

The second door at the back of the hall led to a dining room, complete with a table, three chairs and a dresser made of dark wood. Beyond it was a wide arch into a kitchen, hardly six feet deep, with a few sagging cupboards and a couple of shelves on the wall. She tried the single tap over the cracked sink, but apart from a dribble of rusty water, it was off. So much for Leo's idea that they would just put a new kitchen in and sell for a fortune. She smiled at the thought of her boyfriend's reaction.

There was a bottle of water in her bag that she couldn't face when she had been seasick on the ferry journey, so she could at least clean her teeth and have a drink. Part of her was drawn to the pub overlooking the sea, but the hint of humour on the boatman's face stopped her. *I can do one night in a cold house.* As she turned back towards the door, a small table tucked against the wall caught her eye. No, not a table, a sewing machine.

Bright as a picture, a memory flashed of her mother working at it, stitching scraps of cloth together to make a quilt, treadling with her foot. For a second, she could see her mother so clearly it took her breath away. Most of her recollections of Mum were from studio photographs her father had let her keep. In this memory, her mum's hair was blonde and curly, like her own, but long around her face. She was smiling, her eyes creased up against the sunshine from the kitchen window. *This window?*

Ellie looked at the glazed square, half obscured by ivy and dust. The last of the daylight was pink, and illuminated the sink. She tried to cling to the picture of her mother in her head, but it faded away, leaving her smile until last.

She opened the dresser drawers looking for matches and candles, and found both along with random batteries, string, buttons and odd fixtures. The matchbox had once been so damp it had peeled apart, but it seemed dry now. There were a dozen candles and a couple of wooden holders in the dresser cupboards. She lit one, and the yellow flame made the shadows in the corners seem even darker and flicker like ghosts.

The back door was unlocked and, once unstuck, led to an outside toilet and a garden of tall weeds. She closed the door; she would use the loo in the cottage instead – that one was probably full of spiders.

She checked her phone. Still no signal, but she must have caught some coming up the hill because she had a message from Leo. It signed off with *Love you, call me!* She bolted the back door with a struggle and walked back through the dining room holding the candle. The setting sun painted the sky pink and orange.

Up the precipitous stairs she found two doors, each leading to a dark bedroom, but no bathroom. The front room had an amazing view over the whole bay and the other islands. It also had a large metal bed that looked comfortable enough, although the sheets had been stripped off and dumped in the corner. The back bedroom had a cupboard in it with a couple of sheets, two fluffy blankets and...

She lifted the faded quilt in her hands. Scraps of material unfolded, smelling faintly of flowers and, as she lifted it, a lavender bag slid out. When she crushed it to her face, it still breathed spicy and medicinal and somehow familiar.

Mum.

2

11 NOVEMBER 1940

'There's a storm blowing in,' nine-year-old Patience Ellis said, as she listened to the bulletin on the wireless on the dresser. Mam had put it on so she and her sister could hear the last of *Children's Hour* while their fair hair was twisted in rags for the morning. 'It's supposed to be over the Celtic Sea and the Channel after midnight. They didn't say anything new about German ships, though.'

'Maybe it's too rough for them.' Her mother craned her neck to see between the houses on the quay, in the last of the daylight. 'It does look a bit rough for our trawlers, too. Right, it's time to get Susannah ready for bed, Patsy. Take her out to the lavvy. Make sure she's clean, will you?'

Patience Ellis slid down from her chair and called up the stairs for her seven-year-old sister.

'And you, boys,' she called, sternly. 'Go to sleep, I can hear you giggling.' Clem and William, aged two and three, were already tucked up in the shared room, which just had space for the sisters' bed and the boys' cot.

Her mother slipped out the front door onto the cobbles

while Patience persuaded her sister to use the unheated, unlit outhouse.

'The *Island Queen*'s sailing,' Mam said, coming back inside. 'I don't think we need worry about Dad on *Cormorant*. She'll be back by one, and the forecast says winds force seven to eight. She's weathered worse storms than that, and they'll be in the lee of the islands tonight. Shut the window in Fred's room.'

Patience steered her sister through washing her hands and face at the kitchen sink, cleaning her teeth and mumbling her prayers. Susannah was an amiable, loving little girl but her speech had been slow coming and sometimes she wet herself. Patience took her hand and led her upstairs.

'There's a good girl,' Patience said, kissing Susannah's forehead and brushing her almost-white hair off her face. 'When you wake up, we'll walk along the beach to school, to see what shells have washed up.'

'Night night,' Susie said, and tucked her blanket around her shoulders. 'Window,' she said, maybe because she was in a draught or maybe because she had heard what Mam said.

Patience reached over her to fasten the metal catch, the window barely a foot across and a little taller. The candle flame settled down in its jar and Patience used the light to see her way to the door.

'I'll be back soon,' she said. 'I've just got to help Mam. The pot's under the bed if you need it, and Teddy's under your pillow.' She slipped upstairs to fasten the window in her brother's attic room.

Patience was walking downstairs when she heard her father, George Ellis, stomp the sand off his boots on the cobbles outside before coming in the front door.

'Bit of a blow coming in, chick,' he said. 'But the *Queen* is going out. There's cod around St Piran's headland, I might try for that.' He winked at Patience. 'All for the war effort, hey?' He gave Patience a hug. 'You look after your mam.'

Mam hadn't been right since Patience's older brother Joseph went down with his ship, sunk by a German U-boat last year. Patience breathed in the smell of Dad's rough jumper: diesel, fish and salt.

'I will. Night, Dad. Be careful.'

He dropped down to her eye level, brown eyes gleaming in the light, dark hair slicked back. 'I's always careful, my chick. I never lost a man at sea yet.' He stood tall and lifted his oilskins off the back of the outhouse door, where they hung crusted in salt and glittering with fish scales.

Patience and Mam watched him set off down Noah's Drang, boots clumping on the stones. He greeted Arthur Shore, skipper of the *Queen*, then turned the corner to the quay. The wind lifted the fair curls off Patience's forehead.

'I'll wait up for him,' Mam said, shooing Patience indoors. 'You need your sleep. You've got school tomorrow. But be quiet when you get up; Dad will still be asleep.'

'He doesn't want us to wait up for him,' Patience said, even as she put her foot on the first of the narrow stairs.

'Well, there's no point me going to bed, since I won't sleep. I'll put some dough on. We'll have a mid-week loaf and some currant buns for you children. Set your alarm, although those rascals will have us up at dawn anyway.'

'Love you, Mam,' Patience said. At her mother's height on the step, she leaned forward for a goodnight kiss.

Her mother hugged her fiercely. 'Get along with you. It's a busy day tomorrow.'

Patience woke to a strange shuffling sound, like several people stamping up the stairs with boots on. There were muffled voices, too. She stuck her head around the door to see three men in wet coats lifting two bare legs up to the attic. Her father turned, his face pale in the light of a candle.

'Patsy, get some blankets and towels.'

Patience scrambled into Mam and Dad's bedroom, which was almost filled with their metal bed, and opened the airing cupboard. It was warm from the kitchen flue running inside it. She grabbed two old blankets and a couple of towels and followed the men upstairs.

When Dad stood aside, one man was bent under the ceiling, and one was standing half behind the door. She squeezed in. Her first thought was that there was a dead man on her brother's narrow bed. His naked body was as white as the belly of a fish, the skin around his mouth as blue as the hyacinth she'd bought her mother last Christmas. She almost screamed, and clamped both hands over her mouth, dropping the bedding. Her father beckoned her over.

The young man gasped a breath, and she saw his bare chest rise and fall. Someone had made him decent with a rag, but he looked frozen.

'Good girl,' Dad said, scooping the blankets off the floor. 'Now help your mother in the kitchen.'

She ran downstairs to find Mam struggling with the damper on the stove and trying to heat some water in a wide pan.

'Who is he?' Patience hissed.

Mam looked as grey as old linen.

'The *Island Queen* is lost,' she mumbled, poking at the remnants of the fire.

'Let me,' Patience said, her fingers shaking as she pulled newspaper sheets into twists and added some kindling collected from the tideline. 'What do you mean?'

'The *Queen* is lost.' Her mother turned her faded blue eyes to Patience. She looked strange, her eyes wide, her body shaking. 'Sunk.'

Patience lit a match, caught the first of the twists and a second one to be sure. The simple task occupied her, the paper smoke curling around her fingers before pulling up the flue.

'Did they save any of the crew?' she asked, just as the kindling started to blacken down one side.

'No.' Her mother shook off the strange mood. 'Put a few coals on top. No, they just found the boy, alone, on an old sea chest. A stranger. I don't know him. They think several fishing boats were attacked tonight.'

She didn't say by a U-boat, but Patience imagined the huge, sleek creatures hunting in packs, firing torpedoes then sliding away to secret depths.

The flue was coughing back spurts of smoke, the kitchen window rattling in the wind. Patience concentrated on feeding little scraps of dried seaweed to the fire, not smothering it, just teasing it, like feeding a toddler. When her father stamped into the kitchen, his oilskins rolled down to his waist and his sweater soaked, he nodded at the stove.

'Good girl,' he said to Patience. 'We need to warm him up, he's fearful cold.'

'What happened, Daddy?' Patience asked, although she could see her father was tired. He hugged his wife, and her face curved into his shoulder, making her neck look thin and weak.

'We got a Mayday from the *Island Queen*,' he said, over Mam's head. 'We went out to help but she was gone, just a few bits of net and fuel over the water. We found the boy covered in a wet coat, frozen half to death.'

Patience added a couple more coals, all the smoke going true up the chimney now, the sound of crackling over her mother's heaving breath.

'There, my lovely,' he said to Mam, resting his big hands on her drooping shoulders. 'We've got a boy to save, and I won't let him die if I can help it.'

Mam looked up into his face, searching. 'Who is he, this lad? Is he... one of *them*?'

He stared at her for a long time, and when one of the coals

slipped and caused a shower of sparks to shoot out of the firebox door, Patience jumped.

'His only word was "Dutch",' he said. 'You know we've got Danish and Dutch fisherman out there, so I reckon he's one of them.' He glanced up at Patience. 'That's what we tell people. He's just a boy, he's as cold as a mackerel and he's likely to die. We have to do our best to save him.'

Patience nodded her head solemnly as the unspoken words rang in her head. *Like someone might have helped our Joseph.*

3

PRESENT DAY, 12 MARCH

Ellie pushed open the door to the pub. The lights weren't on in the dark room, but morning light spilled in through deep windows. The beams cut across the low ceiling, so she ducked a little.

A man stepped out of a swing door behind the bar. He was tall, with dark wavy hair, good-looking in a rangy way. He looked about her own age, around thirty. He also looked vaguely familiar, which didn't make sense. All of a sudden, she remembered she hadn't brushed her hair.

'Can I help you?'

'I'm sorry to bother you,' she said. 'The board outside said you did breakfasts.'

'You must be the new owner of Kittiwake Cottage,' he said, looking her up and down. He waved his fingers. 'I would shake hands, but I've been making pastry. I'm Branok Shore, one of the landlords. We do breakfasts, but I don't get much call for them out of season.'

'I'm Ellie.' She looked around. 'Is there anywhere I can get warm? I'm frozen.'

'Come through to the kitchen, then. Eggs and bacon? Toast

and tea?' He pushed the swing door open. 'There's a stool over there by the stove, if you like.'

He walked around the kitchen, put a frying pan to heat on the Aga and opened the fridge. The cooker was belting out heat and she reached her hands to it.

Rashers of bacon lined a pan, and started to shrivel up and spit. A wave of scents rolled around the room making Ellie's stomach growl, which made him smile. He had a nice smile, she thought.

'John said he brought you over yesterday. I thought you would stay here at the pub last night.'

He turned the bacon rashers over, made a space and threw some mushrooms into the pan and put bread in the toaster.

'I wanted to explore the house first. I'm sorry to bother you so early,' she said.

'No bother. I've been up since six.'

'How did you know I was in Kittiwake Cottage?' she asked.

'It's a tiny island and we don't get many strangers out of season. Everyone's been speculating about who was going to inherit Patience's house. You're virtually the only item on the island bulletin board.'

'There's a bulletin board?'

He basted eggs, dished up the food, arranged it neatly with toast and butter and slid it over.

'Not an *actual* bulletin board.' He laughed. 'It's just that everyone knows everyone. There are only a hundred and forty or so permanent residents. There are more in the season, of course, and a lot of second homeowners come over before the holidays start.'

She huddled on the stool and stared at the food. She could feel Branok's brown eyes staring at her as she pulled the plate towards her.

'You remind me of your mother. She had sky-blue eyes, too,' he said softly.

'You met her?'

'Many times. And you, only we knew you as Elowen back then.' He smiled at her, and she couldn't help but smile back. 'Now we're Ellie and Bran.'

'I'm sure it will all come back to me,' she said, spreading butter and taking a bite of toast.

His voice softened. 'I'm very sorry for your loss. I knew Patience – we all did. She was a lovely person.'

Ellie kept her head down, cutting up her bacon. 'I don't remember Patience. I don't recall much from before I was about ten. I didn't even recognise the island.'

'Don't worry about it. Eat your food.' He pushed a mug of tea in front of her.

'Why were you up so early?' she asked, as she mopped up some yolk with a toast crust.

'I'm in training for the world gig championship. We row our pilot gig twice a week, when the tide's right.' He pulled up the other stool and perched near to the stove, holding his mug in both hands. 'So you don't remember any of us?'

'I'm sorry. I was really young when we stopped coming here.'

'I remember you, though. Elowen Roberts, Ysella's daughter.'

'I hardly remember my mother. It was a tough time after...'

'I'll bet.' When she looked up, he held her gaze. 'I was so sorry when she died. I suppose you blocked it out, it was so painful.' He pushed a napkin towards her. 'You have egg on your chin. So, how was the house?'

She wiped her face. 'I spent the night on the sofa. It was freezing when I got there. No heating.' She took a big bite of bacon. Her eyes filled with tears. 'The electricity is off, there's no water, it's freezing cold and there's no indoor plumbing,' she said in a rush. 'It must have been a terrible place for a ninety-year-old woman to live.'

'It was OK with the power on,' Bran said. 'But she had to stay downstairs at the end. Friends offered her a room in the town, or she could have stayed in one of the holiday cottages. But she was independent to the end. She knew she didn't have long and she wanted to get everything in order. For you, I suppose.'

'In order?' She laughed without humour. 'It's a mess. The whole cottage is filled with rubbish and I heard something scratching under the kitchen cupboards. Probably a rat.'

He stood up, his face tightening. 'That was the way she chose to live. She liked everything she needed to hand. I wouldn't be surprised if she put food down for the mice. She fed the birds from her windowsill, too, you know.'

Ellie finished her toast. 'I managed to get a fire going. That was magic, even if it did smoke a bit. I would have been OK, if I hadn't been woken up about four o'clock.' She smiled at the memory, but it hadn't been that funny at the time.

'What woke you?'

'It was so dark last night; I don't think it's ever that dark in London,' she said. 'I'd finally fallen asleep on the sofa when something hit me in the chest, knocked the air out of me. It turned out to be a cat. It took me half an hour to get it out from under the cupboard, and it was yowling like it was possessed. Then the torch on my phone died.' She looked up at him. 'That's when I noticed the sky. The most amazing colours, the deepest blue, each window pane a different shade. I sat in the window seat wrapped up in my coat watching the dawn.'

'I always say that's the best view on the island,' Bran said. 'I used to visit Patience and just sit on the arm of her sofa, staring out. Some people say the lookout is better, but that's my favourite.'

'I've never watched a whole sunrise like that. I didn't realise all the clouds would be quite so pink and yellow. Quite garish. The cat stopped growling and sat and watched with me. He's horribly matted. Do you know whose he is? He's sort of grey and fluffy.'

Bran laughed. 'He's your cat, now. He comes with the house. I think he was quite feral when he was little, but he mellowed. Patience was the only person who could touch him, but he disappeared when she died. His long hair needs a lot of grooming, but he's quite pretty when he's tidied up.'

'After I staggered about, sleep deprived, I realised the outside loo had the coldest seat on the planet and doesn't flush.' She grinned when he laughed. 'I had a quick snack on three inches of bottled water and two chewy mints. That's when I saw a rowing boat coming between the islands. Was that you?'

'Six oars and a cox, that's us. It's a pilot gig. I'm usually up the front because I'm tall.'

'It looked amazing, like you were rowing on silver. Where did you go?'

'Down West Sound to Kettle Rock, around and behind St Petroc's. That's our usual route at this time of the tide,' he said, putting her empty plate in the sink. 'It's a bit more dangerous if the tide's running fast with the wind. We can get swept beyond the island to Founder Rocks. That's where lots of ships have gone down, hence the name.'

'You were going pretty fast. Thank you for breakfast,' she said, as she pushed the empty mug away. 'The food was amazing, and I can feel myself thawing out.'

'Normally I'd have sausages and black pudding but we don't stock up on those until the school holidays.'

She sighed. 'It was perfect. Even the mushrooms tasted like the bacon, and I don't normally like them.'

'You should have taken John's advice and stayed here,' Bran said. 'Now, I have to get these pies done and in the fridge. But stay there if you like, get warm.'

'I wanted to see if I remembered anything about the cottage.'

He glanced at Ellie. 'So, did you dredge up anything?'

She didn't answer for a few seconds, looking away. 'I think I remembered my mother sewing a quilt.'

'On that old treadle machine?' he asked. 'God, I'd forgotten about that. I used to love moving the pedal for Patience with my hands.'

'Did a lot of people know her?'

He nodded. 'Everyone. She was born here and she ran the school for more than forty years. Most of the locals know about you, too, so everyone's going to be curious.' He looked away. 'You have to realise, Patience spent ninety years on the island, taught most of us to read, sing, swim.' He smiled. 'She was a remarkable woman, we all loved her. It was right that she died here, where she was looked after by her own.'

'I wish I did remember Patience, since I have no idea why she left me the house.' She swallowed and looked away. 'After Mum died, my father thought I should concentrate on life in London, so I didn't come back to the island.'

'Patience never got over losing Ysella. She adopted her when she was very young. And she'd only just lost Dutch when Ysella died. Dutch was her closest friend, you see.'

'I didn't know.' She shook her head. 'My father always called my mother Ella rather than Ysella.'

'Yeah, like we called her Ysa for short. Like she called her baby Elowen, Ellie for short. Good island names.'

'I've never used Elowen. I would have been teased at school; I've always been Ellie. How much do I owe you?'

'Call it eight quid, since you didn't get the sausages.'

She followed him through to the bar, where he turned on the till.

'I didn't know anything about Patience,' she said. 'If I hadn't inherited the cottage, I still wouldn't know.'

She paid the bill.

'Well, a lot of people have been wondering where her

family were when she really needed them. So don't be surprised if people are a bit snippy about her leaving the cottage to you, instead of one of her family members. Her brother's still alive, and he has living grandchildren on the islands and in Cornwall. There's a housing crisis on the islands.'

That brought warmth to her face. 'Well, they are welcome to bid for the house when it comes on the market. I'm going to straighten it up, get some proper heating and plumbing in, nice new kitchen and bathroom, and then I'll sell it on.'

He stood back, looking straight in her eyes. With her boots on, she was almost the same height as him.

'Fair enough.'

She banged through the door of the pub before letting her breath out.

4

12 NOVEMBER 1940

After two hours of sleep, Patience half-filled the metal scuttle with the biggest pieces of coal from the outhouse. She dragged it up the two flights of stairs, praying the young man rescued the night before wasn't dead. She paused outside the door to the attic bedroom, where the men had placed him, limp and white as a ghost. When she pushed open the door he wasn't moving but his face was red. She set the scuttle on the tiled hearth and picked up one coal after another to lay on the glowing cinders. As she made a couple of holes with the poker, blue flames started to send up tongues of yellow as they licked around the new fuel. Then came the croak of a breath.

He coughed, and Patience started and turned around. His eyes were half open and he looked at her from under swollen eyelids.

'Hello,' she said quietly, like in church. She took a small step nearer the bed, too scared to get closer. The young man had been laid under the dormer window, one pane cracked open for fresh air. His hair was so short it was almost shaved, just coming through dark. He looked young, maybe seventeen.

'*Wasser*,' he whispered. She didn't understand at first. His hand curved around an imaginary cup. 'Water.'

She turned to the little bedside table and poured some from the jug.

'Here,' she said, offering the small glass at arm's length, wobbling until it threatened to spill.

She took a step closer. His hand was trembling, and he didn't seem so terrifying. She put her own fingers over his to steady the cup, and his skin was hot and dry and different from her younger siblings', or the strong, rough hands of her father. The feeling was disturbing, and once he had lifted his head for a couple of sips, she took the glass away. It was as if all the air in her chest had been sucked out.

'*Danke*,' he said, closing his eyes. 'Thank you.'

'Is that Dutch?' she asked, refilling the glass and leaving it within reach. His breathing was a little easier, less like a creaking door.

'*Ja*, Dutch,' he said, as if he was falling back to sleep. '*Holländisch*.' When the coals crackled, he jumped, and opened his eyes a little. '*Hollander*,' he corrected himself.

'You're quite safe,' she said, wanting to reassure the frown on his face. 'My father says you are a Dutch sailor from a trawler. Is that true?'

His eyes darted from side to side in the room. '*Ja*.' He coughed again, struggling to get his breath. 'Yes.'

Patience tugged at the blanket at the bottom of the bed to cover the bare feet sticking out. She eased the spark guard back in front of the fire – no point saving him from the sea just to burn to death from a cinder – and crept towards the door.

'Your... name?' he whispered.

'Patience Ellis. What's yours?'

'Dutch,' he breathed, and fell asleep.

. . .

Patience looked up from her homework as someone pushed the attic door open.

'It's Dr Hordern, Patsy, just come to see the young Dutchman.' Her mother slid around the side of the bed, making room for the tall man. 'Stay. We might need you to fetch something.'

Patience sat back on the chair where she had been revising French verbs while listening to the unconscious young man wheeze and cough. 'He hasn't woken up for hours.'

The doctor pressed a stethoscope to the boy's thin, hairless chest. Mam helped roll him onto his side so he could listen from the back.

'Pneumonia,' the doctor said. 'It's not looking good. He must have breathed in seawater, and he was very cold.'

'There was a lot of fuel in the water, too,' her mother said. 'It can't have helped.'

The doctor put his stethoscope away and closed his bag. 'The best I can offer is sulfapyridine, but I don't know if I can get it in time. It's restricted to the worst cases. I'll call the hospital from the pub and hopefully they can ship some over before tonight. Meanwhile, it's all down to good nursing. Don't let him get cold, and make sure he has plenty of fresh air.'

Mam stuffed her hands into her apron pocket. 'Is there any hope, doctor?'

He patted her arm as he passed. 'There's always hope. He's very young, that's in his favour.' He hesitated at the top of the stairs and lowered his voice as he spoke to her, but Patience could still hear him. 'The ministry asked me to make enquiries about the lad. They think he could be from a German ship.'

Mam scoffed at the idea. 'What would the Germans want with him?' she said. 'He's just a boy, doesn't look more than sixteen. Anyway, he told my husband he was Dutch and he doesn't sound German. I nursed a lot of them in the first war.'

'They're saying they found a few papers floating where the *Island Queen* is thought to have gone down.'

'I told you. He's a young Dutchman, maybe from a fishing boat sunk by the bloody Jerries. Three ships went down last night. I just thank God the *Cormorant* wasn't one of them.'

Patience knew her father had a theory about a collision between a U-boat and the *Island Queen* from the amount of shredded nets and fuel on the surface.

'If he lives, and turns out to be German, we'll hand him in ourselves,' Mam said.

She showed the doctor out and Patience followed her downstairs. Her mother turned to her with a fierce look on her face.

'We'll turn him every hour,' she said, 'and keep him coughing. I'll make sure he gets Auntie May's balsam, and he can take a bit of broth.'

'Where are we going to get bones to make stock from?' Patience asked, knowing how thin the meagre supplies in their larder were. 'We haven't even seen last week's cheese and meat rations.'

'We can always get something for the sick. If not at the shop, one of the pubs might have something.'

Patience bit her lip. 'What if he isn't Dutch, as he says?'

Her mother shushed her with a gesture. 'Don't even say it,' she hissed, 'or it might come out by accident, or one of the children might repeat it. He's *Dutch*, Patience. We'll call him Dutch until he remembers his name. Go and ask Mrs Kellow at the shop if she's got some bones for the soup.'

Patience took the pennies offered and slipped her outdoor shoes on. As she walked into the narrow lane, a few people were on the cobbles, openly curious. Old Henry Shore, father of the *Island Queen*'s skipper, stopped her.

'He's not dead then?'

She was aware of the door behind her opening, and her mother standing behind her.

'He's just a boy, and close to death.' Patience felt her mother's hands on her shoulders. 'We're very sorry about the *Queen*, and my George is out there on *Cormorant* helping the navy search for the men. We haven't lost all hope yet.'

Old Henry's eyes were red. 'It would give me great comfort if they did find our Artie,' he said. 'But he's likely dead. Him with four children and a baby on the way.'

'They'll all need you now, aye, and his young wife, too,' Mam said, squeezing Patience's shoulders. 'I'll pray for them, and for you, too. You know we've already lost our Joseph to the war, and young Fred is saying he'll join up as a midshipman when he's finished school, God forbid.'

Henry looked older than his sixty years. 'This terrible war.' He nodded. 'Good luck with the lad,' he said, through thin lips. 'I just wish it had been my son your George picked up.'

Mrs Shore stepped out of her door, her eyes also red. 'You be a good girl for your mother, Patience. And pray for our fishermen.'

Patience nodded. Maybe the *Queen*'s crew were lost, but they would do whatever they could for one boy, saved from the sea.

5

PRESENT DAY, 12 MARCH

It isn't my fault the old lady left the house to me, is it?

After her breakfast at the pub, Ellie walked along the quay to the tune of wheeling gulls. She turned to look across to the neighbouring small island, boats buzzing into the channel between them. The wind wasn't as cold as before, and light sunshine was whitening the tops of the waves. The 'big island', St Brannock's, floated a long way to the east, just a grey smudge in the distance behind a layer of haze. Several sharp outcrops of rock stood in the way, and the boats wove their way between them and coloured buoys.

She turned her attention to the buildings along the quay. The houses were different shades of faded colour, each front door individual. One of the shops had its lights on, and a stand outside was covered with nets of firewood and bags of coal. She made her way over to find an impressively stocked store, with a small delicatessen counter as well as a post office, and two women filling up shelves.

'We haven't got any bread yet,' one called out without looking at her. 'The boat's late. Try the café.'

'Oh. OK.' She picked up a large bottle of milk, remembered

she didn't have a fridge, and replaced it with a smaller one. She added a cheese roll from the chiller, a couple of toilet rolls and a box of cereal as she walked around. A small hardware stand held bulbs, fuses, nails and screws, another sold medicines and plasters. The woman looked up and smiled.

'Sorry, I thought you were someone else.' She had a northern accent, sleek grey bob and a badge that named her Linda. 'Can I help you?'

'I've just moved in. Who do the locals call to get an electrician?' Too late, she remembered her phone was dead. 'And is there a phone box somewhere?'

'In the pub. We use the old phone box as a library now.' She stared at her for a long moment. 'I suppose you are taking on Kittiwake Cottage? Welcome to the island. I'm Linda, that's Sue in the back.'

Ellie blushed a little under the scrutiny, and tucked a box of tea bags under her chin, although she had no idea how she would boil water. 'It seems as if everyone knows I'm here,' she said, walking to the checkout.

'There are only a few privately owned properties in the town,' she answered. 'Have you seen the cat? He went missing after Patience died.'

'Actually, he turned up in the middle of the night, almost scared me to death jumping on me,' Ellie replied.

Linda walked away and came back with two tins of Fishies. 'It's his favourite,' she explained, parking them with the shopping.

'I'm not much of a cat person,' she said, staring at the food.

Linda smiled at that. 'He comes with the cottage.'

The animal had been pathetically thin, and Ellie had felt its bones as she grabbed him and threw him off in the dark. She nodded and watched Linda pack her shopping into a bag and add a tide table.

'You'll need this,' she said, tucking it in the top and charging her an extra three pounds. 'Bigger boats only come here two hours each side of high tide. The smaller ferries get a bit longer, but then you have to climb up the quay.'

'I found that out yesterday.' Ellie remembered the rusty ladder and shivered. 'Thank you. Oh, the electrician?'

'There aren't many tradesmen on the island, but try John at number fifteen, along the quay, if he's not working today or driving the boat.'

Ellie thanked Linda and made her way out. She was stopped by an old lady with a wheeled shopping bag who stared at her. 'Good morning to you,' she said with a strong accent from somewhere in Europe; Ellie couldn't place it.

'She was looking for John,' Linda called.

The old lady pushed the bag towards Ellie. 'Well, if you help me for a few minutes, I'll show you where he's working. My house is nearby.'

Ellie smiled and took the handle. 'All right, thank you.'

'Morning, Heike,' Linda called out. 'I see you've got yourself a helper.'

'A packhorse,' she answered. Ellie followed Heike slowly around the shop as she loaded her bag with groceries and paid at the till. 'And three bags of logs, if you please.'

Linda piled three nets of logs into the wheeled carrier and sat the old lady's shopping on top. Ellie dragged the bag, and her own, halfway up the steep road called Chapel Hill, between the pub and the church. The tiny houses looked out over a graveyard. She was just wondering if Patience was buried there when Heike opened her own door. It hadn't been locked either.

'Well, bring it in,' she said, shaking her hand at the hall floor. 'Mind the rug with those wet wheels.'

Ellie lifted it in, and as it seemed expected of her, asked where she would like the logs.

'There's a store out the back,' she said, taking the bag of her groceries and walking through to a kitchen. Outside the door was a courtyard with a timber frame, well packed with logs, and Ellie did her best to pile the fresh wood on top.

'You will have coffee?' the woman called out.

'Um, yes. Thank you,' Ellie called back.

'So, you are Elowen, Ysella's little girl.' Heike looked her up and down with shiny black eyes, like a robin. 'Patience was one of my closest friends. You may call me Heike.'

'I go by Ellie now,' she said, looking around the tiny space.

Heike snorted with laughter. 'I remember you when you used to play with blocks in my garden, and pick my flowers.' The small paved yard was surrounded by raised beds, daffodils nodding in the brisk wind. She poured two mugs of coffee with hands twisted by arthritis. 'You will always be Elowen to me. Here. Come into my parlour.'

They walked into a front room full of antiques, a thick rug underfoot and a velvet sofa next to a rocking chair.

'This is lovely,' Ellie murmured.

'Sit down in the rocker, like Patience used to. She loved that chair.' Heike settled herself onto the sofa.

It was surprisingly comfortable. 'I don't remember her,' Ellie said, staring across at the churchyard through the lace curtains. 'I hardly remember my mother.'

'It was a terrible time, when Ysella was ill,' the old woman said. 'She spent her last summer here, but she lied to your father, said she was well enough to come. She was very frail by then. She spent a lot of time in the garden at the cottage – it was lovely. Now it's just brambles and bracken, but there was once a lawn for you to run about on.'

Ellie could remember that. Stiff grasses under her bare feet, butterflies dancing over the flowers. That was familiar.

'What was my mother like?' she asked, her voice thick with emotion.

'Ysa was one of the lovely people. So funny and so bright. She grew up at Kittiwake Cottage, you know.' Heike stalled, as if she was going to say something else. 'It was difficult for Patience to adopt her, but a joy, too. She didn't have children of her own; she never married, you know.'

'Was my mother related to Patience?'

The old woman seemed to choose her words carefully. 'I heard that maybe she was the child of a distant cousin. Patience was very happy to have her. The island tells a story about how she brought the baby back in a carpet bag.'

Ellie smiled. 'In a bag?'

'On the ferry. She made a little crib out of her hand luggage and laid the baby on top. It was quite a story at the time, I heard.'

'And no one asked where the baby came from?' Ellie was intrigued at the story.

'They must have been satisfied with her explanation as a month later she was reinstated as the local teacher and the baby stayed. It's never easy to get teachers here, you know, especially now we have fewer children. We may be down to just three in September. I don't know what will happen if the school closes.' She put her cup down and folded her hands. 'Your mother adored you. Perhaps you will find out more about her, when you sort through the cottage. It got in a bit of a mess once Patience broke her hip.'

'How did she break it?'

'She fell, in the field above the house. She was trying to help one of Tink's sheep but she slipped over and broke her femur. Afterwards, she could walk about the house with a frame, but she couldn't manage the stairs. I used to get a lift up there to see her, two old ladies clacking our sticks together and playing cribbage.'

'Who's Tink?' Ellie asked, although she presumed it was one of her neighbours. She could hear the sheep over the wall, the persistent cries of lambs and ewes. 'And I didn't know there were any cars on the island.'

'No, no, not really. We have one island car – it belongs to the council and gets used for emergencies. Tink has a bike – I can't remember what he calls it – a bike with four wheels. He does deliveries from the ferry and around the island, and to take old ladies to see their friends.'

'So Tink has a quad bike?'

'He uses it for the fire brigade, and for the farm as well.'

Ellie thought about Patience, breaking her hip in a field. 'What about ambulances – what do people here do in emergencies? How do people get deliveries from the mainland?'

'Tink will pick up stuff from the freight ship for you in his trailer. He delivers heavy stuff over to the shop, too. And the air ambulance comes over when needed.'

Ellie sipped her coffee, and thought about the sheer logistics of living on an island.

'How do you get big things, like furniture?' She wondered how she would get a flat-packed kitchen delivered.

Heike shrugged again. 'People don't bring much. When I came thirty-five years ago, we only had a few bits of furniture. It's a small house and we made do with what was already here, and mended what we needed to. There was quite a lot of woodworm. They like the salty air; it makes the wood damp.'

'If you could just tell me where the electrician is working?'

'His name is John McCullough. He does – what do you call it? Lime plastering. He's working at Lolly's right now. He knows a bit about most things.... Her house is just along from you on the lane. Follow the road – it's the house on the end at the lookout corner.' She stood, bracing herself on the coffee table. 'It's good to see you again, young Elowen. I know Patience would be happy you are at the cottage.'

'I won't be here for long,' Ellie said as she walked towards the front door. 'I live in London, with my boyfriend. I'll have to go back one day.'

'Well, we'll see,' Heike said, following her and smiling. 'This place has a way of catching you in its web.'

Ellie found Lolly's place up the hill. It was a two-storey house with big bay windows and an open front door, despite the cold wind. When she shouted through it, the boatman popped his head around the doorframe.

'Oh, hello,' he said. 'I thought I'd be seeing you today.' He grinned, brushing his hands together.

'I don't have any electricity or water,' Ellie said. 'It's not that funny,' she added, watching him smile. 'I was hoping you would know where the stopcocks and switches are?'

'I drained the system down after she died,' John said. He was trim with greying hair, and was covered in dust. 'I didn't want the pipes to freeze up if we had a cold snap. I can put it back on for you, if you like.'

'That would be great.' Ellie stepped back as he grabbed a small bag and walked out of the house. 'Thank you.'

'Come on, then,' he said, setting a pace along the track that Ellie struggled to keep up with. John turned into the cottage and pushed at the door. 'You locked it?' He turned and laughed at Ellie.

'Oh, sorry, force of habit.' She fumbled with the key and opened the door.

On top of the electricity box was a large fuse she hadn't seen in the dark. It clicked into place and John pulled the switch down with a clunk. The light in the hallway didn't go on, but the one in the dining room did.

'You need a few new bulbs.' He took her out through to the kitchen and turned on a switch under the sink. 'This is for the pump. Your water's from the well out by the back wall.' He turned on the tap, and the pipes banged. Brown water spluttered into the sink for a few seconds before it started to run clear. 'I wouldn't want to drink that straight, to be honest, with the sheep in the field. Run it for a minute or two, and you'd better boil it until you get it tested.'

Ellie looked around for a kettle, but the only one was sat on an ancient cooker with three rusted rings. 'Oh, God.'

'Cheer up. A bit of a clean and it will be fine,' John said. 'Got to get back. I want to finish that back wall before Lolly comes home.'

'How much do I owe you?' Ellie followed him through to the front room.

'Let's call it a pint,' John said. 'If you need any plastering or small building work done, let me know. I'm busy on the other islands in the summer, but I can usually fit in small jobs.' He hefted the bag onto his shoulder. 'I'll be in the pub around eight for that pint. See you then.'

He left Ellie feeling battered by the strong personalities on the island. She remembered to put her phone on to charge. As she filled the kettle, she saw the cat sitting by the back door, staring up at her.

6

15 NOVEMBER 1940

Special Operations Executive

Dear Mr Watkins,

I have carried out an examination of the young man who calls himself Dutch, rescued by fishing boat Cormorant *eight miles SSW of Morwen Island, late on 11 November, 1940.*

Examination of his apparel does not give clues as to his nationality. He spoke little, being very ill with double pneumonia. His appearance was that of a man under the age of recruitment into the German Navy, and he made a few Dutch replies to questions posed, only one-word answers. He was unable to give his full name or any details of his ship. His hosts are both German speakers. Mr Ellis was a POW in 1917 and Mrs Ellis was a nurse in Rouen (No 8 J C France) and learned the language fluently.

Three trawlers (two French, one British) are known to have been sunk, likely by U-boat action on 11–12 November.

Lieutenant Colonel Leigh of the Duke of Cornwall's Light Infantry Battalion has increased air and sea defences on the

islands. Lt. Col. Leigh will continue to monitor the rescued
seaman, and has authorised the use of medication from St
Brannock's hospital.

Yours sincerely,

Laurence Byers, Senior Intelligence Officer, St Brannock's.

Patience walked along the footpath to Morwen School, half
dragging Susannah behind her.

'Don't want to,' the younger girl whined. 'Patsy...'

'You'll be fine when you get there,' Patience said, over the
protests. 'Alice is there, and she'll show you her skipping rope.'

Susie resisted even more, her complaints getting louder,
then stopping. Patience turned to look at her sister, who was
pointing towards the sea. Something was rolling in the surf –
soft, boneless, white. A few scraps of clothing still covered the
lower half of it, but the hands and feet were red and tattered.

Patience put her hand to her mouth, stifling the cry that
would frighten the younger girl. 'It's all right, Susie, it's just
some old rags.'

Susannah whimpered. 'Go back, Patsy.'

'We'll go home. We'll tell someone.' She shut her eyes but
the image remained. Was it Mr Shore, or one of his men? The
idea was dreadful. Maybe it was just a stranger, maybe just a
swimmer who drowned on the mainland.

God, please let it be someone I don't know... Only that's self-
ish, isn't it? The families of the Island Queen's *crew are*
desperate for news. Suppose that was Dad?

'Yes, back to the town,' she said, dragged along by Susie,
who picked up pace down the path.

As she passed the cannery she called out to Mr Bell, who

was outside smoking his pipe, a cloud of acrid yellow smoke drifting around his head with each puff.

'Mr Bell, there's something on the beach,' she shouted. Susie yanked her hand free from Patience's sweaty palm and took off towards home. As she approached him she called out, 'It looks like a body. I have to go, Susie's likely to fall off the quay if I'm not there—'

'I'll get a couple of the men to look. Is it Artie Shore?'

'I couldn't tell.' She sniffed back tears that erupted into her eyes. 'I'm sorry.'

'Go, go, maid, we'll deal with it. Tide's still coming in, it'll nudge it onto the sand.'

Patience took off after Susie, watching her weave across the path towards the quay. She caught her outside the pub crying, Mrs Finch the postmistress holding her. By the time she had taken Susie home and explained to Mam what had happened, Patience just had time to be sick in the outhouse.

7

PRESENT DAY, 12 MARCH

When Elowen arrived at the pub that evening, it was lit by the yellow glow of lanterns, illuminating the sagging beams. The wood-burning stove was alight, and two children were playing in front of a fireguard. The walls were plastered, but in places the bare stone had been left visible. Various bits of old boats were displayed on the walls, including part of the woodwork with the name *Island Queen*. A description underneath said the original ship had been sunk by a German U-boat in 1940.

'Everything lost at sea washes up on one of the islands,' Bran said as he walked over to greet her.

She turned to look at him and remembered he really did have a lovely smile. He pointed at an old man at the head of a long table, telling a loud story.

'That's my dad, Joe,' he said. 'He's the other owner of the pub. It's probably better if you meet him when he's sober, though. He'll be a nightmare to get home tonight.'

'Where's home?' she asked as she read a chalked menu.

'We live in a tug on the quay.' Bran pointed up at the specials board. 'My mystery pie, with a secret ingredient. You get a free drink if you identify it. They've sold well but no one's guessed it yet.'

Ellie ordered the pie, bought a glass of wine and found a small table by the end of the bar. From the way people were looking and talking, she was sure they knew how her first day had gone.

The food was delicious. Buttery mash, greens, crunchy pastry and some creamy, herby filling, with chunks of tender pink meat. It reminded her of something from childhood, but she couldn't pin down the memory.

Bran walked over as she was scraping up the last of the mash.

'How was that?'

'That pie was amazing, thank you.'

'Now,' said Bran, 'you have to guess the special ingredient or you don't get your free drink.'

People started shushing and turning to look at her. She put her head on one side. 'Um. It was delicious. Some sort of game meat?' She thought back to a distant flavour in the past. 'Is it rabbit? It is the best pie I've ever had.'

Bran laughed and the pub clapped and cheered. 'It is! Rabbits from Tink's field, behind your cottage, with wild garlic. Patience gave me the recipe.'

'I have tasted it before, then.' Ellie smiled at the thought. 'People keep saying "Tink" as if I should know who he is.'

'You used to play with him; he's about a year younger than you. His surname is Ellis. His grandfather has the biggest fishing boat on the quay.'

'The big blue ship?'

'No, the blue one is my dad's home, *Porpoise*. The big red boat is the trawler. Tink is trying to make a go of farming in the fields behind your land. He looks after the sheep.'

'Is that where Patience broke her hip?'

'Exactly,' he said. 'Tink and his partner Corinne have a

micro-farm and some polytunnels in the fields behind your cottage. The greens in the pie came from there, too.' He smiled. 'Well, I think you deserve that drink. Order when you're ready.'

Another round of applause and laughter filled the pub and she smiled.

'They'll think I'm going soft,' Bran said. 'You're an incomer, emmet, grockle. We're supposed to overcharge you, but I can't quite do it.'

'Because you knew me as a child?' she teased, emboldened by the warm food and wine.

'I'm a year older, remember.' He smiled. 'We played together.'

She laughed and looked around. 'Where's the best place for a mobile signal? I need to call my boyfriend. I don't get a signal at the cottage.'

His smile faded a little as he looked at her, his eyes narrowing. 'In front of the gift shop,' he said. 'But there is a landline in my office. Get some privacy. This lot are the nosiest people in *the whole world*.'

Laughter rippled around the pub. She smiled back at him. 'I must admit, I wasn't looking forward to standing out in that wind.'

'Take as long as you like.'

'Thank you. He's sent me all these messages. I only get them when I walk down the hill. I realise now, I go straight past the gift shop. I'm hoping to get a landline put in, but I can't see any phone sockets or wires from a telegraph pole.'

She walked through to the office, put the lights on and sat at the desk. When Leo eventually answered, it sounded like he was at a party, with people laughing and shouting in the background.

'Ellie, *finally*! Didn't you get my messages? I've been worried. The last time we spoke you were dying of seasickness.'

'There isn't much signal here,' she said, tears pricking at her eyelids. She felt so far from anything comfortable or warm, and the idea of walking back up alone in the darkness was daunting. 'What are you up to?'

'I'm out with the office gang,' he said. 'They knew I was a bit down without you, so they invited me out.'

'Are you feeling down?' She pushed the chair back a little so she could see the quay, streaks of rain cutting through the streetlight.

'Of course I am. I'm missing you.' His voice took on that growly quality that she'd always loved. 'You don't have to stay there every single night, surely? You could have a weekend off for good behaviour.'

'You know what the will says. I have to stay a whole year.' She rubbed a hand over her tired eyes. 'It's not as modernised as we'd hoped, but a detached cottage on the island must be worth half a million once it's done up.'

'So we can buy our first proper home together.'

'Don't,' she said, blinking a few tears away at the thought of the dream she'd had for years. 'You're making me cry.'

'Hold that thought. Oh. Sorry, I have to go. Love you.'

'I love you too.'

'Call me later when I get back,' he said, and joined in some cheering.

'I don't get a signal at the cottage—' Ellie started, but he had already gone.

'How's your boyfriend?' Bran asked, pulling another pint at the bar.

'He was at a party.'

'I've got a pint of Selkie ready for John, for putting your electric on.'

Ellie could see the boatman chatting to an older man. She

paid the bill and lifted the pint. 'Could you do me a black coffee? I don't fancy the walk up the hill just yet, it's cold.'

'Patience bought a couple of electric radiators, but I don't know where she kept them.'

'I'll look for them, thanks. I've got some logs in the porch, so at least I can light a fire. I'll have to find somewhere that sells bedding. All I have is some blankets and an old quilt. And I need an electric kettle.'

Bran pushed the coffee in front of her. 'I can lend you a duvet and a couple of pillows. We keep a lot of spare bedding for the letting rooms, but we're not booked up yet.'

'Thank you, but I'll be OK.' She bit her lip, looked down into her coffee. *I'm being an idiot. I don't want to sleep on that old sofa again.*

'Oh, shut up,' he said, half smiling. 'Just say "thank you" and I'll bag some up for you. Honestly, you're practically a child-hood friend. Don't suffer if you don't have to.'

'Thank you. I'll just deliver this beer.'

John was kind and funny, and the whole table cheered when she ceremoniously handed him the pint.

'You'll get to know everyone soon,' he said.

'Thank you.' She smiled at John, and walked back to her coffee. By the time she had finished it, Bran had brought down a bag of bedding and propped it by the door. A lot of people were staring as she pulled on her jacket.

'There you go,' he said.

'Thank you,' she said, lifting the bag. 'You've all been very kind.'

His face looked conflicted, like he wanted to say something but couldn't.

'Watch those wet cobbles,' was all he said.

8

24 NOVEMBER 1940

Patience studied the inside of the church, listening to the eulogy. She had failed to get the image of the flopping, rolling body out of her head, and couldn't help imagining it in the coffin. Five island men had died in the storm, but they had found only one: Artie Shore.

The funeral was for all of them, and many of the island's four hundred residents were present, crammed into the pews and the aisles. The vicar seemed a little overwhelmed by the size of the congregation, and had opened all the side doors so people could crowd in and listen.

Dutch had been left at home, sat in the parlour with a blanket over his knees. The islanders were still unsure of him, and a few rumours were still circulating that he was a spy. The medicine had worked, but the Dutchman was skin and bone, still coughing. His bed was right over Patience's room, and she could hear him struggling to breathe at night.

Old Mr Shore had gone up to read the next passage.

His face was red and his hand shaking. 'Who killed my Artie, and the sons and husbands of the *Island Queen*'s crew? Who's to say you haven't got a German in your attic, Ellis?'

'Now then, Henry,' Reverend Whittle said, but Mr Shore shook him off.

Dad stood up, his hair flat where he had taken off his Sunday hat.

'You know, Henry, the fisherman we picked up isn't German. The ministry is issuing him temporary papers and will be verifying his identity through the Red Cross in Holland.'

Patience knew that was a lie. The most the young man could remember was that his name was Janssen, a name that could be Dutch *or* German. He hardly spoke, even when he could breathe.

'Who is he, then?' Shore's face was shining with sweat. 'If he can't even remember his name?'

Dad looked at them all squashed together on the pew, the youngest boys on Mam's lap. Patience found herself standing up, trembling in the face of such hostility.

'His name is Piet Janssen,' she stammered, making it up on the spot. She had already studied the big atlas in the school library. 'He's from Groningen, in Holland. He's a fisherman like Dad. When his country was invaded by the Germans, he joined a trawler to help the British fishing fleet. He's on our side.'

The imagined backstory she'd created for him was out there, now. Anything to stop the wave of hatred hitting the young man they had fought to save.

'That's enough,' Mam hissed, pulling at her coat. 'Quiet now.'

'Is it true, George?' Mr Shore shouted at her father.

'True enough, I reckon,' her father replied. He turned to Henry Shore and his voice changed. 'We are here to honour Artie, Henry. A brave and honest man. A good skipper and a fine trawlerman, a husband, son and father. That's who we're talking about today, and the fellows who risked their lives to sail with him.'

The vicar stood up and spoke in the direction of the piano.

'Hymn 102 now, I think, Miss Elstree.'

> Above me hangs the silent sky;
> Around me rolls the sea;
> The crew is at all at rest,
> And I Am, Lord, alone with Thee.

Dutch improved at the Ellises' home for another month, before being found temporary lodgings and papers at the seamen's mission on the big island of St Brannock's. When he was fit to work but still reed thin, he joined the crew of the *Lucky Lady* there. Once a month, he visited Morwen Island to have dinner with the Ellises and share his news in improving English.

His parting gift from George Ellis had been a Dutch–English dictionary purchased by post from a bookshop in Bristol. Patience would make an effort to talk with him, teaching him English, and he teaching her a little Dutch. The book was old, written at the end of the eighteen hundreds and had common phrases at the back.

'Dutch is a bit like English,' she said, reading a phrase slowly. '*Mijn hond heeft honger*,' she read. 'My dog – hound – is hungry. Has hunger.'

'*Maar wil niet eten*,' he added. 'Will – not – eat.'

'Do you think it's like German?' she said, glancing up at him.

He looked away. 'I know small German,' he said. 'Live close to Deutschland. Duitsland. But Nederlandse man.'

'See,' she said, smiling. 'Man is the same in both Dutch and English.'

His smile was crooked. 'Tell me of school.'

Patience could always make him laugh about the children's

antics, and she tried, making it up when it wasn't funny. But today he was sad. 'What's wrong?'

He shrugged, his bony wrists pushing out of one of her father's old shirts. 'Tired today,' he said. He looked better, his hair dark and thick, growing through from the close cut he'd had when rescued, brown eyes watching her. She felt very young next to him; he looked more like a man than a boy now.

'You must miss your family,' Patience said, feeling a lurch in her chest. 'And your friends.'

'I don't remember any friends,' he said, frowning. 'You my friend, now.'

'Exactly,' she said, smiling. 'And you can come to my tenth birthday next month. You missed Christmas with us; you must come and have some cake.'

'If tide—' He wrestled for the words.

'If the tide is right,' she finished for him. 'We won't have cake until my father is back. Thirteenth of February, it's a Thursday. Birthday.'

'Birthday,' he said. 'Good word.'

'When is your birthday?' she asked, looking up from the book. He stared at her, blank. She looked away. 'Don't worry. You probably still can't remember.'

'Just sad,' he said. 'Maybe talk to...' His voice trailed off. He looked through the dictionary but didn't settle on anything.

'The Red Cross are looking for your family, aren't they?' she prompted.

'Not know things,' he said, then hit his knee with a bony fist. 'Not full name. Just Janssen. Not house place, or birth date. Age even.'

'What did your parents call you? Do you remember them?'

He thought, then shook his head. 'My mother call me *Junge*, like – boy. Maybe son.' He smiled at her then, from under his dark fringe. It would soon be time for Mam to cut his hair again. 'I like Piet, Pieter. You gave good name.'

Patience knew the question she dared not ask him, because she felt he would tell her the truth. 'You must stay here,' she said slowly, 'and work hard. After the war – it can't be much longer – you can contact the Red Cross and they will help you find your family.'

He nodded. 'After war.'

9

PRESENT DAY, 12 MARCH

Ellie walked up the hill from the pub. There were no streetlights on the lane, and she stumbled a few times on the grass between the ruts. She had left a light on in the cottage's living room, mostly so she could find it in the dark. Unlocking the door was a challenge, too, trying to juggle her phone's light and the big key, but eventually it gave. She wasn't leaving the house unlocked, whatever John said. A laptop loaded with data from a work case had arrived and she would work offline, looking for evidence of fraud.

She was warmed by Bran's pie and the loan of the bedding. She debated lighting a fire before bed but decided exhaustion would win out before she could enjoy it. She found the heaters in the cupboard under the stairs, right at the back, and plugged one in in the front bedroom. It stank of burnt dust for a while, and the fittings looked suspiciously antique, so she resolved to turn it off before going to sleep. It was difficult to believe an old lady had been living in these conditions.

She made the front bedroom comfortable with Bran's duvet and sheets and added the patchwork quilt for good measure. It looked more homely. There was an old-fashioned sink in one corner of the room and, after a few minutes, she managed to run clear water through the single brass tap to clean her teeth. She put the old sheets in the kitchen, made herself a cup of tea and sat in the living room. The cat wound through the broken pane in the front window and started meowing. Not the endearing sound of a happy cat but a screeching wail, with growls like it was possessed.

She walked back to the kitchen, found a tin opener in the dresser drawer and hacked into a can of Fishies. It smelled vile, but the cat stopped yowling and stared at her. It was mostly grey with a few areas of dirty white, and had chunks of matted fur hanging from its neck.

'Here, cat,' she said, wielding a fork to chunk the food onto an old plate. She put about half the tin down and, after a minute, the cat moved towards the food, never taking its eyes off Ellie. It growled until she backed away into the hall, then began eating. She started exploring.

A dark wooden sideboard ran along the front-room wall. It was crowded with old photographs, fogged with dust, but she didn't feel up to looking at them. Part of her didn't want to see a picture of her mother yet. The sideboard had two drawers filled with useful bits, like string and brown paper, and a few folded cloths. Two cupboard doors below were locked and immovable, and Ellie couldn't find a key.

There was a bookcase in the far corner, the shelves bowing under the weight of hardbacks, stacked in rows then horizontally above to fill the space. There were several copies of the same book in different editions: *Animals and Plants in British Rock Pools*, and she was surprised to see the name P.M. Ellis. She took one off the shelf. It was illustrated with pen and ink sketches. She looked inside the front cover to find the copyright was held by Patience Martha Ellis. She settled on the sofa with more interest, finding a whole section on seabirds and dolphins.

The door scraped open and the cat walked in. It paused,

looked at the sofa that Ellie was sitting on for a long moment, then stalked to the other one. It sat on a cushion and tried to groom itself, tugging at knots and mats. Ellie had noticed a jug on the sideboard full of pens and some scissors; she grabbed what looked like the sharpest pair, and sat at the very end of the cat's settee. The animal stared at her, and she stared back. Finally, she reached out a hand and the animal sniffed it.

'Hello,' she murmured.

It didn't growl, so Ellie tried stroking its head, the only bit she could reach. The cat observed her coldly, but eventually rubbed its face against her fingers. Ellie pounced, grabbing the cat by the scruff of its neck, and pressed it down onto the cushion. She managed to cut half the felt swinging from the cat's throat before she was skewered by ten claws and the cat was on top of the bookcase. Ellie washed her scratched hand in the kitchen. It felt good to help the reluctant animal. She couldn't do anything for the old lady, but she might be able to save her cat.

When she got back to the living room, the ungrateful animal was right where Ellie had been sitting, and it flattened itself, making the hellcat noise again. She collected the old book, which smelled a bit like a museum, and retired to bed.

After a better night's sleep, Ellie walked down to the Quay Kitchen café and arrived just as a woman in her thirties came to the door.

'Are you waiting for us?' she asked. Fresh faced and pretty, she had her hair tucked into a ponytail and was tying apron strings around her waist. 'We're just getting ready but you can wait in the warm if you like. I'll be five minutes.'

'Thank you.' Ellie smiled, stumbled up an unexpected step and discovered an old room, painted apple-green and white, with tables and chairs. The timber-framed walls were filled in with old brick and patches of stone. It smelled like coffee and freshly baked cakes.

She sat at a table and hung her coat on the back of the chair. She could hear laughter from the kitchen, and a couple of faces appeared as if to check her out.

The woman reappeared with a notebook. 'Hi. Are you Elowen, Patience's relative? I'm Lucy, I own the Quay Kitchen.'

'I go by Ellie now,' she said, immediately hating the prissy way it came out. 'But I suppose Elowen is fine. I don't think we were related, but Patience did leave the house to me.'

Lucy took her order of a large latte and a cooked breakfast, and recommended the home-made marmalade which sounded delicious. Lucy hesitated at the counter before coming back to the table.

'While Amy cooks your breakfast, could you help me with something? I need a hand moving some garden furniture.'

Ellie agreed and followed Lucy to the back of a café and through a glass door.

'We open the garden in the spring,' she explained, walking up concrete steps and looking back over her shoulder. 'Angie, our gardener, is going to pressure-wash the steps and patios today and I need to move everything onto the gravel for her. I won't have time later – we have a few bookings this morning.'

'Of course,' Ellie said, feeling the slippery algae under her soles.

The skeletons of shrubs and plants punctuated nooks filled with tables and garden chairs. Spikes of bulbs were everywhere, daffodils making a haze of yellow, and blue flowers burst from pots. A few leaves were starting to open on the trees around the stone walls.

Lucy stacked chairs beside the tables and Ellie copied her. 'Now the big wooden one,' she said, lifting her end with ease. 'I was really sorry about Patience. She came in regularly. She helped me get the café off the ground in the early days.'

'So, you haven't been here long?'

'Four years,' she said. 'But I made the mistake of moving in late in the year, after all the visitors had gone. Patience helped me get people in here. She even set up a book group. It kept me going, otherwise I wouldn't have been able to take on staff. We employ six people all year round, more in the summer.'

Ellie moved more chairs to a stone wall covered with ivy. 'I can't remember meeting her. What was she like?'

'Oh,' Lucy said, looking surprised. 'I thought you came here as a child.'

'I don't remember much. I stopped coming here when I was quite young,' she said.

'Patience was lovely, and super smart,' Lucy said. 'She didn't suffer fools gladly, and she could be brutally honest, but she was always kind.' She brushed off her hands. 'We had people back here after her funeral, the ones that didn't go to the pub. Pretty well the whole island went – they opened up the church specially for the burial. We had a ferry load of people from the other islands as well.' She looked down at the gravel. 'The service was really moving. Angie did all the flowers and lots of evergreen leaves. Dozens of people spoke. She was the oldest person on the island and everyone knew her.'

A girl pushed open the garden door. 'Hi, Lucy.'

'Oh, Connie,' Lucy said, smiling at her. 'I was just talking about Patience's funeral.'

'Oh, it was lovely,' Connie said. 'Patience taught me to swim, down in Seal Cove. She used to take us on night hikes and camps around the island. We loved them. She was strict, though. There's a full English waiting indoors, Lucy, and the ferry's just coming in.'

'Thank you for helping with the tables,' Lucy said to Ellie. 'Come inside and get warm.'

Ellie followed her in and asked the question that had been

bothering her. 'Did someone else on the island expect to inherit the cottage? People seem a bit surprised by my arrival.'

Lucy hesitated in front of her table where a mug brimming with coffee-scented foam waited. 'I suppose her brother's grand-children might have expected something. Maybe not expected it, but hoped, maybe. She was very close to Tink, her great-nephew.'

She was interrupted by a taller woman carrying a tray.

'There you go,' she said, putting it down. 'Do you want any sauces or anything?'

Ellie asked for ketchup and, while the other woman went to get it, Lucy bent lower. 'Look, you should ask Amy about the cottage before we get busy. She's lived here her whole life, she knows a lot about the town.'

'I might do,' she said, as a group of older women came in, talking loudly and laughing. 'But it looks like you're busy already.'

As she walked back up the hill, the idea of Patience's family intrigued her. Maybe there were papers in the house that would explain her connection to the old lady.

She reached Kittiwake Cottage just as a woman with a mass of white hair tied up in a bun walked from the porch, carrying a large red bag.

'There you are!' she said, as if she knew her already. 'You're Elowen, aren't you? Patience told me all about you. I'm Maggi, the post lady on the island. I've left a few letters for you.' She smiled warmly at her. 'And I needed to talk to you anyway.' There were tears in her eyes when she squinted up at Ellie. 'Can I come in? It's so windy out here.'

'Of course.' She fumbled in her pocket for the key. 'I'm sorry it's a bit of a mess.'

Maggi stepped around her and opened the door, and Ellie noticed it hadn't been locked.

'I'm sorry, do you have a key? Were you in here?' Her voice was sharper than she'd expected, and Maggi stepped back.

'I just put the letters inside. There was a parcel as well. I always put the post indoors in case it rains.' Her voice faltered. 'I'm sorry, was that wrong? I knew you were out.' She pointed back at the porch. 'There's a key behind the woodpile – lots of people use that. Let me get it for you.'

'No, it's fine.' She felt bad seeing how distressed Maggi was as she retrieved the key from the porch and waved it until Ellie felt she had to take it. 'I'm just not used to how friendly people are around here. London's not like this. Please come in.' She found herself ushering Maggi into the dining room. 'Can I get you a cup of tea or something?'

Maggi sat at the table and nudged the stack of letters. One was a large envelope that looked crammed with papers. 'I don't want to be a nuisance,' she said, subdued. 'Tea would be lovely, though. I left this house until last, hoping to meet you.'

Ellie put the kettle on and heard a scratch on the door. She opened it and the cat slunk in.

'Oh, he's all right! He's very thin, poor darling,' Maggi said. 'We thought he might have died, but then Linda said you had bought cat food in the shop. I was so relieved.'

'I can't get the knots out of his fur.'

She froze. 'You touched him?'

Ellie placed a mug in front of her. 'I had to – he was matted all over. He let me do a bit.' She showed her the backs of her hands. 'He got me a few times, but he lets me fiddle with the scissors while he eats his food.'

Maggi smiled. It was like the sun coming out.

'Well, that's lovely, well done you. He won't let most people touch him. His name is Bertie, by the way.'

Ellie opened the smaller letters – just bills and condolence cards. The large packet was from her father; she recognised the heavy handwriting scratched into the paper. He was probably trying to bully her into breaking the legally restricting entail again.

'What did you want to ask me?' she said, pushing the packet to one side. Maggi was looking around the room.

'I wondered if you had noticed one of Patience's pictures is missing? Over the fireplace.' Her hands were clasped together so hard her knuckles had whitened.

There was a square of less faded wallpaper in the living room.

'I did wonder. I thought she must have given it away.' Ellie was puzzled, by the older woman's agitation as much as anything.

'Only, it was painted by my husband, before he died,' she said, with a rush. 'I didn't know anyone was going to move in here, and I thought it might be thrown away—'

Ellie held up a hand. 'Wait a minute. Maggi – is that short for Margaret?' She retrieved the creased solicitor's letter from the dresser drawer. 'Margaret Maginnis, is that you?'

'It is.' Maggi stood by her side, looking down the crumpled list.

'I have to arrange to give things to these people. This came with the will.' Maggi was number seven of eighteen names. 'Look,' she said, '"Margaret Maginnis, to have her choice of my pictures". I suppose she knew which one you would like.'

Maggi was pale. 'Pete, my husband, died a few years ago. Patience did offer me the picture after he died, but I loved coming up here to see her. I would make us a cup of tea and we would chat. I loved looking at it. It was meant for that space, lit by the reflection off the sea.'

Ellie nodded; that made sense. 'Where is it now? We could have a look upstairs if you like.'

'The thing is,' Maggi said, and took a deep breath. 'I was

here after she died. I looked at the picture and – well, I just couldn't leave it to be scrapped.' Her voice was thick with sadness and Ellie could see how bright her eyes were. 'Peter was quite celebrated as a local artist,' she said. 'I used to dabble as well – we both had paintings in the gallery.' Her face changed. 'Then he died.' Her voice was utterly bleak, and for a moment it touched the frozen emptiness Ellie still carried from her own mother's death. 'He died at home, at least. Well, of course, Patience did, too. It's what she wanted. I found her, you know, after...'

'I didn't know that,' Ellie said, her voice soft.

Maggi shook off the sadness. 'So,' she said, looking straight at Ellie, 'I took the painting. I stole it. It's been on my conscience terribly. I feel like a criminal, and I've never stolen anything in my life.'

'But it's yours anyway,' Ellie said, starting to smile. 'Patience wanted you to have it. *I* want you to have it.'

'You're very kind,' Maggi sniffed.

'I just wish I remembered her. And more about my mother.'

'Have you looked at her pictures?' Maggi looked around. 'There's a nice one on the sideboard...' She disappeared to the living room and returned with a heavy silver frame, dusting it off with a tissue. 'There you go. This was one of her favourite pictures. Patience, Ysella and Dutch.'

A dark-haired older man was sat on the living room sofa next to a woman with a strong face and pale curly hair, with Ellie's teenaged mother perched on the arm of the sofa beside them. The man's arm was around the girl.

'Who was Dutch?'

'Patience's dearest friend.' Maggi tightened her lips as if she wanted to stop herself saying more. 'He was a wonderful man.'

'He seemed very close to my mother, too.'

'Dutch was like a grandad to all the kids on the island. He had a romantic story, actually. He was almost drowned in the war, but was picked up by a local trawler after the Germans sank his fishing boat. He was just a boy then, seventeen or so, and the islanders took him in. He was the only survivor, and all he could say was "Dutch". His real name was Janssen. His grave is in the churchyard. You should go and see it. Patience was buried in the same plot with him.'

'So, they were really close.'

'He was her love,' Maggi said simply. 'I don't know why they didn't get married. Of course, he was much older and, back in those days, she would have had to give up her career as a teacher. It was like nursing, you had to be single.'

'But they could have got married later, when she retired?'

Maggi shrugged. 'I suppose so, but they didn't. She'd adopted a little girl – your mother – but when Ysella got married and left the island, that was a huge wrench for her. But you came along and they were the golden years.' Maggi smiled. 'She was a lovely person. My boys loved Ysella reading to them when she babysat. She used to make up stories. Oh, I'm going daft – you must know that better than anyone.'

Ellie sat back, her mind sifting through dark clouds of memory. 'I remember her reading books to me,' she said slowly. 'Did she write stories as well?'

'She used to make little comics for the school, for those children who weren't reading yet. She trained as a teacher, too, you know.'

Ellie was stunned. 'Did she? All I know is she grew up on an island and married my dad.'

Maggi finished her tea. 'She did. And now you are here in her house. *Their* house, Patience and Ysa's.'

'I'm not sure of the relationship between Patience and my mother, just that she was adopted,' she said.

'Being a grandmother is an act of *choice*, not biology. I've got three grandchildren, two step-grandchildren and one we just adopted because we love him,' she said, picking up her mailbag.

'Patience was your grandmother. You should talk to Clem Ellis. He lives on Noah's Drang, off Fore Street. He was Patience's youngest brother and I'm sure he'd love to meet you. Now, I'd better get on.' Maggi looked at her. 'You really don't mind me stealing your picture?'

Ellie smiled back at her. 'I'm glad she had such a good friend. She wanted you to have it, so it all worked out fine.'

Maggi reached up and lightly touched the side of Ellie's face. 'You do look like Ysella,' she said. There was a sadness in her eyes as she turned to leave.

'Wait!' Ellie shouted as Maggi passed the rusted gate. She grabbed the spare key and put it back in its little niche, behind the logs. 'I'll leave this here,' she said, feeling a little shy. 'Just in case you have something to deliver that can't get damp.'

Maggi laughed. 'See you soon, my lovely.'

10

11 AUGUST 1941

Patience knew she should be proud to have passed the eleven-plus exam for the grammar school, but the idea of travelling to Truro, thirty miles by train from Penzance, was terrifying. To have her own bed in a dormitory, and to only come home for the holidays didn't seem possible. Not hearing the sea before she went to sleep, not seeing it every day as she walked to school. How would her mother, who was looking more tired and thin every day, cope with the boys and Susannah?

'You must look forward to this adventure,' her mother said, sitting on the end of the bed. 'You deserve it. You'll have some time on your own, to work hard. You were always a clever child. Miss Cartwright says you could study to become a nurse or teacher, if you want. Think of that.'

'I'll miss you,' Patience mumbled, and the tears came. Curled into Mam's arms she started to cry. 'How will you manage without me?' she asked. 'With Susie and the boys?'

'The boys are nearly old enough for school,' her mother answered, stroking her head. 'You know, I always thought your hair would go darker as you got older, like mine did. But it's so fair, it bleaches white in the sun.'

'What about Susie?'

Her mother kept smoothing her hair. 'Susannah will have her own life. It's likely that she will go away to her own school one day. A place for children like her, where she can learn how to look after herself.'

Patience pulled away. 'A lunatic place? That's what they say at school, that she's a loony.' She dashed her hand over her wet face. 'Mam, you couldn't.'

'You said yourself, we can't always manage her.' Mam put a strong hand under Patience's chin and pushed it up. 'Let Dad and me look after her, and the school will look after you.'

Patience felt her lower lip wobble. 'What if I hate it? What if I'm not as clever as all the other girls?'

'You'll be cleverer than many of them.'

'Will I see Grandma Moore?' Patience saw her mother's mother once a year, when the whole family made the long journey by train to the middle of Cornwall, and stayed in a hotel in Penzance on the way back. It was the closest thing to a holiday they ever had.

'She will be happy to have you at the half-terms, and, if you get permission, you could visit her on a Saturday now and then.' She paused. 'Grandma's not as young as she was. She lives in a boarding house. But she has room for you.'

Patience said, 'I'll miss everyone here horribly.' She would miss Dutch, she thought.

'You will write every week,' Mam said. 'And you'll be back for Christmas, Easter and the summer. The time will fly by.'

Patience fiddled with the books in her suitcase, borrowed from Grandpa Ellis. 'You can tell me all about the family, and our friends, like Dutch. Maybe he will write to me.'

Mam took a long time to answer. 'I'm sure I'll write when I can. But Dutch will be busy working with your father. And he's courting a nice girl from St Brannock's.'

Patience was shocked, but didn't want to Mam to see how much. 'Is he?'

'Marie somebody, I forget her surname. She's a nice girl, a bit older than him, works in the harbour office over there. Mind you, he's filled out so much you might think he was twenty-five now. He's a young man, with a full life ahead of him.'

Patience felt an unfamiliar pain inside her chest and a dryness in her throat. Her friendship with Dutch seemed far away.

11

PRESENT DAY, 19 MARCH

A week later, Ellie's daily phone conversations with Leo from the spot outside the gift shop were beginning to feel strained and awkward. The calls were getting shorter, and she sensed that he was getting impatient, although she had explained why she couldn't just come back to London.

'But it's my birthday in two weeks,' he grumbled. 'For God's sake, Ellie, you can come home for a few nights. Who would even know?'

'Everyone in the town,' she answered. 'Probably everyone on the islands. We can't risk it, it's valuable. Why don't you come here for your birthday instead? I'll book you a great room at the pub, overlooking the sea. We'll explore the whole island together. We could make a proper holiday of it.'

She waited for Leo to reply. She could hear him sighing.

'But everyone at work's coming, even my new boss. It won't be the same without you there. It's my *thirtieth*, you can't miss a milestone like that.'

'Leo,' she said, trying to keep her voice light, 'it's half a million pounds on the line, it's the deposit on a house. When is this big bash, anyway?'

'Wednesday night,' he said quietly. She could hear the hurt in his voice.

'OK. So you could come down on Thursday or Friday and stay for a few days, or even the week. Surely you can get some time off? I mean, it *is* your thirtieth.'

She could hear his breath, hissing in frustration. 'I miss you,' he said, his voice soft. 'I can't sleep without you.'

She melted. 'I know, Leo. I can't sleep without you either. Well, that and the mice scratching.'

'Can't you just get an exterminator in?'

'I've explained this,' she said. 'The nearest one is in Cornwall.' She caught sight of the post lady power-walking along the quay on the way back to her cottage. 'Hi, Maggi!'

'Hello, darling,' Maggi called back, puffing a little as she slowed down to pass her. 'How's Bertie?'

'Good, thanks.'

'Who's Bertie?' Leo asked.

'I told you about him,' she said patiently. 'He's the cat. I've been cleaning the cottage up, and the view from the bay window is brilliant. You will love it, too. It looks over the sea.'

'I just hope the cat hasn't got fleas,' Leo said. 'Look, Ellie, we can't do this whole year by phone.'

'Just come to the island,' she cajoled. 'It's got white sands, blue seas. It's different here.'

She glanced over at the heaving grey sea, just touched by the last light of the day.

'OK,' Leo conceded. 'I'll ask the senior partners. But will you stay at the pub with me?'

She knew she couldn't, but she desperately wanted to see him. They could work out the details when she got here.

'I love you. Of course I'll stay with you whenever I can.'

He made a suggestion of what they could get up to in the pub bedroom as two people approached.

'That would actually be *lovely*,' she said, in a low voice. 'But I am in a public place.'

'I expected a bit more enthusiasm,' Leo said, his words sharp. He snapped 'Goodbye', and they ended the call without the usual 'I love you'.

This impatience had to be the result of only communicating by phone, Ellie thought. There was a poor signal some days, and there seemed to be no rush to get the phone line and Wi-Fi set up at the cottage. She texted him a *Good night, sleep well* message, but there was no reply.

She walked along to the pub to find a music session in full swing. Three men, bearded and long haired, were playing something lively. A half-circle of other musicians of assorted ages and genders were playing along on instruments ranging from an accordion to a cello. They were good. In fact, they were *really* good. A lot of people were nodding or tapping their feet along to the music and the room was crowded. When they finished, there was a raucous round of applause and shouting.

The barman, Max, offered a single nod and a menu. While Ellie squeezed onto the end of a crowded table and waited for her pasta, she listened to the music. There were people she didn't recognise and, as she caught fragments of conversations, she realised some were staying at their holiday cottages.

A boy of about six or seven was standing in front of the musicians with a finger in his mouth, spellbound by the playing. The tallest guitar player, balding and with a formidable beard, leaned down as the song ended on a wave of cheering and stamping. He gestured to people to shush and the place fell quiet.

'Do you want to sing?' he asked the boy. The child nodded and pulled his finger free. 'Do you know any songs?'

The boy leaned up and said something. The player nodded, and with complete solemnity turned to the musicians.

'Right, five verses of "Wheels on the Bus", key of A.' There was a cheer from the musicians and laughter rippled around the spectators.

The boy stood in front of them all, turned to the audience when the musician prompted him, and sang the first line in a thin voice. The musicians joined in, in a raucous, rollicking version of the song.

Ellie found it strangely moving. She felt like she'd never forget it and neither would the child, who ended his song with every adult in the pub singing along.

Max slid the hot plate onto the table in front of her. 'There's a quieter table by the skittle alley, if you want some peace.'

'I'm fine, thanks,' Ellie answered, trying to imagine how Leo would cope with the crowded pub. Over by the bar, Bran smiled and lifted a glass to her, and she nodded and smiled back. For the first time, she felt less of a stranger.

She became aware of four older men staring at her from the corner of the pub, by a low window overlooking the quay.

'Hi, Ellie,' Bran said, as he took her empty plate away. 'How are you settling in?'

'Fine. I mean, I've never really been so cold before, but it's OK. And I found the cat.'

'So I heard,' he said. 'At least he came home for you. Can I get you anything else? We have a couple of slices of apple pie left, or there's a cheesecake.'

She ordered the cheesecake and a soft drink, and when he brought the order out he leaned over the table. She could smell his aftershave, feel his breath on her hair, and it seemed strangely intimate.

'Can I ask you a big favour?' he asked, his words just above a murmur. 'Can you very loudly ask me out for a drink? It's to wind my dad up. He keeps staring at you.' He smiled down at her. '*I* know you have a boyfriend in London, but he doesn't. It will really annoy him. He's always trying to match me up with one of the local girls.'

Ellie smiled and drew on a year of high-school drama classes to speak up.

'I was wondering if you fancied going out for a drink? Bit of a busman's holiday but—' She was aware that everyone around them had stopped talking and was listening in. She could feel her face heating up.

'I'd love to,' he said, equally loudly. 'My day off is Friday. I can show you the big island, if you fancy it. There's a lovely restaurant down in the port.'

'It's a date then,' she said, just glancing at the table by the fire. A thin, grizzled man looked like thunder, and the others looked like they were trying not to laugh.

'I have to do some shopping over there if you actually want to come,' he added in a low voice. 'Or you can give me a list.'

'Actually, I'd like to come,' she said. 'I haven't worked out the ferries yet and there's lots of things I need. An electric kettle would be helpful, and I need to get my own bedding. A tour guide would be great.'

'But I'll buy my own lunch,' he said, eyes twinkling. 'The boat will go from the quay about eight thirty. Is that too early?'

'I get up with the sun, now,' she said. 'Between the thin curtains, the sheep and the cat, I'm up by seven most days.'

'Great,' he said. 'I'll just leave the old man to think about that. I should have told him you were sleeping in my sheets, that would have stirred him up.'

He rolled his eyes as he left.

12

16 APRIL 1944

In her first three years at boarding school, Patience had grown five inches, and her skirts were becoming too short. The girls were taught how to extend their clothes and unpick and resew seams; clothing was scarce even if you had enough coupons.

Far from feeling different at school, Patience found herself in a group who came from all over the country, many displaced by the war. Friendships formed around interests, and everyone was lonely and missed their families. Only a handful had experienced boarding before.

Every time Patience had made the long ferry journey from Cornwall to Morwen, she noticed that Dad was a little greyer, Mam was thinner and Susannah was more unruly. Susie had started having strange episodes where she seemed very distant and would sometimes faint; the doctor called them fits.

She found the island had changed, too, the fields dug up for vegetables. Even Mam and Dad had a few chickens, which were fed on fish trimmings and clucked around the newly planted and pruned orchard opposite the house. The school was relying more on porridge and bread than meat, and she missed butter. At least going home meant enough eggs, and fish for variety.

In her third year at the boarding school, a letter came from Dutch.

I am granted temporary British Citizenship, his letter said. *I no longer have to account for all my movements. I can apply for permanent residency in five years. I have learned lots of English and have new job as pilot at the harbour on St Brannock's. I have cottage now, rent eight shillings, with kitchen and bedroom.*

Your English is much improved, she wrote back. She noticed he didn't mention Marie. *I am learning lots of geography and history. I hope to study to be a teacher like my grandmother. I expect I will be just like Miss Cartwright and have a cottage next to a little school on an island, and be very happy with many books and cats.*

Schoolteacher is a noble thing, to teach little children about the world. And how read and write, he answered back. She loved that, and couldn't wait to correct him. *I am pilot now for naval ships, as well as cargo. My job keeps me very busy, but I sail on* Cormorant *two or three tides a week.*

I miss the sea, she replied. *Now the weather is warmer, I especially miss paddling and swimming. Is Susie swimming yet? My father always said we should teach her. I miss her, and the boys.*

There was no reply for several weeks, until her mother's letter came.

My dear Patsy, Dutch told me you have asked after Susannah. I didn't know how to tell you at first, but Dad has told me to explain the whole situation. Susie has been enrolled in a special place in Penzance, a nice place, more like a school than a hospital. She has gardens to play in and lots of children just like her.

Patience cried at that. No one knew Susie better than they did. She was like *them*.

Her fits have become much more common, and she was

getting silly with the local children, Mam continued. *She will be home for some of the holidays, if she is well enough and it won't upset her too much. I am visiting her once a month and she seems to be settling well.*

The letter ended on a different note. *My darling Patsy, there is one other thing that you should know, even though Dad says not to bother you. I am having an operation in Plymouth next month, one which will make me quite unwell for a little time. I may not be able to write for a few weeks. Grandma Ellis will look after the boys and the house, and our neighbours will help. I shall be as right as rain by the summer.*

13

PRESENT DAY, 20 MARCH

Ellie hacked her way through a blackened bramble as thorny as razor wire, and caught her hand on a hidden barb. She swore as she put her finger to her mouth. The area of ground at the back of the cottage (she couldn't seriously think of it as a garden) was a mass of nettles, thorns and scrambling bushes.

'Hi there.'

The voice made her jump, and she turned to see a woman about her own age looking over the wall at the back. She had dark skin, a colourful scarf wound around her head and dangly earrings with feathers blowing in the breeze. She was very pretty.

'Oh, hello.' She swiped the back of her hand across her sweaty forehead, finding a gritty smear of mud.

The stranger's smile widened. 'I'm your neighbour, Corinne. My partner Tink and I own the field back here, the one with all the sheep.'

Ellie heard the ewes and lambs as often as the gulls that called overhead, and she thought of them as part of the background noise, like the wind.

'Oh, great. Hi, I'm Ellie. I was just tackling...' Her words failed her. 'To be honest, I don't know what I'm doing. Or how to get rid of the bits I've cut down. I can't drive it down to the tip.'

Corinne pointed at the pile of sticks she'd cut. 'Well, in permaculture terms, that's all useful and fertile mulch. Why don't you hire Tink to come and brush cut the whole lot? You'll be able to get to the shed, which is buried in there somewhere, and Tink will take the brambles away for you.'

She smiled. 'If it's all useful mulch, maybe he should pay me.'

Corinne laughed. 'Good luck telling him that,' she said. 'I don't think Tink will find it easy to tackle that thicket, even in his chainsaw trousers. It's all a bit no-man's land back there.'

'Seriously, would he be able to do it?' She held up a pair of rusty secateurs she had found in the porch. 'I don't quite have the tools.'

Corinne nodded. 'He's fishing on the *Gannet* at the moment, helping his grandad on the trawler. I'll get him to pop in and give you a quote. As you say, all that lovely mulch.'

Ellie looked up at her; it would be lovely to have company. 'Have you got time for a cup of tea?'

Corinne looked back into the field. 'I'm just clipping feet, but I can spare a few minutes. I'll come around the front. Coffee for me, though, if you have it. Black.'

By the time Ellie had made the drinks, Corinne had pushed open the front door and was standing on the threshold.

'It seems strange not to walk straight in,' she said, her voice shaking. 'I expect Patience to be sat on the sofa, ready for a cuppa and a chat.' She hunched her shoulders and looked at the hall floor. 'We used to look in on her, even before she had her fall. Tink's known her all his life; I'm just a blow-in, but we both loved her.' She looked up and waved a hand at her face. 'Not many island farmers look like me. She was always welcoming and supportive, even when I was new.'

Ellie handed her the cup. 'Weren't you welcome otherwise?'

'Not at first. Can we sit in the dining room, would that be all right? I'm not quite up to the sofa yet.' She sat at the table. 'I don't have a problem with being black here, but they're living in the nineteen fifties with their ingrained misogyny. The islands are largely run by old men with very fixed ideas about women.'

'That's awkward.' The cat walked in the open back door waving his fluffy but ragged tail. 'Food time, Bertie?'

'I'm glad he's OK,' Corinne said.

The cat wove himself around the chair Ellie was sitting in, and she was able to stroke the cat's head. Corinne started laughing.

'You've tamed him! I thought he would only go to Patience. Maybe he senses you're family.'

'But I don't think I am,' Ellie said. 'I can't find any link to Patience. I think she adopted my mother out of kindness.'

'You should ask Tink. He played with you as a kid, only he remembers you as Elowen.'

A green-eyed boy with a mop of brown curls popped into her mind. 'My full name is Elowen,' she said, 'but my friends call me Ellie.'

'Well, Tink only used his real name at his college graduation; even the lecturers called him by his nickname. That's where we met. He was doing agriculture, I was studying aquaculture – fish farming. Seems funny now, such a lot has happened.'

'And you've been together ever since?' She filled a saucer with the disgusting fishy paste.

'I went into the navy for four years afterwards, but yes, we stayed in touch. How about you?'

Leo. She sat down and picked up her cup. 'I've got a flat in London. I share it with my boyfriend. Once the cottage is ready to sell, we can put a deposit down on a house closer to our jobs.'

'Nice.' Her voice was subdued. 'You must be missing him. When are you going back?'

'Not for a while,' she said, the words coming out bleak and hard. 'It's a stupid technicality of the will. I'm supposed to live here for at least a year before it's mine.'

Corinne looked astonished. 'Why would Patience do that?'

'I have no idea. Everyone tells me what a nice person she was, but I don't understand why I have to stay here. It's damp, the kitchen is a nightmare, there's no indoor bathroom and there are mice.' The words tumbled out in frustration.

Corinne looked calmly back at her.

'Well, she was the brightest, kindest person I knew. She clearly has a plan for you.'

Ellie sorted through magazines and articles Patience had decided to store, and it turned out she had been a real Second World War buff. Ellie wondered if there was a museum that would want the materials. Her family must have lived through a lot of hardship, and Patience had kept a comprehensive archive on how the islands kept going despite redeployed fishing boats, lack of food imports and sightings of German ships and submarines. A garrison and a small group of spotter planes on St Brannock's waged war on the U-boats that sank freighters and trawlers all along the Atlantic coast.

The sideboard cupboards were still locked, but Patience had kept many personal letters in boxes. A folder from the dresser was a goldmine of information about her teaching work. It contained hundreds of notes and cards from all over the world, all from grateful students. Australia, South Africa, Scotland, America – Ellie read through them, stacking them in piles around her on the floor.

Dear Miss Ellis... She was astonished at the warmth Patience had generated. She must have had a gift for unlocking the potential of these kids. *I never would have graduated/enjoyed reading/become a doctor or professor or mathematician without your encouragement and inspiration...*

They recalled night-time walks to look at stars and planets through a telescope, lighting bonfires to warn ships about the Armada, camping in the fields to watch shooting stars or owls or bats. They recalled the time Catriona got mosquito bites and Michael got stuck in the fence. She taught them to swim, enjoy nature, study science and create art.

Ellie could feel tears building as she thought about the difference between her academically focused school and these children's experiences. She was triggered by flashes of memories: looking at the stars from an old telescope, the smell of baking on a floured apron, identifying birds from old books. *Nana Pat.*

A battered box file was covered with stuck-on flower pictures and marked, simply, 'Ysa'. Ellie hesitated, feeling pressure in her chest; she was almost frightened to open it. The box was warm from the sun, inviting her to fall into the past. She lifted the lid.

It was full of papers and photographs. Right at the top was a picture of a beautiful young girl, maybe in her teens, looking off to the side and laughing at someone. She wore her pale curls short, just a mop, probably very fashionable at that time. It was a big photo and taken before it was properly focused, just a joyous moment where she looked like she was still moving. Ellie's eyes welled up, a knot loosening somewhere in her chest. She could hear her mother's voice, light and musical.

'Elowen, look...'

There were more pictures from Ysella's past, little black and white ones and a few brightly coloured school photos. Patience was often at her side, her own blonde curls almost white, cropped short like a man's haircut. She opened school reports, exam certificates, hand-drawn cards to 'Mummy', all Ysella's.

In the middle of the pile was a large envelope, and she was shocked to see her father's blunt, black handwriting. The address had been scored into the paper, almost cutting it. The postmark was about six months after Ellie's mum had died. The packet had been opened, and the contents slipped into her hands: a pile of envelopes of all sizes and colours. They were all glued shut, and were addressed to Elowen Roberts in the same neat hand. She was sure she'd never seen them before. She took a deep breath, and started to open them.

> *My dearest Elowen, I hardly know what to say to comfort you. I hope you will have a wonderful birthday and I hope to see you soon. I think about you and Mummy every day, love to you, my darling girl. Nana Patience.*

There was a card with a child sailing in a little yacht, and inside, a crisp five pound note.

She opened letter after letter, all postmarked 2003 and early 2004: pocket money, a Christmas present (a child's book of astronomy, which she would have loved), little chatty letters. Under all the letters there was a large sheet of paper in her father's hand.

> *Please do not attempt to communicate with the child. She is already deeply distressed, and a psychiatrist has advised that she should concentrate on new friendships and school. Any association with her mother's memory causes intense grief and is best, on medical advice, avoided.*

She was stunned into paralysis, her chest frozen with pain. Her mother, and Nana Patience... She remembered that they were suddenly gone, wrenched away with the sunlit days of childhood. Her distress had been amplified by feeling abandoned by the island people, as well as the agony of missing her mother every day. She had buried Morwen Island with Ysella, and covered it with grief and rage.

Under the package were more pictures. Ellie on Ysa's lap, as a toddler. Children at a birthday party: two little boys and herself competing to blow out four candles. Tink. She remembered the younger boy now, and his bossy older sister. Tink was the little one who followed them around, got dunked in the paddling pool, was tied up and bawled to be rescued, who climbed onto the wall and fell into the field behind – the very field his sheep were now roaming in.

She looked around. *This is where I was last happy as a child.* Her sadness leached away, to be replaced with anger at her misguided and selfish father. He must have been jealous of Patience's influence over Ysella and Ellie, and lashed out after she died.

She put her arms across her stomach, suddenly cold, and tears started to come.

I will never forgive him.

14

7 MAY 1945

I shall be right as rain afterwards, Mam had promised.

But she was never well again, and Susie never came home to the island for the holidays. By the time Patience was fourteen, school had become a sanctuary of peaceful study from the nursing, housework and cooking at home. She decided to leave her plans to train as a teacher behind. Her duty was clearly at home. Mam was mostly confined to a chair or her bed and Dad had taken to drink when he could get it. When drunk, he shouted at everyone, including his sick wife.

Mam still loved to talk, and they often sat in the kitchen, Patience cooking a casserole and baking some bread or scones for the boys, or frying fish if Dad had brought some home. Dutch had faded from their lives, although occasionally Patience got snippets of news about him. It was just something else she had lost from her bright childhood memories.

The trawler went out less and less, partly because Dad couldn't get fuel or help. Money was so tight Patience had to get a job in the cannery, gutting pilchards when they came in. Like everything else, the fish were in short supply. She loathed the stink on her skin and hair, and it lingered no matter how often she washed.

Patience walked out along the quay, striding up to the southern lookout as she did most evenings. She passed the last cottage on Long Lane and went to sit on the rock in front of the coastguard cottages. She wrapped her arms around her drawn-up knees, her sandals flat on the slope. It felt as if she could slide forward and fall to the sea below.

When she looked up from staring over at the endless water, Dutch was standing there. Something felt different. He was lanky as always, his dark eyes narrowed against the sun on the horizon. She noticed the breadth of his shoulders, the muscles in his forearms below his rolled-up shirtsleeves. Her heart jumped and her throat went tight.

He sat down beside her, his shoulder brushing hers. Her mouth curled into a smile by itself.

'Your father said you were up here.' His dark hair was almost black in the evening light. His gaze travelled over her face. 'You've changed.'

'Well, I'm grown up now,' she said, leaning her cheek on her knees to look up at him, squinting into the sunlight. 'Why are you here?'

'I came to tell you the war's over,' he said, holding out his hand. 'It's over, finally, in Europe anyway. They said so on the radio. All I could think of was telling you.'

Patience stared at his fingers, her insides feeling hollow, the elation gone. 'I suppose you'll go home now.'

He shrugged. 'Where is home, really?' he asked, dropping his hand. 'I don't know any more. I can hardly remember. Even Groningen.' He grinned at her. 'I can't believe you made all that up.'

'Better than the whole island wondering if you were

German,' she replied, feeling angry when she should be happy. But the end of the war wouldn't put Mam and Dad back where they had been before the war, it wouldn't bring Joseph and Susie home. 'Mam said you were courting a girl on St Brannock's,' she said, hearing the jealous note in her voice.

'No girls,' he said. 'I don't plan to settle down yet. I'd like to have my own ship one day.'

She looked east towards the misty shapes of the distant islands. 'I don't want to get married either.' She stretched her feet flat and looked at them. 'I wanted to be a teacher like Miss Cartwright, and go travelling to places like Italy and France in my holidays. I thought I would, after everything goes back to normal.'

'The war isn't over yet in Asia.' He leaned forward. 'I think nothing will go back to the way it was.' He looked sad when she glanced at him. 'Germany, the Netherlands, Belgium – they are badly hurt.' He shook his head. 'And the Jews...'

'Some came to England, at the beginning. There are a few in Plymouth. We raised money for them at school.'

'The news is terrible,' he said, tears in his eyes, making them glisten. 'People are starving and homeless. It is hard to fight a war, and even harder to lose one.'

Patience felt held in the tiny jewel of an island far from anything. Sometimes things were difficult, fish were scarce, money was tight. Patience hardly ever had new clothes or books, but there was always food on the table. She couldn't imagine what it would be like to go hungry, day after day.

'Maybe you should stay. You could save up and buy a share in a fishing boat.'

He shook his head, his shoulder bumping hers. 'They won't want me once the men come home from the war.' He sounded so sad Patience felt a lump form in her throat. 'I will just be "that foreigner".'

'You're *our* "foreigner".' She leaned against him. 'You could help Dad. He's sick.'

'I know what hurts him.' He frowned now. 'He worries about your mother.'

'But drinking doesn't make him better, and now we don't have money for the doctor.' The drawer where Mam kept the housekeeping money was down to a few shillings and a handful of copper for the boys.

'But the doctor keeps coming,' he said. 'The fishermen's mission pays for her medicine.' He sighed. 'He's a proud man – charity hurts, too.'

'If she gets any thinner, she will die,' she whispered, afraid to even say the words. 'She's only forty-three.'

'You must go to college and become teacher,' he said. 'A good teacher, and live on the island and work at the school.'

Patience looked away. 'I can't. There's too much to do. I have to look after Mam and the boys. And we can't afford the college fees, anyway.'

'You will find a way to go. If you really want something, you will makes it happen.'

'*Make* it happen,' she said, 'not makes.'

'Yes,' he said. '*We* will make it happen.'

15

PRESENT DAY, 23 MARCH

Ellie didn't sleep well after reading the letters her father had kept from her. She was filled with rage, grief maybe. There was love there, too; love betrayed, because she had trusted him. After a restless night, she fell asleep only to be woken by a banging on the front door, rattling the bedroom window.

She pulled on a dressing gown and shuffled down the stairs.

'I'm coming!' she shouted. She unlocked the door and wrenched it open. 'Do you know what the time is?'

'Eight fifteen. You wanted a quote for your bramble fest?'

Emotion overwhelmed her as she recognised the brown curly hair and merry face of the boy in the photos.

'Tink!' she cried, and when she held out a hand he grabbed it and pulled her into a hug.

'I didn't think you'd remember me,' he said, laughing, thumping Ellie on the back before letting her go.

'I've been going through old pictures.' She stared at him, at his stubbly beard and bright green eyes. 'You grew up.'

'Yep, that's me, twenty-eight next birthday. You're invited, if you pay for the drinks.' He pushed past Ellie into the hall. 'Sorry about the old lady. I loved her, you know? She was the best auntie ever. But the garden got pretty overgrown in the last few years. She didn't care, said it was good for the wildlife.' He walked through the kitchen and opened the back door. 'Yep, brilliant for wildlife. You can hardly see the wall.'

'Can you sort it out? I mean, I can pay. Some, anyway.'

Tink turned and grinned, the same broad smile she remembered from childhood. 'I would love to say don't bother, but me and Corinne are broke at the moment. I'm having to do the odd shift on the family boat and I hate it.'

'I thought your family were born to work on the sea? You were always in it, or on it, as I remember.' She had found photographs of a trip around the islands with Tink, Patience and her mother. She must have been eight or nine, and they fished for mackerel which overflowed from a basket at her feet. She could still remember the cold, metallic shininess of them.

'Shallow seas, sure. Oceanic fishing, no. I'm trying to farm the land but it's uphill, no pun intended. I have a small flock from another farmer. I bring his ewes over for the spring and summer, and we share the profits of the lambing. We've got a polytunnel up in the field and no-dig veg beds. We're mostly supplying the pub and the hotel, but we've just got a contract for micro-herbs and greens for a restaurant on West Isle.' Tink pushed at the ten-foot shrub that was growing out of the cracked concrete patch behind the house, making it sway. 'Nice big elder. I can get rid of that so you can get to the shed. It used to be full of Dutch's stuff.'

Dutch. That name again. Ellie filled the kettle and put it on the only electric ring that reliably worked. 'I'm making some coffee. Do you want some?'

'Sure. Go and get dressed, I'll make it.'

Ellie pulled on fresh clothes upstairs and wondered how she was going to do laundry. She'd already been reduced to washing underwear, socks and a couple of T-shirts in cold water and washing up liquid.

By the time she got back downstairs, Tink had helped himself to mugs and made coffee for them both.

'Milk?' he asked, raising an eyebrow and taking the bottle off the windowsill.

'Thanks.' Ellie sat at the dining-room table and pulled on her thickest socks. 'So, how much to beat the jungle out there?'

Tink raised his coffee cup. 'A hundred quid and I'll shred and mulch the lot for you. Corinne's the plantswoman. She can advise you on what's a plant and what's a weed. I just do what I'm told.'

'That would be great, thank you.'

They drank in silence for a minute. Finally, something Tink had said registered with Ellie. 'You mentioned Dutch? I've heard a bit about him and I've seen pictures.'

'Oh, yes. It was sort of an open secret that Dutch and Patience were an item. They hid it pretty well when she was working as a teacher, but once she retired, they weren't so discreet. Either that or he was too old to walk down the hill. My mother used to say he slept up here most days in the years before he died.'

Ellie got the silver-framed photo off the dresser. 'Is this Dutch?'

'Yeah, that's him. Lovely old bloke. He used to collect model trains, and he let me and my sister play with them. Patience was my great-aunt, you know. My Grandad Clem's older sister.'

'I'm not sure I'm related to her at all,' Ellie said quietly. 'My mother was adopted, but there are no papers.'

'You need to talk to Grandad Clem. I think he knows more than anyone else.' He sipped some more coffee. 'Which reminds me – and this is Corinne wanting to know – did you really ask Bran out?'

Ellie smiled. 'Yes, but only to annoy his father.'

'That will be Joe. He used to run the Island Queen but he had a stroke, so he got Branok back from London to run the place and look after him. Bran hates it. He left a successful career as an artist behind.' He put his cup down on the table, grinning. 'So, you're not going, then?'

'Oh, I'm going,' Ellie said. 'Just not on a date. I need to do some shopping. Clean clothes, some things for the kitchen. By the way, do you and Corinne have a washing machine I could run a few things through?'

Tink laughed. 'You really don't get this micro-farming lark, do you? Corinne and I live in the back of a converted army lorry and earn almost nothing. We take our dirty clothes down to the pub, until the laundrette opens at the campsite at Easter. Ask Bran, he'll do a load for you, clean and dry for five quid.'

Ellie was astonished. 'You're living in a lorry?'

Tink shrugged. 'There's a bit of an old barn in the back field. We're hoping to get planning permission to convert it into a house one day. The truck was left over from the war – we just tarted it up and converted it into a campervan.'

'I'll have to come and have a look.'

'Any time. Actually, if you're going to be around for a few months... We have a tiny volunteer fire service, just a water tank, a shipping container with our gear in and a training programme. We need volunteers, you could help us out.'

Ellie could feel the hairs on the back of her neck prickle. 'I'm not really hero material.'

'And I am? You're young and healthy, and you're here all the time. We have two others besides me: Ed and Lolly. Have you met Lolly, proper name Loveday? Ex-lifeboat crew, genius firefighter, helps up at the school and teaches canoeing. But seriously, mostly we put out chip-pan fires and bonfires, deal with the odd gas incident and install smoke alarms in holiday cottages. We pumped out a flooded basement last year, too.'

Ellie couldn't help smiling at his enthusiasm. 'I'll think about it. But, I warn you, my idea of fitness is running paperwork through the shredder.'

'The training will be a workout, then.' Tink stood up. 'It's great to see you again. Look, maybe at the weekend we could all go out for dinner at the hotel, really catch up? You should get to know Corinne, she's amazing.'

'I'd like that,' Ellie said, a warm feeling spreading. Most of her social circle was made up of Leo's associates, but this was a proper old friend she had known from childhood. 'I'll even pay for the wine, as it will be your twenty-eighth birthday.'

'I'd love to say it is, but it's in August,' Tink said, grinning.

'Early present for old times' sake.'

'I might let you,' Tink said, 'for old times' sake. You should bring Bran,' he added at the door, a sly grin on his face. 'Since you two are *dating*.'

16

By the time Patience was twenty-two, she had trained as a teacher. Her mother was buried in the churchyard, her dad was stern faced and sober, and her brothers were growing up. Thanks to scholarships organised by the grammar school and the teacher training college, she had been able to take an accelerated programme to help meet the shortfall in new teachers after the war.

After two years as a probationary teacher, she obtained a post in a girls' school in Taunton, living in accommodation attached to the school. There were other young teachers staying there; some had been land girls or worked in munitions. The saddest were the ones from the families that had been torn apart by the bombings, or evacuated from their homes.

When she visited the island she rarely saw Dutch, who was working on the deep-sea trawlers off the north coast of England. But every time she received a letter from him, her heart still skipped a beat.

She travelled home via Penzance for each school holiday, her hands sweaty and dusty from the train, her hair smelling of coal and steam as she reached the ferry. This time, the first person she saw, in a smart purser's uniform, was Dutch. She swayed with shock, a smile bubbling out.

'Dutch! I thought you were in Whitby!'

'I'm back. Welcome aboard the *Islander II*,' he said, his smile widening to a grin. 'Let's get you home.'

Patience caught her breath. Dutch had always been tall, but now he had filled out. His dark hair had grown longer, too, and she was suddenly shy. He held out his hand.

'Mind the gangway,' he said softly.

She put her hand in his strong fingers, feeling the familiar shock of his skin. She was back in the cottage's cold bedroom for a second, listening to the fire crackle and his rasping breaths, holding a glass for the half-drowned boy.

He steadied her as she stepped onto the gangway.

'Thank you.' Her voice sounded like a little girl's.

He let go slowly. 'I will come and find you, once we sail,' he said, his voice soft.

She nodded, and found a seat on deck, resting her ankles on her leather case. The wind was blustery and she kept her coat on. She could still feel the tingle of his fingers on her skin.

Dutch. How long had she loved him? He had been her closest friend somehow, all through the war and beyond, through all the changes in their lives. And she held his secrets, all the things she knew about him and some of the things she suspected. During the last few years she had thought she was cold to men, holding herself a little aloof from her friends' brothers. She had started to think she was like Miss Cartwright, destined to be an educator rather than a wife or mother. But, now and then, she would take in a feature film with a friend and be carried away by the romances, the love stories that made her wonder what it would be like to be swept off her feet, maybe by Dutch leaning in to kiss—

'Patsy.' He sat beside her, so close she could smell his soap and hair pomade.

'It's good to see you.' She leaned back so she could really see him. He had a few deep creases in his tanned face now, from squinting into the sun.

'I have been waiting for weeks to see you. Ever since your father said you would come home for the summer.' His smile faded. 'Your mother would have been so proud of you.'

'I think she would.' She missed her mother's letters; now she only got notes from the boys, or the occasional message from her father. 'How is Dad?'

'He will be happy to see you.' He looked away, as if he was trying to find the words to tell her something.

Patience grabbed his sleeve and shook it. 'Tell me, Dutch. I need to know. Is he drinking again?'

'No, nothing like that.' He put a warm hand over hers. 'But he is seeing a woman in St Piran's. A nice woman, a war widow.'

Patience felt the world swirl around her head. She gasped like a landed fish. 'My mother...'

'Has been dead five years,' he said, squeezing her fingers before letting go. 'A long time to be alone.'

She stared out over the rippling ocean, dark in the shadow of a few clouds, blue in other, a shade darker than the sky. 'What about the boys?'

'They seem to like her,' he said. 'They love her pies. Her brother is the butcher on the big island, so they get extra meat.'

Patience liked the idea that her father was at least well fed. 'I know I shouldn't be jealous...'

'Look,' he said, pointing over the water, the ship stretching out its lead against the tide now, away from the harbour. A few grey shapes surged out of the water ahead of the bows.

She smiled. 'Oh, I missed the dolphins. What do you call them?'

'*Dolfijnen*,' he said, 'in Dutch.' He turned serious. '*Delfine* in German.'

'And *morhogh* in Cornish,' she added.

'Yes,' he said, smiling again. '*Morhogh*.' He even rolled his tongue correctly.

She leaned against his side, sheltered from the wind.

17

PRESENT DAY, 25 MARCH

On Friday morning, Ellie walked across the quay to go shopping on the big island with Bran. She shrugged the collar of her wool coat around her ears against a wind that was coming across the Sound between the islands. The sun was up, but it had little warmth. She couldn't see the ferry yet.

Bran was waiting by the timetable board outside the pub, and gave a little wave when he saw her. She had decided to wear heels today, knee-high boots in black leather. Not the easiest to wear on the cobbles, but she had fancied dressing up.

He was dressed smartly, too, in crumpled chinos and a shirt under his padded jacket. She said so, and he laughed.

'I'm running out of clean clothes,' she said, looking up at him.

He frowned a bit. 'Oh, for goodness' sake, Elowen! Bring them around to the pub, run them through our commercial machine. It's quick and I don't charge much. We do half a dozen people's laundry in the winter.'

She hesitated. 'It just seems strange getting someone else to wash my stuff.'

Bran looked over the water. 'You could redesign your

kitchen over time. Get a washer-dryer.' He waved at Maggi waiting for the post bag and walked over to the ferry landing.

'I was wondering if they do hot drinks on the ferry,' she asked.

'Not today.' She followed his pointing finger to the tiny red and black speck chugging towards the island. She could feel herself pale.

'That's not a ferry. That's smaller than the boat John brought me over in.'

'Well, he was just available on his way home. If he hadn't been, you'd have been stuck on the big island all night.' Four teenagers turned onto the quay and gave them a wave. 'Some of our local kids are doing college interviews this week.'

As the ferry approached it looked even worse and its red paint was streaked with rust. The pilot brought the boat along-side the quay and tied it up. One of the teenagers jumped forward to help, looping a rope over a bollard. The pilot carried a post bag up, and handed it to Maggi.

'Thank you, Birdie.' Maggi turned to Ellie. 'I hear you two are off to have lunch somewhere. I can recommend the Slipway Bar. Pete and I always went there for the fish of the day.'

Bran smiled and glanced at Ellie. 'Very romantic.'

Ellie laughed, but her cheeks heated up anyway. 'No, we're just doing some shopping.'

The young people scampered over to the boat and stepped aboard via the lurching gunwale, sitting on the bench seats.

Ellie stared at the pitching ferry. 'There isn't room for us, surely.' She turned to Birdie. 'Seriously. How many people are you allowed to take?'

Bran laughed at her nerves. 'There's loads of room. Budge up, kids.'

He placed one foot on the side of the boat, then trod down the two steps into the ferry. He sat next to the students and moved up to leave room for Ellie. 'Come on, it's fine. It's pretty calm today.'

Birdie reached a hand out to Ellie. 'We're licensed for eight,' he said, grinning. 'Eight fat ones.'

Ellie slipped on the bottom step and ended up half falling onto Bran's lap, but he pushed her onto the seat and patted her arm. 'See? Loads of room.'

She looked over her shoulder at the water, which was two feet down from the edge of the boat. 'OK,' she said. 'If you say so.'

'I've never sunk the ferry, or ended up in the water and drowned everyone yet,' Birdie said kindly.

'Hang on to my rucksack,' Bran said, rummaging in his pocket for money. 'I'll pay for us both this way, you can pay on the way back.'

Birdie cast off at the stern, revved up the engine, and one of the girls unhooked a rope at his command. Bran passed a bank note to the boatman.

Ellie started to smile. 'I was thinking of a cosy seat in a saloon, and a morning latte.'

He laughed. 'The ferries run for the tourists are much bigger but, honestly, no coffee or saloons. A bit of shelter if it's raining, that's all.' One of the kids had a large art folder, which caught his attention. 'How are you guys this morning?'

A slim girl with a huge smile and flying plaits grinned at him. Ellie recognised her as one of the waitresses from the Quay Kitchen. 'I'm escorting this motley bunch over to the mainland for college interviews.'

'Is that your portfolio, Connie? Can I see it?'

Connie nodded, and passed it over. Bran unzipped the leather case. The colour palette she had used was lovely, high-lighted by the yellows and pinks in the morning sky.

'Wow,' Ellie said, staring at each page as Bran slowly turned them.

'I'm hoping to study fine art with printmaking,' Connie said to Ellie.

'That really reminds me of the view from the cottage,' Ellie said, staring at one print.

The shape of the roofs echoed the heaving, restless sea, and Connie had captured the current that went against the tide close in to shore. The islands beyond looked like fog banks floating on the water.

'It's a screen print,' Connie said. 'From the ridge behind your house.'

'It's beautiful,' Ellie said. 'I'd love to buy it.'

'I'm just showing my portfolio at the art college,' she said. 'Nothing's really finished yet.'

Bran looked up. 'Be ready to talk about process as well as materials and design, and don't be too specific about outcome. It could be your first commission sale.'

Connie smiled. 'I'd love that, but I wouldn't know what to charge. I'm just a student.'

'Two hundred quid is fair,' Bran said, sliding a glance at Ellie. 'Say, one pound a square inch divided by two because you're a student, but it is hand printed. It's a bargain. Elk would frame it for you for another eighty or so. One day a signed print from Constance Chenoweth could be worth thousands. What do you say, Ellie?'

Connie had gone bright pink with pleasure. Ellie grinned at her. 'OK. It can hang over the mantelpiece, cover up the faded bit of wallpaper.'

'Pete's picture used to hang over the fire,' Bran said, passing the portfolio back. 'What happened to it?'

'Patience wanted Maggi to have it.'

She looked back at the island, growing smaller as the wake curved away. When she looked back, they were chugging in the currents around the end of the Sound, and close to the island opposite. A few cottages were scattered along a path but there was no quay on this side.

'That's St Petroc's?' she said, leaning forward.

'Yes. They have a lovely beach, you'll see it when we round that stack. It's called Kettle Rock, but it's lethal if shipping comes in at night.' A column of stone soared out of the water, with a few broken boulders at its base. One grey shape moved, turned its head to look at her with black, liquid eyes.

Ellie pointed. 'Look!'

'Grey seals,' Bran told her. 'They're just finishing their breeding season, so we only get a few, but they love that spot. They can fall into the water there and be carried right to their breeding beach at the right time of the tide.'

As they rounded the rocks, Ellie could see the longer coastline of the big island in the distance, a few blotches of colour, ships tied up along the quay. The higgledy-piggledy houses were stacked in tiers up the hill.

'The port's bigger than I expected,' she said, as the boat wove between buoys towards St Brannock's.

'It has to serve all the islands,' he said. 'Our supplies and the tourists need to be able to get here.'

It took several more minutes to make the approach to the landing pier.

When they stepped onto dry land Bran laughed at her relief. 'Do you still want that latte? I know a great place, opens early.'

She agreed, and he led her through quaint, crowded streets.

A car horn made her flatten herself against a wall as a delivery van crawled past. 'I'd almost forgotten cars,' she said.

'This isn't too bad. Penzance is always a culture shock for me when I get there.'

'You know a lot about art,' she said, as they walked past the tiny shops on the hill.

'I studied Fine Art at Goldsmiths,' he said curtly. 'I ended up doing ceramics for a while.'

He didn't elaborate. 'What happened?' she asked, finally, as he pushed the café door open.

He shrugged his jacket onto the back of a chair and sat. 'I was building a career,' he said. 'Then my dad had a stroke, so I took a couple of months off to help him and somehow it was six months and then a year and the moment was gone. It's over.'

She didn't seem to be able to stop herself. 'Over, how?'

'You get one chance at a gallery show alongside a world-famous artist, and that's it. I sold most of my pieces so I had nothing left to show, my marriage folded, I moved back. That's it.'

'I'm sorry. I didn't know you were married before.'

'Briefly.' He winced a little smile.

She looked down at the menu. 'Sorry. I'm being nosy, I know. You're managing the pub and you do it brilliantly.'

'Well, I was brought up to it,' he said lightly. 'I was born there.'

She took a deep breath. 'Which reminds me. Tink suggested you might like to join him and Corinne for dinner at the hotel. With me, obviously. Just as friends.'

His ears went pink when he was embarrassed, which was endearing.

'Corinne already invited me. I think Tink's hoping I will come in case you talk all evening about fashion and shoes.' He grinned. 'Which you won't, but it would be good to get away from work. Especially with the pub up for sale.'

'Really? I had no idea.'

Bran took his time answering. 'I'm just waiting for Dad to finally accept an offer and then I'm gone,' he said, with a crisp snap in his voice. 'And I'm *never* coming back.'

18

14 AUGUST 1953

Three weeks later Patience sat, her ankles crossed and tucked under the chair like the Queen, in front of the school board on Morwen. She had been the only candidate and she knew she had answered the committee's questions well.

The head of the board smiled at her. 'Well, we are all agreed that you are an excellent candidate, and we are happy to offer you the position. Even if you are a little younger than we expected.'

'I am twenty-two. And there is a national shortage of teachers,' Patience said.

The mousy secretary, Miss Plumley, nodded. 'How wonderful to have one of our own students taking over the school.'

There was a smattering of applause as Patience smiled politely. Inside, she was so happy she wanted to shout it out. Maybe kick off her shoes, run down to the harbour and tell Dad. She resisted.

'I will do my very best, Governor Wenstead.' The head of the school board always liked his title being used. He was the most prominent cannery owner on the islands and one of the most prosperous employers. Decades before, he had been educated at one of the tiny island schools.

She smoothed her head, to flatten any unruly hairs. She had started braiding it and pinning it close when she got her first job as a teacher. She almost wished she had glasses to hide behind, to look older.

'Now, the terms,' he said. 'As advertised, we normally supply the schoolhouse, but since you are presently living in your father's house...?'

'I will need the schoolhouse,' she said. 'My father is about to remarry and is living with my three brothers. I will need time and space to create lessons, prepare materials and make written reports.'

'Of course, of course.' He glanced at Miss Plumley. 'We did think the cottage might be used to house local families...'

'It is only two rooms,' Patience replied, clutching her hands together to keep her voice firm and level. 'It has been the teacher's accommodation for many years. Indeed, the salary reflects it, and it was mentioned in the advertisement.'

She knew the school board could barely afford her wages as it was. 'Very well, as you wish,' Wenstead said. 'We just thought, as you are so young, that living alone might be... lonely.'

Lonely? Spending time with eleven children would leave her little time to indulge in loneliness. 'I should relish the challenge of the position even more, and Miss Cartwright found it helpful to live so close to the school.'

The board looked at each other, exchanging glances and pursing lips, which made Patience even more curious about why the previous teacher had left. Of course, she was of retirement age.

'We are very aware of your youth.' Miss Plumley said. 'And of your reputation, as a young woman living alone...'

'I assure you, I am a respectable woman, whether I live

alone or not,' Patience said, knowing her face was glowing pink. She couldn't wait to be alone to read, to watch the wildlife, to gaze up at the night sky. 'I was accustomed to lodging alone at my previous post.'

'Of course,' Mr Wenstead said, looking at the other members of the board. 'So, that's settled. We hope you can take up your post in plenty of time for the September term, and the cottage will be ready for your use from the end of August.'

Two weeks later, Patience carried the first of her boxes of books into the cottage. It smelled damp; the new whitewash on the walls was probably still drying. The roof had needed repairing, too. But the furniture was very familiar, and Miss Cartwright's books were in pride of place on the large bookcase. The governors hadn't replaced the curtains but her mother's sewing machine, carried up by her brothers the previous day, should sort that out.

'Here, maid,' her father said, puffing up behind her with a tea chest, 'what've you put in here, lead weights?'

'Just a bit of china and my telescope,' she said.

The instrument, although second-hand, had been a gift from her previous school and was very precious. She had bought an old microscope, too, and hoped to enhance the teaching of science on the island, a subject Miss Cartwright had mostly overlooked.

'Maybe you'll be able to see the fish coming in,' he grumbled. 'Haven't had a good catch in weeks. Mostly saithe and flatties.'

'People are glad of any fresh fish,' she said, getting out of the way for Clem, now fifteen, who was carrying her box of treasures from childhood. Mam had always said the children needed somewhere private of their own, so all of her brothers and sister had one, hand-made by her grandfather. She wondered if Susie still had hers in her hospital.

'Well, if the catch don't improve, we'll be selling the boat to pay the bills,' he grumbled. She knew he was joking; he'd rather sell the house, but it wouldn't come to that.

'The new allowance will help,' she said, knowing the islands had signed up to National Assistance.

'Aye, well, we'll see.' He looked around the small room. 'This is it, then? You'd have company if you stayed with us. Missus would be glad to have you. She'll be outnumbered, especially with her own boys as well as mine.'

It was a kind thought, but Patience knew he hardly had room for the family as it was.

'She's very kind, but I will visit regularly,' she said. 'But this is where I can work, as well as live. I have to get up early to light the stove in the school, and stay up late marking books.'

He leaned his head to look up the stairs. 'Bedroom, I suppose?'

Patience led the way up to the simple room, just a square yard of landing and a door. She was surprised to see Miss Cartwright must have taken the bed, because a new, narrow cot filled the space over the stairs and a chest of drawers was tucked under the window. A few empty hangers rested on a hook on the back of the door.

'It's simple and clean,' she said to her father. 'It's all I need.'

He grunted some sort of agreement and bent to look out of the window. 'You need curtains, my lovey,' he said. 'You don't want the children seeing you in your skimpies.'

'I have linen,' she said primly. 'I will make some.' She looked at him again. 'Pa, can you tell me what the big secret is about Miss Cartwright?'

'Ha. Well, I don't think you need to know.'

'Of course I do,' she said. 'Teachers learns all sorts of secrets.

Children tell us everything,' she prompted him. 'Henpecked husbands, unmarried mothers, beaten wives, criminal pasts—'

'All right, all right.' He sat on a chair she hadn't noticed, in the corner of the room. 'We all thought she were a single lady, her betrothed killed in the first war. She had his picture up in the parlour, you recall.'

Patience did remember, although she had never asked about it. She had always imagined it was her brother. 'Was she?'

'Maybe so, maybe not,' he said, placing his scarred and stained hands on his knees. 'But she had friends, lady friends who came to stay. *Slept over*,' he added for emphasis.

'Well, that was all right, wasn't it?' Patience frowned at what he was trying and failing to tell her. 'I remember Miss Bright, she was nice. She took us on nature walks sometimes. She knew the names of all the butterflies.'

'There was only one bed,' he said, tapping the side of his nose.

Patience couldn't see the problem. 'It was a big bed.' Experience of the girls' dorm unfolded in her mind and she couldn't help smiling. 'You mean, they were... affectionate?'

'Well, we weren't there to watch, but the landlord of the Mermaid's Purse saw them kissing after too many sherries one Christmas.'

Patience could feel a bubble of laughter expanding in her chest. 'Oh, Dad,' she said.

'You may find it funny,' he said, 'but it's unnatural, and her looking after kiddies.'

'I'm sure it was quite innocent. I never saw anything untoward.'

'Well, when Miss Bright left and Miss Forge moved in with her trousers and men's jackets, we knew it had to stop.' He nodded to her. 'That's when they advertised the job and told Miss Cartwright that it was time to retire. She was sixty-odd, you know. Hanky-panky at her age.'

That made Patience laugh out loud. 'I can assure you, there will be no hanky-panky when *I'm* in charge.'

His smile faded. 'I always thought you carried a bit of a torch for Dutch. Just a girlish fancy. Your mother thought there was something there.'

Her heart lurched for just a second. 'I'm a grown woman now, Dad,' she said quietly. 'I'm not worrying about all that nonsense now.'

'Only, your sister won't have children, and with Joseph gone and William is in the sanatorium... I was hoping to have a grandchild or two.'

She smiled at him. 'There will be time for that. Clem is courting already. And William and Freddie have lots of time to settle down. Who knows, in five years I might meet a nice man and give up teaching.'

He nodded, stood up and patted her on the shoulder on his way to the landing.

'Well, you're pretty enough, even if you do tie your hair up tight as fish in a net. Your mam would be proud of you,' he said, looking back. 'You've turned into a proper lady.'

Patience smiled, even though her heart had taken a little skip when he had mentioned Dutch.

19

PRESENT DAY, 25 MARCH

The following morning, Ellie's kitchen looked a lot brighter with an electric kettle and a toaster, even if they did trip the electrics if they were on at the same time. Bran had known all the shops, and had been a charming companion. They'd spent a lot of time laughing, and he'd helped carry the bundle of linens she'd bought.

'A microwave's out, then,' she said to the mouse, who was scratching behind the sink somewhere.

The cat stretched, and walked out of the open back door to the garden. Tink had done an amazing job, clearing it right down to the wall and throwing the branches, some several metres long and covered with huge barbs, over into the field. Corinne had fed it through a noisy chipping machine, releasing clouds of blue smoke and the stink of fuel.

The revealed outbuilding was the size of a double garage, and the corrugated roof had collapsed against the stone wall at the back. It was padlocked and one edge of the door was reinforced with a heavy metal strip. Tink had left a few heavy items, like bolt cutters and a crowbar, and had offered to help, but Ellie felt a strange impulse to tackle it herself. Maybe she was protecting Patience's privacy, she reasoned, since everyone thought so highly of her.

The cat leapt onto the wall and watched her attack the padlock with the bolt cutters. Finally, she creaked one half open, scraping over the concrete, and the morning sunlight poured onto a pile of old blankets and tarps.

She dragged layer after layer off until several mouldy boxes and containers were revealed. Beside them were the headlight and handlebars of an old motorbike. When she dusted off the nameplate, she could see it was called a Vincent, a make she didn't know. It seemed like a vintage bike, but it was clean of rust except where the metalwork had been exposed at the back. The leather saddle was well worn, split in one place, with horse-hair erupting out.

The name had sparked a memory and she went back indoors to consult the list of individual bequests. *Mitchell, Vincent.* Who was Mitchell? She decided to take a break from working to ask Lucy some questions.

She was halfway down the lane before she remembered she hadn't locked the front door.

The café was full inside, so Ellie was shown to a table in the garden surrounded by spring flowers and a few trees in blossom. Lucy bustled out to take her order.

'Do you know someone called Mitchell?' Ellie asked.

'Do you mean Mitch Tate? Everyone calls him Elk. He lives right on the north corner of the island. He's more a pub person, so we don't see him in here much. Amy knows him better than I do – ask her.' She paused, as if trying to find the right words. 'His bark is worse than his bite but he would do anything for Patience. He was one of her pallbearers. Tell him you're her heiress if he's a bit unfriendly.'

Amy came out with her food and coffee. She always seemed shy but came to life when she started talking about Elk.

'He was in a famous band in the eighties, called Case Shot. We have all sorts of pop stars visiting him now he makes guitars. He's a bit quiet until you get him talking about music or motorbikes.'

'How do I get to his house?'

'It's not really a house as much as the old canning sheds right down at the bottom of Lighthouse Hill,' she said. 'If you walk past the pub along the shore road towards the hotel, there's a gate on the way, that's Mitch's property. The red door, that's usually where he is. Ignore all the No Trespassing notices.'

'Does he live there?'

Amy smiled. 'Officially he just has a workshop and studio. But I think you'll find he's been sleeping there for years. There aren't enough houses for residents on the island. Don't mind him being rude, he's just not very good with new people.'

Ellie walked along the path Amy had described. Apart from having to keep away from the odd nettle, it was a good track, a stone wall running between her and the sandy beach. Opposite, a barbed wire fence enclosed a triangular field, and beyond it, a corrugated shed had a faded red door next to a row of shacks. A gateway in the fence was jammed shut with a large stone, and Ellie had to ease it away before she could open it. It petered out to little more than a rabbit path towards the buildings.

'Hello?' she called towards the red door, then cleared her throat and tried more loudly. 'Hello!'

A baritone growled from behind the slightly open entrance. 'Leave the package at the gate and go.'

'I'm not delivering anything. I need to ask you something.'

When the man came out of the shack, Ellie was a little less confident. He was the lead singer from the pub, very tall and broad, his belly hanging a little over old jeans covered in paint splashes.

'You're trespassing and I don't like visitors,' Elk growled. Some grey hair straggled down his back in a ponytail, his beard fell onto his chest and a pair of glasses were pushed back on his forehead.

'I'm Elowen Roberts,' Ellie said. 'Patience left me Kittiwake Cottage.'

'Good for you.' The growl had something else in it, curiosity perhaps.

'She mentioned you in her will,' Ellie said.

'Come in and say what you need to say. Then leave me alone. Patience spent the last years of her life obsessing over you, even made me track you on social media so she knew you were OK. You couldn't have picked up the phone or dropped her a letter once you grew up?'

'I didn't remember she existed,' Ellie said softly. 'I mean, I was only nine when my mother died, and my father made it impossible to make contact with her. I hardly remembered my mum, let alone how to find Patience.'

'You were like a grandchild to her. When her daughter died, she lost you as well.'

The uncompromising words made Ellie feel guilty, and angry at the same time. 'Well, whatever. She left you something in her will.'

'I don't need her money,' Elk said, turning to go back in his shack. 'Give it to charity.'

'It isn't money. It's a motorbike. An old one, a Vincent.'

Elk looked at her over his shoulder. 'What?' He shook his head like a wet dog. 'You'd better come in. Just don't touch anything.'

Beyond the shack's rambling exterior was a complete timber cabin, the walls lined with panels of tools, shelves of spray cans and instruments. There were guitars on worktables, hung on the wall, on stands in rows. Two benches, a stool and a keyboard filled the middle of the space, and a curtain half-screened an armchair and a sink.

'Wow.' Ellie could guess at the identity of a few unusual instruments, a lute and maybe a mandolin. 'You make guitars?'

'I'm a luthier, yes. I make a lot of instruments. I've just made my first violin. I've been working on it for a couple of years.'

'Someone said you used to be a musician.'

'I'm still a musician, that doesn't stop. I just don't play in a band for money.' The floor was covered with wood shavings and sawdust. 'I didn't move to the island until Dutch was old. I knew he used to have a bike, but I thought it was long gone. What's it like?'

'It's surprisingly OK,' she said. 'I think it was wrapped up in tarps the whole time.'

Elk waved Ellie to a bench. 'That's so Patience,' he said, and he smiled crookedly, making him look less intimidating. 'So she's got you to hand out her belongings to her friends?'

'I think so,' Ellie said. 'I gave a picture to Maggi already.'

Ellie could only remember a few names but Elk knew some of them.

'Graeme – is that Graeme Hiscock? He's a boatbuilder on the big island now. His kids go to school with my grandson. Lottie could be Charlotte Midwich. She's in a home in Cornwall now. Jayne is probably the teacher at the school.'

'It's hard,' said Ellie. 'Mostly it's just first names.'

'You should ask at the pub. Joe knows almost everyone and he knew who Patience cared about.' He nodded to Ellie. 'I wish you'd come home in time to meet her. She was haunted by Ysella and little Elowen, like they both died together.'

That struck Ellie in the heart. She looked away. 'In some ways, they did.'

20

21 JULY 1954

Every month, Patience made the trip to visit Susannah, and had tea and scones with Dutch in Penzance on the return. Their friendship had blossomed, but they always met in public and sometimes Patience wondered if he was even interested, but then he would look at her in a way that made her heart race.

One morning, not long after her first full year of teaching, Patience received a telegram. The postmistress had decided that with five boys, George Ellis didn't have time for the defective daughter living in a hospital, and all news about Susie came straight to Patience.

WITH REGRET WE MUST TELL YOU SUSANNAH ELLIS DETERIORATING. WOULD URGE IMME-DIATE VISIT. CALL PENZANCE 353.

Thank goodness it was already the holidays. Patience walked swiftly down the hill to the post office to use the phone. After a few minutes, she was put through to the ward.

'We are concerned about Susie's convulsions,' Matron McCaffrey said. 'She had one in the bath a few months ago, so we've been giving her strip washes, but the other day she fell and hit her head on the sink. She was quite knocked out, poor girl. But she came around before we had to send her to the general hospital.'

'I see.'

'But since the incident Susie has been having more fits. Maybe twenty or thirty a day, and some of them leave her insensible. She has to be watched all the time.'

Patience shut her eyes and tried to remember what Susie had been like when she saw her at Easter. 'I will come and see her,' she said.

'Well, you will be very welcome. But...' The matron's voice tailed off.

'But what, Matron?' she asked, crisply, in her teacher voice.

'Some of the staff are of the opinion that this new development might be a kindness. Perhaps Susannah will slip gently away.'

Patience could feel her heart racing. 'Susie is twenty-one years old. When I saw her last time, she was lively, enjoying life. We went into the town for an ice cream; she was so happy.'

'Well, I suggest you visit her now and we can talk further.' Matron's voice was calm. 'These fits can be dangerous, which means we should increase her medication. But the sedation restricts her activity and her appetite. She has lost quite a lot of weight.'

Susie had always been slight, even slimmer than her sister. 'I will come tomorrow and stay in the town,' Patience said, heart hammering in her throat. 'Please tell her I am coming.'

'I will, but I doubt she will understand,' Matron said.

After the call ended, Patience stood in the small kiosk in the corner of the shop beside the post office counter, eyes shut, tears crowding her throat. She dialled a familiar number and got through to the ferry office.

'I wonder if you could leave a message for Mr Janssen?

Patience Ellis. Could he telephone the post office at his earliest convenience, and message me when he is available to take a call? One of my relatives is ill.'

She rang off, feeling shaky. After Mam, she just couldn't lose Susie.

She was working in her garden when a lad shouted for her. 'Miss Ellis!'

'Do you have a message for me?'

'Mr Janssen can wait another twenty minutes, miss, but then he has to sail on the tide.'

Of course he did. The postmistress could have written that down for her but now the whole island would know.

'I will come at once. Tuck your shirt in, Michael. Your mother wouldn't like it hanging out like a puppy tail.'

Patience started down the hill as fast as she could. She walked into the shop to find the postmistress standing by the phone. 'We kept it clear for you,' she said, breathlessly.

'Goodness,' said Patience, in her best teacher voice. 'Such a drama.' She rang the ferry office and Dutch answered himself.

She shut the kiosk door and tears started to fill her eyes. She turned her back on the glass door.

'Dutch, it's about Susie. I need to go and see her tomorrow on the ferry. I'll have to stay in a hotel in Penzance. Could you get me a room in the town? I know it's short notice, but you will be on the mainland tonight and could find a room.'

'I know a good one, very respectable. Most of them are busy, though – it's the holidays.'

'I don't care what it's like, I just need somewhere to stay over while I sort this thing with Susie out.'

'The ferry leaves at twelve fifteen. Can you get a boat to St Brannock's before that?'

She thought quickly. 'I'll go over on the tourist boat. That should be there in plenty of time.'

'I've got a shift on *Islander II* tomorrow,' he said. 'You can tell me all about it on the ship.'

Patience felt lighter just from hearing his voice.

21

PRESENT DAY, 9 APRIL

Corinne called through the house. 'Hi, Ellie? Elowen!'

'I'm here,' she mumbled. She'd dozed off on the sofa over a complex account on her work laptop.

Corinne put her head around the door. 'You're still coming to the hotel tonight with Bran, right?'

'Of course.'

I've told Tink it is *so* not a date. He does know you have a boyfriend in London.'

'I have, and Leo's coming over for Easter so he can meet you all. He's taking a helicopter, though. He doesn't travel by sea very well. His boss has paid for a ticket for his birthday, to save him getting sick on the ferry.'

Corinne looked surprised. 'Nice birthday gift. And Bran has sorted you both out a room overlooking the sea.'

'I won't be able to stay,' she said, blushing a little.

'Why not? The upstairs rooms are lovely, much more modern than the bar. Bran's mother did them up before she died.'

'It's not that,' she said. 'I told you about the will. I have to stay here every day for a year.'

Corinne stared at her. 'What happens if you don't?'

'Then it goes to Patience's nearest relations. The grandchildren of her siblings. Somebody Morval, Gemma Lovelace and Daniel Ellis.'

'Beatrix Morval,' she said, looking away. 'Tink's sister, Trixie. She's got twins, lives on West Island. Gemma's a nurse in Cornwall. I don't know her well.'

'Well, I intend to stay here for the year anyway. I'm enjoying it. It's a break from my usual life.'

Corinne's face was tense. 'You'll get a packet selling it for a holiday let.'

Ellie nodded, wondering why she looked so upset. 'Leo's been talking to estate agents. Maybe we could keep it, rent it out, make some money but still visit.'

She couldn't imagine turning her back on the house just yet, with memories whispering in every corner. Maybe in a year's time she would be sick of the place, especially after a winter, but right now she loved it.

When she looked back, Corinne was standing by the door, her hands clenched together.

'Tink,' she said. 'Tink is Daniel Ellis, Patience's great-nephew. You'd think, if she was going to leave it to anyone, she would split it between you all, or just leave it to him.'

Ellie's memory lit up like someone had pressed a switch. Of course, Daniel. She'd only ever heard him called Tink but if Daniel was Clem's grandson...

'I didn't realise,' she said. 'But Patience obviously had her reasons.'

'That's what Tink says. He's not angry, not jealous, not anything. But I'm a bit hurt for him.' She winced. 'It's not your fault, I don't blame you. I kind of blame Patience a bit, though.'

'But if I missed a night at the cottage, you might tell a solicitor?'

Corinne shook her head. 'God, no. What do you think I am? It's just, we're living between his grandfather's attic and a clapped-out old truck. Sadly, I think of you as a friend now, and Tink never forgot you from childhood. So, if anyone rats you out, it won't be us.' She stepped forward, and hugged her. 'We're practically cousins, now. We'll call for you about seven, we can walk down together. Do you have anything smart?'

She nodded. 'Literally the last thing I brought that is still clean.'

'It's all OK, Elowen. You can do us one favour, though.'

'OK. What?'

She punched Ellie lightly on her arm. 'Come to Grandad Clem's for Sunday lunch. He's dying to meet you.'

'I haven't been invited.'

'Oh, for God's sake! They're a bit offended you haven't already banged on the door. I'm inviting you. I'll let Nan Sarah know. You'll be so welcome. But until then, we'll see you tonight, OK?' She reached forward and unexpectedly kissed her cheek. 'Don't look so surprised. You're part of the family now.'

Later that evening, after a lovely meal, Corinne tucked her arm into Ellie's and switched on a powerful torch to light the way from the hotel.

'That was delicious,' she said, looking back at Tink and Bran, stumbling along behind them.

'It was,' Ellie admitted. 'I didn't think I liked crab but that was amazing.'

'Robert's such a good cook,' she said. 'He could go far on the mainland but he's absolutely hooked on the island, they both are. Of course, he grew up here – Justin's the blow-in. But their daughter, Merryn, is keeping hope for the island's school alive. She's only four.'

They walked down the gravel track. 'You've been so kind to me, all of you,' Ellie said. 'Especially with the will being the way it is.'

'When I told Tink, he wasn't quite as Zen about it as I thought,' she said, a giggle in her voice. 'He did swear for about five minutes. But then he said something I don't understand and he won't explain. Perhaps you can get it out of him.'

'What?'

'He said – I'm quoting here – "So Grandad Clem's stories are true."' She stumbled on a big tuft of grass and clung to Ellie until she got her balance back. 'I knew I shouldn't have worn heels.'

The darkness over the Sound was lit by reflected moonlight and a few flickering lights from cottages here and there on St Petroc's.

'What stories?' Ellie asked.

'You'll have to ask Clem. Have you noticed, islanders do that, like it's none of our business? My mum reckons they are all drug dealers or smugglers, that's why they have so many secrets.' She squeezed Ellie's arm. 'Come to Sunday lunch tomorrow. You'll get a warm welcome and Nan Sarah does the best gravy on the island.'

'Even though I get the cottage? While you all have two jobs and can't buy a proper house?'

'You know someone who only has two jobs on the island?' she said, mock outrage in her voice. 'We all have half a dozen at least and live on a pound a week, everyone knows that.'

Bran and Tink had caught up with them. 'You have a pound a week?' Tink said. 'Half of that's mine.'

Ellie laughed, the four walking astride more easily as the path widened past Elk's shack. 'It seems strange now,' she admitted. 'My flat costs nearly two thousand a month.'

'Where is it?' Bran said. 'I lived in a studio apartment in

Finsbury Park. Nine hundred pounds a month and I got burgled twice in one year.'

'Bermondsey. Crowded, busy, loud, but we like it. We share with two other people. Well, Leo was a sharer at first but now he's moved in with me. It's a big room but we don't have enough space for clothes.'

'Shoes,' Bran said. 'I didn't realise there were so many shoe shops in the world until I went to London.'

Tink staggered forward and looked back at them. 'I have three pairs of shoes,' he announced, clearly more drunk than the rest of them. 'Two have holes in. I also have two pairs of steel-toecap wellies.'

Corinne let go of Ellie's arm and grabbed her partner's. 'I know. And very fetching you look in them, too, but I'm really glad you didn't wear them to the hotel.' She pulled him along in front.

Bran took Ellie's arm and she suddenly felt shy.

'How long were you in London?' she asked, watching Tink and Corinne pull away.

'After Goldsmiths,' he said, matching his steps to hers, 'I got an apprenticeship at a ceramics studio, working as an assistant. Then I started developing a small collection of my own. I had to leave when Dad needed me.'

In the dark she could hear the sadness in his voice. 'How is he now?'

He hugged her arm as if he was cold, although the air was almost still. 'Dad moved onto the boat six years ago, after my mother died. He spent two years doing it up. It's really nice inside. I thought he would go all macho but he kept a lot of my mother's stuff. It was great until he had his stroke. He sleeps in his recliner most of the time now, in the saloon. He likes it because he can see the water the moment he wakes up. I take the bigger cabin downstairs.'

'I thought you lived at the pub?'

'Occasionally I don't fancy the ladder, if the tide's low, so I've got a room behind the kitchen. Or, like tonight, if I've drunk too much wine.' He fell silent and they came into the light of the first of the streetlights on the cobbled quay. 'He's angry all the time. But he needs me to help him to the loo. The floor was awash with water and daffodils the other day, and the vase was full of pee, because I had a late night at work and slept over at the pub.'

'Why doesn't he get carers?'

Bran sighed. 'He won't have them on the boat, even if we could find some. If I help wash and dress him, a couple of men from the pub help him over. Sometimes I persuade him he's missed the tide and put him in my room, but he sees that as defeat. I love him, but he's difficult. The stroke has made him impulsive and he has meltdowns if he doesn't get his own way.'

Their footsteps changed as they walked up to the pub on the rounded stones. 'That's how I feel about my dad,' she confessed, in the dark. 'He wants me to break the entail and sell up. He thinks I'm losing too much seniority taking time off.'

'What do you do?' He stopped in the pub's porch, staring at her. 'How can you afford to take a year off from your job?'

'I'm a forensic accountant at a London firm. I am working, just offline to protect the evidence from hackers. I'm going to be doing more work at the cottage over the next few months, once I get back on the internet.'

'You probably earn megabucks,' he said. 'We should have made you pay for the seafood platter.'

'Hardly megabucks,' she said, smiling at the thought. 'Not much work to cover a whole year and I'm paying my share of the rent back home.'

'Home,' he said, his eyes gleaming under the light on the quay. 'Where is "home", really?'

Corinne walked up and hugged Bran, as he pulled away from Ellie.

'Goodnight, Bran. This was so much fun. I had a lovely time, I almost forgot we have the vet coming tomorrow and I will have to sleep with him to pay the bill.' She kissed Bran's cheek.

Tink smiled. 'The vet is a woman in her sixties, if I remember correctly.'

Corinne laughed. 'I love a challenge. Night, Branok.'

Bran walked into the back porch of the pub, pausing to wave over his shoulder.

Ellie set off up the hill with Tink and Corinne and they finally reached the porch of Kittiwake Cottage. 'Corinne told me about the will,' Tink said. 'It's OK. I never thought she would leave it to me. I thought, to be honest, she might leave it to Grandad Clem, but he doesn't need it.'

'So why *did* she leave it to me?' Ellie said, exasperated. 'My mother was her unofficial adopted daughter, but she wasn't a blood relation.'

'Ysella needed a home for some reason and Patience offered. Who could be more respectable than a spinster schoolmistress with an unimpeachable reputation and no children? She adopted Ysa and no one thought it was wrong, and she adored her. The Ellises are a big family. Any one of them could have got pregnant, had a baby out of wedlock.' He sounded like he was going to say something but stopped.

'Do you know something?' Ellie asked, trying to see Tink's face but it was very dark now.

'You need to come to lunch tomorrow, meet Grandad Clem. He can probably tell you everything. We could really be distant cousins. We can keep the cottage in the family.' Tink clapped Ellie on the shoulder hard enough to make her stagger. 'When the farm takes off, we'll convert the barn and it will be great. We'll be neighbours. Unless you sell up, obviously.'

'I'm thinking about keeping it,' Ellie said impulsively, the words warming the cool darkness. 'Maybe Leo and I will be regular visitors, and make a fortune renting to holidaymakers.' It was a good thought, but a splinter of doubt shot through the words even as she said them.

Leo.

22

Patience waited for Dutch to find her on *Islander II* the following afternoon, when she travelled to Susie's hospital. She had packed a few days' clothes, and Dad had given her over two pounds for some decent accommodation and sent his love to Susie. She hadn't told him Dutch had booked her hotel room; for some strange reason she felt awkward discussing him with Dad now.

'There you are.' Dutch looked smart in his uniform, never really handsome with his crooked smile and grey eyes, but tall and broad shouldered. Patience noticed a woman her own age give him an approving look. 'Come aboard. It's quiet today, we can talk.'

One of his colleagues was sweeping the wooden decks and emptying out the ashtrays in the saloon. Dutch waved her into one of the booths and sat opposite her at the table. 'What now is happening?'

She didn't feel like correcting him. 'It's the fits.' She shut her eyes at the thought. 'I'm worried they are just going to give her so much medicine, she will "slip away".'

He put one of his hands over her clenched fingers on the

table top. 'In Germany, before the war, there were many children like Susannah,' he said, and she opened her eyes. 'Some not as bad as her, but the government took them away.'

She looked down at their hands. 'What happened to them?'

'They all died. They were put down like dogs.'

She gasped. 'That couldn't happen here, surely?'

He shrugged, releasing her hands. 'I doubt that people thought it could happen in Germany, either.' She stared down at the table. His brown fingers were crisscrossed in scars from the ropes; her father had many similar marks.

'Dad stopped visiting after he married Missus,' Patience said. 'Susie's my responsibility now.'

'I will come with you,' he said, his voice so low and deep she almost felt it. 'I have the rest of the day and tomorrow off. I can travel up on the bus with you. I managed to get you a room at the Sunflower guesthouse.' He hesitated. 'It's a double room, it's all they have left, but you will be comfortable and I can help if it's too expensive.'

'Thank you,' she said. 'Was there a problem?'

He half smiled. 'Don't be angry,' he said, patting her hand for a moment. 'But I had to let them think I was Mr Ellis booking for his wife to visit her sister in the asylum. They don't like single ladies staying in a family hotel.'

She smiled, a moment of lightness. 'Are you sure I'm not Mrs Janssen?'

'I don't suppose they would approve of a foreign couple either,' he said, wincing a little. 'They are a very respectable guest house, they said it three times. No, you will be Mrs Ellis and I'll go home. But I'd like to speak to Susie's doctor with you, if I can.' He swallowed, and she could see his Adam's apple bobbing above his tie. 'Susie's an innocent. She needs people to protect her.'

'Thank you,' she whispered.

. . .

Sitting in the hospital waiting room at four o'clock, Patience jumped to her feet when she saw the shuffling figure in a daisy-print dress. She had made the garment for Susannah last summer, but now it hung off her. The nurse who was holding her hand smiled at them as Dutch stood up.

'See, Susie, here is your sister all the way from Morwen Island. Shall we go in the day room before tea?'

Susie didn't even look up. Her hair was lank, falling over her prominent collar bones. Just when Patience was feeling helpless, she felt Dutch's hand cup her elbow.

'That would be good,' Dutch said. 'Come on, Patience. Let's follow Susie.'

Susie did glance up at the sound of his voice, but she looked blank, as if she didn't recognise either of them.

'Oh, Dutch,' Patience whispered.

'It's all right,' he murmured to her, his breath just touching her hair. 'We'll sort this out.'

It wasn't easy to improve Susannah's situation. The nurse had described her as incurably epileptic, and the doctor had diagnosed a deteriorating condition. Susannah sat on the chair she was put in, but sagged sideways. Matron came over with a little spouted cup.

'Susannah's medication,' she said, offering it.

'Susie, sit up, maid,' Patience said. 'Here's your medicine.'

Her sister's blue eyes, so much like her own, stared back, puzzled. She closed them as if to shut Patience out.

'It's Patsy,' Patience said, pulling her chair very close and putting an arm around to support her. The matron slipped the spout between Susie's lips and tipped the cup back. Susie flapped her hands a little, but swallowed.

'Patsy?' Her voice was like a small child's, dragging Patience back to their childhood bed, to Teddy and Raggy doll and the miniature china tea set in a box on the window seat.

'Susie,' Patience said, relieved. 'It's all right, we've come to see you. Do you remember Dutch?'

Susie held up her head long enough to look, then shook her head.

He crouched down beside her. 'Do you remember "Fishy, fishy, in your dishy"? We used to sing it.'

'Fishy, fishy,' Susie parroted. She reached up with a small hand and touched his hair.

He grinned up at Patience. 'There you are, little sister.'

He looked back at Matron. 'I think Susie just needs to spend some time with her family. We can get her eating again.'

'That won't stop her fits, Mr Ellis. As the doctor will explain tomorrow.'

'He's Mr Janssen,' Patience said. 'I'm sorry, I've quite forgotten my manners. He's a friend of the family; he's known my sister since she was a child.'

'Not at all,' the older woman said. 'We all care very much for Susannah, and you may be able to help. She has been declining since these fits increased. If you spend more time with her she might improve.' Her face changed. 'And if she doesn't, at least she can have a happy few hours.'

'I'll do what I can, before term starts again, anyway.'

When her tea came, they could only tempt Susie into eating a few nibbles of cake and a little juice in the cup, like a baby.

As they walked out of the hospital, Patience started crying, the tears tickling her face. Dutch held her against his coat for a few moments.

'People will think I made you cry,' he finally said.

'I've left her too long,' she said. 'I should have come much more often.'

'You heard the nurse. She's been having more... seizures. Is that the word?'

She patted her face dry with a clean handkerchief, then blew her nose. 'Sorry. I'm a bit of a mess. Your respectable hotel might not let me in.'

He stood back to search her face for a moment. 'You'll do,' he said. For a sudden moment his gaze dropped to her lips and she thought he wanted to kiss her.

'Dutch,' she said, uncertain.

'Let me get you settled in,' he said, looking away, holding her case as well as his bag. The moment had passed. *I must be mistaken.* But it was nice having an arm to lean on and the feeling of being small. Patience was five feet nine in her sensible flat shoes, but Dutch towered over her.

As they stood outside the dark red, rather forbidding exterior, he put her bag down. 'I bought this for you.' He reached into his jacket pocket and brought out a tiny sliver of gold. 'It's just a second-hand one. But it should make you seem more like a married lady.'

It was a plain band. 'Oh.' Patience didn't want to take it at first. 'I don't think I should.'

'Don't be silly,' he said, reaching for her suddenly weak arm. 'Hold your hand out.'

He slipped the ring onto her finger. It felt significant; she caught her breath. He leaned forward and kissed the top of her head.

'There. Mrs Ellis, respectable lady visiting her sister.'

She leaned towards him. 'Dutch—'

'Don't say it,' he said, looking down. 'Let me get you inside and I'll disappear.'

'Where will you stay?'

'I'll walk home. It's just a mile. I will be back tomorrow to meet with the doctor.'

'Eleven o'clock.' She had to press her fingers together to keep the ring on. 'This seems deceitful.'

He rested his hands on her shoulders for a minute. 'We're not doing anything wrong.' He nodded his head and smiled. 'Chin up, shoulders back. That's what you tell the children. Let's get you checked in, Mrs Ellis.'

23

PRESENT DAY, 10 APRIL

Ellie walked down with Corinne and Tink for Sunday lunch at the Ellises, apprehensive about how she would be received. A very short lady opened the door and beamed at them.

'Come in, Elowen. It's lovely to see you after all this time. My, don't you look like your mother!' Clem's wife, who everyone in the town seemed to call Mrs Clem, reached up and hugged her. Ellie felt very tall, as Mrs Clem was about four feet eight and plump, with streaked grey hair stuffed into an untidy bun. 'You can call me Nan, I'm Sarah Ellis.'

'Thank you for inviting me.' The cottage was so small Ellie felt like she needed to duck through the doorway. Tink and Corinne had already squeezed in.

'Well, you're always welcome. It must be lonely up at Patience's cottage. I always thought it was a wild place, overlooking the sea.'

Noah's Drang was a row of houses in a small alleyway between Warren Lane and Fore Street, parallel with the quay. The terrace looked over an ancient wall surrounding a green area filled with trees. A couple of chickens scratched around the front door and there were more between the trees.

'Oh, you little monsters. They kick up my gravel and eat my pot plants.' Every green space in the row was overflowing with spring bulbs and potted heathers. 'Come in, come in, the boys are in the yard.'

Through the tiny living room and past an area almost entirely filled with a table and a mismatched collection of chairs, was an open door onto a stone patio. A few steps led up to a square of lawn, washed with sunlight. There were a few people she didn't recognise, and Tink was putting out more seats.

An old man with a barrel chest and with legs stretched out from a garden seat stared at her from under massive, yellow-white eyebrows. He had a pipe between his teeth and the garden smelled of tobacco smoke.

'Well now, young lady. Welcome to my house,' he said around the stem. He had the thickest accent of anyone Ellie had met on the island, and didn't smile.

Tink waved to a chair. 'Sit down, Ellie, I'll get you a drink. We have bitter, lager or would you prefer a coffee?'

It seemed very early for a drink but everyone else had one.

'Hi,' said a man in his forties, holding out a glass. 'I'm Mark, Trix's husband. Nice to meet you.'

'Hi. Uh, a lager would be great, Tink, if that's OK.'

'Sunday tradition.' Tink sprang down the steps and vanished into the house.

'Well. So, you're Ysella's daughter, young Elowen,' the old man said. He looked her up and down. 'Welcome back. I'm Clement Ellis. Everyone calls me Clem; I suppose you can, too. I can see your mother in you. Your father, too.'

'Yes, sir.' Ellie took the glass Tink held out to her. 'I was wondering if you know anything about my connection to Patience? I've been unable to find any useful papers explaining my mother's adoption.'

Clem didn't answer, just sucked hard on the pipe and blew

a cloud of blue smoke over his shoulder. 'She left you the cottage, maid. That's the connection.'

Ellie stared into her glass. She felt there was a pretty strong 'mind your own business' feeling in the air.

'It's just...' she said, still looking down. 'I don't really remember much about my mum.' It was embarrassing, the way tears prickled, even after so long.

'That were a sad business,' Clem rumbled. 'She was still young. The apple of Patsy's eye, that was for certain. Such a bonny baby, too.' He coughed something that could have been a laugh. 'Not like you, a little rat of a baby, like a shaved ferret in a bonnet.'

'You saw me back then?'

Clem rumbled with amusement. 'Ysa came home to Kitti-wake Cottage to recover from her operation. Your dad came, too, but he could never stay away from London long. Island living didn't suit him, and he had a job. I remember you, snuggled up on my shoulder, fast asleep. You liked to be carried all the time.'

Ellie slowly digested this. Operation? She hadn't known her mother had had a caesarean. Looking at Clem in his thick jersey, she could easily imagine a baby would be warm and comfortable.

'How long did we stay?'

'I don't remember. A few weeks, maybe. She took you home to London and we didn't see you again until the summer. Then you were a different baby. You got bald, fat, like Chairman Mao. Eh, Sarah,' he shouted towards the open door, 'do you remember young Elowen when she was a baby? Like a little Buddha.'

Tink grinned. 'Don't worry, they do this to me, too. Apparently, I was born with hair all over my back like a monkey. It's pretty well the first thing they ever say about me.'

Clem puffed another cloud of eyewatering smoke, the wind spinning it around their heads. 'Tink cried all the time. A sad monkey.'

'Come in for dinner,' Corinne said, leaning around the back door. 'We're at the gravy stage.'

Tink jumped up. 'Nan's gravy is legendary,' he said to Ellie, then lowered his voice. 'Just don't mention that she overcooks the meat every time. They like it brown all the way through.'

The dining room was off a small kitchen, and was packed. At bewildering speed, Ellie was introduced to Trix Morval, Tink's older sister, and her twin boys Alfie and Ben, who immediately merged into each other scrambling for seats.

'Boys on the stools,' their mother shouted over their heads. 'Here you go, Elowen, sit in the chair in the corner. That way no one will ask you to get anything. Tink, sit next to her. Ben! Sit down or no pudding. Corinne, do you want to sit between the boys, stop any food wars? Mark, can you get a chair from the garden...'

The whole experience was immersive, snatches of conversation over Ellie's head, everyone friendly and relaxed. She was sitting so close to people that knees rubbed and elbows clashed. Mrs Clem, who insisted again that Ellie called her Nan since she had apparently walked her up and down in a steamy cottage through a bout of croup, served up plate after plate of food. There were a lot of in-jokes, teasing and jostling until the gravy was poured, then the room grew quiet.

The food was lovely, the gravy was the best she had ever had, but there was something else. Every time she caught someone's eye, they smiled at her. Even Clem lifted his fork in a salute. The teary feeling was back, so Ellie concentrated on the food. The meat might not have been pink but it fell apart, delicious. The horseradish was home-made and nearly burned through her sinuses. The roast potatoes were gold and crunchy, fluffy in the middle. She recognised purple sprouting broccoli that Tink and Corinne had grown, and baby carrots.

'This is the best roast dinner I've ever had,' she announced, surprising even herself.

Corinne smiled. 'I said exactly the same thing when I first came here,' she said. 'Pass the horseradish, please. I feel like my head's still on my shoulders and we can't have that, can we, boys?' She heaped a spoonful on her plate.

'We grow the horseradish ourselves,' Tink said. 'It's been great. We've got orders from the pubs and hotels on several islands.'

'We'll need the fire brigade if it gets any hotter,' Clem said. 'And you are joining the brigade, Elowen? Tink told us you might.'

'I'm thinking about it,' Ellie said, turning warm and probably pink.

Mrs Clem, who ate delicately and slowly, smiled at Ellie. 'So, how has it been in Patsy's old cottage? It must be a bit grim – she was never very house-proud.'

'It's OK,' she mumbled, then swallowed her mouthful. 'Sorry. It's...' All the complaints she'd been telling Leo crowded to the front of her mind, then faded away. 'It's sort of magical,' she found herself saying. 'I get up when the sun comes in the window. It's a simple life, you know? Very different from London. I wish I had a proper kitchen and washing machine, though. And an indoor bathroom.'

A chorus of offers to do her laundry and a standing invitation to pop in for meals overwhelmed her. One of the boys – Alfie, she worked out – earnestly recommended dinner on Wednesdays when Nan cooked sausages and made cake. Her offer to help wash up was accepted, and at the end of a mammoth heap of dishes, she found herself alone with Mrs Clem and the twins.

'Go and play,' Nan said to the boys, handing them each a bottle of bubble solution. She took the damp towels from Ellie and hung them over the front of the stove. 'I'm guessing you want to talk about your mother.'

'If that's OK,' Ellie said.

'I didn't know her as a child,' she said, putting a kettle on. 'I'm the second Mrs Clem. I married him about thirty years ago.'

'Oh. I had no idea.' She was surprised, it seemed like she'd always been 'Nan'.

'I'm an island girl, though, just not this one. We all heard the rumours about Ysella, of course. Patsy was teaching at the school here. She'd trained over Cornwall way. She was overqualified to teach a handful of little kids, but that was Patsy. Suddenly she took a leave of absence from the school to look after her sister.'

'I didn't even know she had a sister.' Ellie leaned against the worktop, watching Nan put out mugs from hooks under a plate rack on the wall.

'The older boys were Joseph, who died in the war, Frederick, then Patience. After her came Susannah, William and Clem. William died of TB. Susie wasn't right in the head, if you know what I mean, so she ended up living in a sort of hospital for people like her after her mother died. Her dad couldn't cope with her and the little ones.' She refilled the kettle after pouring water into the first few mugs. 'After Martha died, Clem's dad married again, and she already had three young boys. No one was surprised when Patience went to the mainland to look after her sister because no one else could go.'

'What was wrong with Susie?'

She pursed her lips and lowered her voice. 'I don't know, something mental. She was in an asylum and had fits, poor girl.

There weren't proper medicines back then, and people just got locked up and left. People were really shocked when Patsy came back with Ysella in her luggage, snuggled in a carpet bag on a pile of baby clothes. The family said the baby belonged to a cousin of her mother's who couldn't bring the babe up, so Patience took it.'

'That must have caused some speculation?'

'Well, back then you couldn't have a baby out of wedlock and teach innocent children.' She looked quite shocked. 'My goodness, not then. But she explained what *had* happened to the school board. I don't know for sure what she said, but they let her carry on teaching. She went back to work, and the first Mrs Clem and a minder in the town shared the childcare.' She leaned closer. 'Of course, people suspected the baby was Susannah's all along. The hospital had boys as well as girls. It would be a nasty thing for a girl like that to get in the family way.'

'So, my mother might have been Susannah's baby?' The idea was uncomfortable.

'Maybe,' she said, picking up two mugs of tea in each hand. 'But Clem doesn't like talking about it. Getting a girl like that pregnant, very sad.'

Ellie managed to lift the last three cups. 'Where are we going?'

'To the parlour,' she said.

The living room was more than cosy, it was crammed. Tink was sat on the arm of the sofa next to Corinne, who was squashed in next to Trix and Mark. They seemed grateful for the tea, and Ellie sat on the window seat watching the family. They looked as sleepy with food as she felt, the residual taste of apple crumble in her mouth, acidic and spiced with cloves.

Clem cleared his throat and sipped his tea. 'So, I suppose you want to know a few things about your mother, maid?'

'I didn't even know she had a caesarean,' she said. The room fell quiet and she could hear the clock on the mantelpiece ticking. 'You said she had an operation.'

'She had you normally enough,' Clem finally said. 'But she had an operation for the cancer straight after you were born.'

'What? No, she found a lump when I was eight.'

'That was the second time,' Clem said. 'No, she found it when she were four, five months gone with you. Patience was beside herself. Ysa came home and they talked about it with my dad and your father. Ysella stood firm. She was having her baby and to hell with the cancer. She waited until you were big enough to be born, a month early. Then she had the surgery straight after.'

Ellie couldn't believe what she was hearing. She felt sick.

Tink sat forward. 'Is this OK to talk about, Ellie?'

She put her arms around herself, trying to keep her composure. She swallowed the lump in her throat. 'Yes. Of course. So, the surgery worked?'

'Oh, that and all the drugs she had.' Clem's voice was soft and rough. 'But she always said you were the best treatment. We all looked after her, and you, the little scrap in the middle. Patsy went up to London for months at a time, to help out when Ysa went home. Your mother recovered so well she was back on the beach the next summer, rowing with the girls, showing you off to all her friends.'

These people had known more than she had. How was that even possible? 'What about my father?'

'Well, he had his work so he didn't come as often. She came all summer and most Easters. They sometimes visited for Christmas, too. He usually stayed at the pub or rented a house for you all. I got the impression he didn't get on with Patsy. She had her opinions and Malcolm didn't like sharing Ysella with anyone.' Clem shrugged. 'He'd come down for a week here and there, he learned to sail and used to swim off the beach.'

'Here, lovey, drink your tea,' Mrs Clem said soothingly. 'It's all a long time in the past. No matter how sad, it's all over.'

Obediently, she drank her tea. It wasn't until she got up to leave that Clem put a hand on her shoulder. 'You're family. I'm not sure exactly how – my father wouldn't talk about it. But my sister brought you home and that *makes* you family. Patience chose you to inherit the cottage and we respect that.'

24

'Mrs Ellis' found she had more confidence than spinster Miss Ellis, and Patience was outside the hospital to speak to the doctor by eleven. Dutch joined her at the gate and they walked in together. As they got to the door, she slipped her hand into his.

'Don't worry,' he said, looking down at her. 'Whatever you have to deal with, you can do. *We* can do.'

The door was unlocked by a nurse, and they discreetly let go.

Patience was distracted by her own reaction to his skin, his fingers entwined in hers. She had carried a childish admiration for him that had blossomed into a girlish crush. But now she was intensely aware of his every movement in the chair, his deep voice, every breath. She could barely concentrate on the conversation, even though it was terribly important.

Dr Carlton smiled a lot as he delivered his devastating verdict. Words like 'weak corpus' and 'feeble constitution' made no sense in her mind. In her memory Susie raced along the coastal path, shrieking with laughter, chasing a butterfly or a puppy. This was Susie who would listen to the story of the fairy queen in the oak tree over and over again. She could patiently cut out little pastry flowers and leaves to decorate a pie, even though she could barely write her name. *Suʒanah*.

Patience bent forward, holding on to her tears. She took a deep breath and looked up. 'What will happen if you reduce these sedative drugs?'

'She would be more agitated, and the seizures would increase. These long fits are very damaging to the brain.'

'But she was stable enough until she hit her head in the bathroom.'

The doctor sat back in his chair. 'She fell because she had a fit,' he reminded her.

'The nurses knew she was vulnerable to falling,' Patience said, trying out her new sense of power. 'Yet she was allowed to fall so badly that she was injured.'

The doctor gave a patronising smile. 'We don't know if she was injured by the fall. Sometimes people are unconscious for hours after a fit. She bumped her head a little but I wouldn't call her *badly* hurt.'

Patience sat up straight in her chair. She could almost feel Dutch cheering her on. 'But Susannah's fits have been worse since this – incident.'

'That may be so,' he said, sounding very doubtful, 'but it's in the nature of her illness to suffer deterioration. Her behaviour has been harder to manage; she has become frustrated with some of the staff and other patients.'

'So, you drugged her.'

'We did everything we could to treat her agitation and, incidentally, reduce the severity of her illness.' He looked as if he'd eaten something sour. 'I'm afraid I do not appreciate the accusatory tone you are using.'

'I love my sister,' Patience said passionately. 'Susie shared my bed, went to school with me, played with our toys. I can't believe she has become so difficult.'

The doctor turned slightly towards Dutch, smiled faintly. 'I'm afraid the situation is that as young girls develop, they mature into women. Hormones affect their disease, as this leads to escalations and also – forgive the indelicacy, Miss Ellis – *sexual* behaviour. Susannah has, on occasions, been immodest with male members of staff, such as our groundsmen and porters. This is a natural instinct, and not moderated by any understanding of moral behaviour. When frustrated, this can lead to aggression. And morally insanitary behaviours.'

Patience realised she was expected to blush and yield to his greater knowledge. Instead she stood abruptly, leading both men to follow suit.

'I wish my sister to be moved to another institution,' she said, using her best teacher voice. 'Could you please suggest some other places where Susannah can live her life as she is, rather than how you think she *should* be? And if that means being attracted to men, and having the fits God gave her, so be it. But sedated, drugged into starvation, hardly able to recognise the people who love her? No, Dr Carlton. She needs care and affection, not this slow death.'

'I very much doubt you will find a place as progressive as this one,' Dr Carlton said. 'Especially with Susannah's diagnosis.'

Dutch squeezed Patience's wrist for a moment. It gave her confidence.

'We will seek other expert advice,' she said. 'A second opinion. Thank you for your time.'

Patience swept out on a wave of anger, but as it faded in the hospital gardens, she started to feel sick. Susie was sat on a blanket picking at the grass, cared for by a young nurse. Patience looked down at her.

'What have I done? I'm not even her guardian, Dad is.'

'You have loved her, and revealed their neglect.'

She glanced sideways at him. 'What was he talking about, Susie being "insanitary"?'

It was Dutch's turn to flush. 'I think he means that she touches herself, that's all. It's natural enough, but she doesn't know not to do it in public.'

Patience was humbled. 'I don't know enough about any of this, do I?'

'We can learn together,' he said. 'Come on, she's seen you and I think she recognises us.'

That was heart-warming, and they sat down on the grass to entertain her. Patience could see how much intellect she had lost, and while they were sitting on the rug she suddenly went blank and slid sideways. Dutch caught her shoulders in time to stop her head hitting the grass. A few twitches later, she was muzzily looking up, licking her lips and grimacing.

'She needs specialist care,' Patience said. 'We need to find somewhere better. Will you help me?'

Dutch nodded, looking into her eyes. 'Always.'

25

PRESENT DAY, 11 APRIL

Ellie had ordered supplies for repairs, ahead of Leo's visit. She wasn't bad at DIY and had been encouraged at school to learn the basics. She could see that the top kitchen cupboards were mostly salvageable. After deciding to paint them all, she had ordered primer and undercoat, and some fresh timber to replace the wormy battens holding them to the wall.

She had sorted out the contents of the dark, varnished dresser and washed them. She had brought back linens for the bed, tea towels and bath towels from her trip to the big island, and basics like a clothes airer and an electric radiator, which had all had to be balanced on the little ferry with Bran's help.

The campsite had opened for the spring, and she had paid the sum of one pound for a ten-minute shower and five pounds for a load of washing.

When the ferry company were going to deliver her supplies, she asked Tink to take the quad bike and trailer down to the quay to help her pick up the tins of paint, lengths of planed timber and a large box of various screws.

The gift shop on the quay had been closed for the winter,

the windows obscured with paper. Now, the door was open and a middle-aged woman was watching, leaning on a stick.

'You must be Elowen,' she called, smiling at her. She had a friendly, open face, a mop of blonde curls and a local accent. 'My husband told me about you.'

'Oh?' Ellie struggled to pile planks of timber, taped together, in the back of the trailer.

'He drives the boat sometimes. John McCullough. I'm Judith.'

'Oh, hello.'

'We were wondering how you're getting on with the cottage?'

She stacked the box with the tins of paint in a corner of the trailer as Tink lifted some planks. 'I'm working on it. It's slow.'

'I knew Patience. She was part of our art group.'

She stopped and looked at her properly. 'There's an art group?'

'In the church hall. We've got a few artists on the island.'

'Are you an islander?'

'We haven't been here long, about seven years. John said the plaster at the cottage was in bad shape. The render outside is blown in places, as well. Did you know he was a lime plasterer?'

'I did.' Ellie noticed more people crossing the quay to have a nose at her shopping or to talk to Tink. 'I know, it falls off every time I do anything to it.' *Or bang a door, or stamp on the floorboards.*

'Lime plaster is better for old buildings because it breathes,' Judith said patiently. 'You don't get moisture building up behind it, loosening it. It's got a lovely finish, too.'

Ellie nodded. 'Maybe he can come and chat to me about fixing it up?'

'I'm sure he will. It's even older than our house, and John's completely replastered ours. We're next to the gift shop, the tall house.' She waved to someone in the doorway. 'Poppy, come and meet Elowen.'

'You must be Patience's heir.' A tall woman with paint-spattered overalls came over. 'Tell me what you're going to do with that kitchen,' she said, with an unexpected intensity.

'Oh. I'm not quite sure,' Ellie said, flustered. 'I was going to try and save some of it.'

'Good idea. What about Patience's dresser? Because if you don't want it, I'd love to buy it.'

Judith laughed. 'Stand in line, Poppy. I might make an offer, too.'

Ellie smiled weakly as a good-natured, virtual auction started around her ears. 'I was going to paint that, too,' she interrupted.

Poppy turned that intense gaze on her again. 'Good for you,' she said. 'We're just sorting out the new art gallery. You'll have to come to the opening.'

'I'd love to,' she said, a little overwhelmed. As Tink made their excuses and started the quad bike, Ellie walked beside the trailer, steadying the timber.

'We'll all be invited,' Tink said, over his shoulder. 'And if we don't go, the art mafia will want to know why.'

'I've got a lot to do,' Ellie said, grabbing the shelves as they turned the corner. Her hand stung as she got a splinter. 'And Leo is arriving on Thursday.'

'They're trying to get Branok involved but he won't do it,' Tink said as they slowed at the corner.

'What do they want Bran to do?' The whole trailer bumped and rattled over the ruts.

'Judith used to be his art agent. She wants him to get a few pieces out of storage for the gallery.'

'It's a shame he didn't keep doing his art,' she prompted, curious.

'Apparently he was loving it, although he had separated

from Lizzie by then. Then his dad had a stroke and Bran rushed to his bedside. Now he's looking after him on the boat and running the pub.'

'It seems odd that they can't get help.'

'It's really hard getting carers on the island, and Joe absolutely doesn't want anyone else doing it.' Tink pulled up outside the cottage. 'Bran stopped talking about going back after a few months. But now they're selling the pub, maybe he'll go back to it.' He switched the engine off and jumped down.

The idea of Bran moving off the island gave Ellie a stinging feeling of loss. She started lifting paint tins. 'I haven't heard anything about people viewing the pub.'

'I don't think Joe wants it to go an off-islander who doesn't understand the importance of the pub to the town. The building's got some structural problems, too, and not everyone wants to do a complete refurbishment. It would cost a fortune, and close the pub for months.'

Ellie could see that would be a disaster for the island, and for her personally. In the cold evenings, the pub was a lifeline – a hot meal and a warm welcome just when she needed it. She now knew how many people dropped older relatives off for lunch and company. It was a day centre for several people, including Bran's father.

She looked forward to seeing Bran, his big smile whenever he saw her. *He's become a friend.*

She lifted one end of the timber and Tink carried the other, laying it down in the hall. Tink smoothed the peeling wallpaper. 'John will give you a fair price for replastering.'

'So people keep telling me,' Ellie said, going back for a box of painting supplies and the tins of paint. 'It's all like that. I've stripped most of the wallpaper off upstairs and the plaster comes with it. I think I can squeeze a bathroom up there between the bedrooms, so it will need re-doing then.' She ran her hand down the wall. 'Not to mention rewiring. Indoor plumbing, some heating, and the roof.'

'John could teach you the basics and you could help,' Tink suggested as he dropped a bag of brushes and sandpaper on the floor. 'There you go.'

'How much do I owe you?'

Tink scratched his head. 'I feel bad charging my neighbour, especially as I need you to do me a favour.'

'What favour?' Ellie wasn't really listening; she was putting the tenner back in her pocket.

'I need you to babysit the sheep for a night.'

Ellie felt a cold shudder start at her neck and run down her spine. 'You are kidding?' She looked Tink in the eye. 'I can't keep houseplants alive. And I don't know one end of a sheep from the other.'

'Poop at the back end, baa at the front end,' Tink said promptly. 'There are about ten people on the island who know more about sheep. You can call on them.'

'Why not ask one of them to do it, then?' Ellie could hear the lambs in the field behind, calling to their mothers. In her imagination, they were now screaming for help. 'How do you know one hasn't broken his leg or got stuck in the fence?'

'Oh, you'd know,' Tink said. 'Everyone else works, Ellie, they don't have time. You're the only work-shy layabout who's around in the day.' He walked through to the front door. 'Also, it will make Corinne very happy. I'll pop around on Thursday morning to show you the ropes. It's very simple, you just count them in the evening, make sure they've got food and water, and check on them again in the morning.'

Ellie was literally speechless, and Tink had already gone when she remembered Leo was arriving on Thursday.

26

23 JULY 1954

As Patience and Dutch walked back from the hospital, her head was spinning. The hotel looked even less welcoming in the late afternoon sunshine, the paint peeling off the window frames. She didn't know how to get a second opinion for Susie, and badly needed to talk to Dad.

'Mr and Mrs Ellis,' the landlady greeted them. 'I hope you will be joining us for dinner, Mr Ellis, and won't have to rush off to your ship?'

'We have time for dinner,' Patience said, glancing at Dutch.

She needed to talk over the day. She also wanted him there. If only she could broach the subject of the feelings that seemed to twine around them like invisible string. Their bodies seemed to lean together, her fingers tingled when they touched his. She slid her hand into her pocket to catch the slim band of gold.

They hung their coats up. 'I could take that up to your room for you?' the landlord said, smiling, reaching for Dutch's duffel bag. Patience was too tired to make up a reason why he shouldn't, and agreed.

The menu had a very limited selection. 'A choice of two

dinners and one pudding,' she said, in a low voice. 'Or coffees. Very continental.'

He laughed. 'You have an optimistic idea of continental food,' he said. 'Except France. Oh, my, what food!'

They both chose the steak and kidney pudding. 'When did you go to France?'

'My father took me to Paris when he attended some sort of big meeting. Conference, that's the word, isn't it?'

She looked at him, at his deeply tanned face with its familiar irregularities. 'I always wanted to go to Paris. I thought I'd travel in the holidays, like Miss Cartwright used to.'

'Well, she always travelled with a friend,' he said. 'It's probably cheaper to share a room.'

Patience laughed at that. 'Did everyone know about Miss Cartwright and her lady friends, except me?'

He straightened his cutlery. 'They weren't hurting anyone. People don't have the right to dictate where and how people can love.'

Patience put her head on one side. 'You sound like you feel very strongly about this.'

'I do. People should take love where they find it.' He put his hand over hers. 'You look like a robin when you do that, I've always loved it. It makes you seem so small.'

'Well, I'm not,' she said, shy. 'I'm too tall, too boyish-looking. Look at my chin, it's as big as my father's.'

'I love your chin,' he said, dropping his gaze to her mouth. 'I love your little teeth, and freckles, and your beautiful blue eyes. Like forget-me-nots. I had never seen eyes that colour before I met you.'

She held her breath, and let it all out with a sigh when their food arrived. He released her hand. Pretending to focus on her dinner, Patience moved soggy cabbage, grey mash and a slice of what looked like kidney pudding around her plate. When she dared to glance up, he was staring at her.

'I am trying to tell you I love you,' he said simply. 'This is all the grand, English words I know.'

'Dutch, please,' she said faintly, aware that her face was hot. 'This isn't the place...' Even as the words emerged she knew how stupid they were, but by the time she looked again he was trying to eat his food. She leaned forward and whispered, 'I have always loved *you*. From the moment Dad carried you up those stairs.'

The smile creased his lips although he didn't look up. 'This is not the place, *liebling*...' he whispered.

A woman at a table nearby looked up and Patience folded her hands in her lap. 'Dutch,' she said. 'Careful.'

'I will call you *lieveling* if I choose to,' he said loudly. 'That is Dutch for sweetheart, you know.'

She could feel a nervous fizz of laughter building in her chest. 'Eat your dinner,' she said sternly. 'Even though it's mostly gristle and gravy.' She couldn't help smiling. He *did* love her.

'We need to talk,' he said. 'Can I come upstairs? I have to get my bag, and at least we'll be alone.'

She laughed then. 'Of course you can.' Because he was still Dutch, and he was the same, kind man that he had always been.

Things felt different in the bedroom. Dutch followed her in, shut the door behind them and looked for his bag.

'I should leave,' he said. He looked awkward, his shoulders bent. 'This isn't proper.'

'But in private, where everyone thinks we are married, we can say what we like,' she said. It was as if her body was speaking without thinking, because she yearned for him, she ached for something she couldn't express. 'We can do whatever we want,' she said boldly.

He straightened up, his head brushing the fringe of the single pink lampshade. 'You don't know what you're saying.'

She almost stamped with temper. 'I'm not a child, you know.'

'You still feel like that clever little girl to me.' He looked down at her lips. 'Sometimes.'

'But I'm not a child,' she said, stepping so close she had to look up. *I love that he's so tall.* She put her hands on his chest. 'I've never been kissed by a man,' she said. 'Not properly. Kiss me.'

He bent down, and as they touched lips she held her breath. The electric feeling was back, even though his kiss was as chaste as a child's.

He pulled away. 'What do you mean, "not properly"?'

'There was one time,' she said, then kissed him again. This time was different. She felt exhilarated and he was shaking. His arms slid around her waist and pulled her closer. She could reach up and put her arms around his neck, like in the movies. 'It was my schoolfriend's brother,' she murmured as he kissed her again, this time like he would never let her go.

He buried his face against her neck, mumbling, 'Was it like this?'

She threw her head back and laughed. 'No! He bumped his teeth into mine and his lips were wet.'

He seemed to like it when she crept close against him, leg to leg, body to body. He still pulled his face away enough to say, 'Patience, this will go much further if you don't stop.'

She looked up at him. *I'm about to become a fallen woman.* The idea made her smile, her whole body tingle, and she had an irrational wish that he would touch her the way she'd seen couples embracing in the shadows by the ferry port.

'Don't stop,' she said, and pulled him closer again.

27

PRESENT DAY, 12 APRIL

Ellie had discovered that walking further along the lane to the south brought her to the footpath that looped around the back of the island. It was time to think about Leo, how she had missed him, but now there was a comfortable feeling of anticipation. The island people, especially her new friends like Tink, Corinne and Bran, seemed so vivid and real. *Bran.* She paused to think about the way he made her feel off balance.

She was on the highest part of the track, with cliff views over the open sea, a walk many islanders made every day. There were places where the footpath branched down to the shore in steep coves, or had been patched up after winter storms. The wreckage of jetties ravaged by the relentless sea dotted the coast. To the west of the island, the landscape was much steeper and rockier, in places just a cliff rising out of the water at high tide, so she could only walk on the sandy shores on the falling tide, from beach to beach. She struggled to bring Leo to mind, as if the distance had faded him entirely.

She started up the rocky coastal path at the base of the cliffs. It was steep, rocks hanging over a few nasty drops, until it branched down narrow steps into Seal Cove. She rested for a minute at the top, watching black dots at sea, seabirds that were too far away to identify. A cormorant popped up close to the shore and stared at her until she felt compelled to move on. Behind a rusted bit of barbed wire fence, she could see a few fat seals on the rocks at the base of the cliffs, wet and glossy like polished stones. Footsteps behind her made her jump and she spun around. Bran.

'Oh.' She hadn't heard him approach. She took a deep breath at the sight of him. 'Hi.'

'Ellie.' He turned away. 'Sorry, I didn't think anyone would be out in the middle of the day.'

'Who's running the pub?' she asked, wondering why he looked so grim.

'Max is. My dad is being chair-lifted off his boat for his lunchtime drinking session as we speak.' He sighed, a deep, frustrated release. 'I was just walking up to Lighthouse Rock.'

'Is Joe OK?'

'Not really. It's a bit easier now he's lost so much weight.' A tear ran down from the corner of one eye, to be dashed away. 'It's windy.'

'Do you want to talk about it?'

He stared at her as critically as the cormorant had. 'Can you keep something quiet? I mean, a proper, mainland secret. Here, the quickest way to get something around the archipelago is to say it's confidential.'

'Definitely,' she said, waving him to a bench overlooking the amazing view. 'Everyone here knew everything about me before I got here. Some of it was even true.'

He sat down, undid his jacket in the sunshine. 'When my dad had his stroke they did loads of tests to check why. I mean, he's not that old, he's sixty-nine.'

'OK.'

'They found he had advanced prostate cancer,' he said. 'He used that to blackmail me to run the pub. Everyone thinks I'm stopping the sale, but it's really him. He can't let it go. He can't let *me* go.'

'Oh.' Ellie stared back out to sea, to give him some privacy

'These are angry tears,' he added, dashing another away. 'I could kill the old bastard most days. I've started to hate him. I haven't stopped loving him, though, and he is *dying*.'

'I'm so sorry.' She searched in her pocket and came up with a creased tissue.

'Thank you.' Bran blew his nose. 'I'm glad I bumped into you, but no one must know about the cancer. I only cope by bossing everyone around. How about you?'

Ellie looked at her hands. '*My* father can't believe I want to stay here. He's trying to get me to break the terms of Patience's will. But it feels sort of disrespectful now I'm starting to get to know her.'

'*Could* you break the terms of the will?'

She shrugged. 'I don't want to find out. I'll do my year because it's what Patience wanted.' She leaned back into the seat, getting a little pocket of shelter from him. 'When my mum died, I was crushed. My father cut me off from Patience, who I must have had a good relationship with. She sent me letters, presents, birthday cards, but he wouldn't even let me see them.' Ellie took a deep breath. 'He parcelled them up and sent them back with a cold little note, telling her to leave me alone.'

'God, that's harsh. She adored you.'

She turned to look at him. 'If those letters are anything to go by, she was essentially my grandmother.' She smiled. 'You would have loved my mum.'

'I *did* love your mum,' Bran said. 'We all did. I was a year older than you when Ysella died, I remembered her being carried off the ferry that last time. She was skin and bone, but so full of laughter. She had freckles and the bluest eyes.' He smiled at Ellie. 'You have her eyes, you know. I think that's why we all forgive you for getting the cottage. It's what Ysa would have wanted.'

'I wish I remembered more about her. Dad buried all that emotional stuff. He sent me off to boarding school, and that was the end of that.'

'End of what?' His voice was soft.

'Sunshine, sand, island friends. I've started to remember bits and pieces. Doughnuts – I don't know where we had them – and chips on the beach. Boats racing, this really fat dog with brown fur, ice creams we bought from a cart on the quay.'

Bran nudged her shoulder with his. 'It will come back to you. Give it time. Everyone who was here back then remembers you and Ysella.' He took a deep breath. 'Now, I have to get on. I have a load of grumpy old men to feed.' He stood, fastened his jacket. 'Bring Leo to the pub when he arrives.' His tone had changed, was cooler. 'I've reserved a sea-view room for you both.'

'That's very kind...' she started to say.

He shrugged her words off. 'Enjoy being a tourist for a few days.'

28

Patience lay close to Dutch, a hand on his chest. Her fingers played with the curls there until he looked at her and smiled.

'Don't start another storm,' he said softly.

She smiled back, still revelling in the sensation in her body. Tired, a little sore, a little ache here and there. And a feeling that nothing in the world would ever be wrong again.

'Maybe I want another storm,' she said back, teasing. 'A tornado.'

He pulled her to lie in his arms and for a long moment she just breathed in and out, all the tension and grief of the last days gone. Susie's illness was still there, to be touched and flinched away from, like a wobbly tooth in childhood.

'I love you,' she breathed, not caring if he could hear her or not.

'I love you too,' he said, almost as quietly, as if he didn't want her to hear. 'You know I would marry you if I could.'

'I believe you.' Sadness dropped onto her, and she felt cold. She pulled the blanket over her shoulders. 'But why can't you?'

'I am ashamed to tell you.' Another minute ticked by, the

silence so deep she could hear her watch clicking from the bedside table, with its moulded glass vase and plastic flowers.

'There is nothing you have done that I wouldn't understand,' she said with some conviction. 'Just say it.' *He's going to say it, he's going to tell me he's not Dutch.*

'I am already married.'

The words were a shock, like a wave of cold water. She pulled away, and stared at him. 'When? Was it someone on the islands?'

He turned to look at her, his eyes shimmering with tears in the shadows from the street light outside. People outside were talking loudly as if they were drunk, someone laughing like a donkey.

'It was when I was young, seventeen. Before I went to sea.'

She cautiously settled back into his body, his arms tightening about her fiercely. She could feel his words rumbling from his chest.

'She was sixteen. Her name was Erma Schuster. I didn't like her much but she was my friend's sister and I saw her every day.'

'You married her?'

'It was Belsnickel's night, the sixth of December. We, all the young men and boys, dressed up to scare naughty children. We were drinking, and at each house more people joined us, and brought more beer. She was there.' He sighed, shut his eyes. 'My friend Justin had brought some rum. We tried to make *feuerzangenbowle* but the sugar wouldn't burn.'

'What's... why wouldn't the sugar burn?' She just wanted to keep him talking, to explain why they couldn't spend every night together like this. Her thoughts were racing.

'It's like, what do you call it, punch? But we drop a big block of sugar into the rum, light the alcohol. But it kept blowing out.' He moved his head so he could see her. 'We drank it all, anyway. That much alcohol, wine, rum... it made me dizzy, everything was loud and funny.'

'And she was there?'

'She held my arm, pulled me behind the blacksmith's store, and kissed me. It was nice, I wanted to keep kissing, but then she undid my trousers and—'

'You and her. You did that thing, that we just did.' Her voice came out small and hard. She could feel jealousy tightening her chest and making her breaths shallow.

'No!' He shook her a little bit. 'Never think that. With you... I have never done that with anyone.' His voice was rough. 'With her it was just like two animals.'

She sat up and swung her feet to the threadbare rug beside the bed, clutched a fold of sheet over her. The image his words had created wouldn't go away.

'Patience, that was what I did with Erma, or rather, she did with me. I was drunk, she grabbed me. I was a boy.'

'But then you married her.' She was shaking as she tried to understand. She *did* understand. How many times had her own brothers been over to the big island, got drunk and did who knows what? Their father always warned them against loose young women. 'She was pregnant?'

'By someone. She told her mother she was expecting a baby. What could I do? The whole village hated me, blamed me, as if I had seduced a good girl.'

'I was a good girl. People will say you seduced *me*.' She was thinking aloud. 'What am I now?'

'We seduced each other. Two people who love each other.'

She couldn't help hugging his arms to her. 'But why we can't get married now? What about a divorce?' She turned to look at him.

'When my ship went down, she was told I died. I found out after the war that she married again, had children.'

'Your child...?'

'A boy. I wrote to my mother two years after the war ended. She told me never to write again, that I was dead to the family, a traitor. She wasn't even going to tell anyone I was alive.'

He rocked her a little. It was strangely comforting, his naked body against her back. 'What happens if I become pregnant?'

He was silent for a moment. 'I made sure you wouldn't,' he said finally.

A wave of irrational agony went through her and took her breath away. She had never wanted a child, never needed to cradle her own baby. Now she didn't have the choice.

'You would lose everything,' he said, to the back of her head, his face buried in her hair. She could feel his breath lifting the hair around one ear. 'Your reputation, your job, maybe even your family.'

'But I would have *you*. And our child.' She let the idea run, like a flame touched to a newspaper twist. 'We could pretend we were married, move far away.'

'Patience.' He let go, leaving her naked back suddenly cold. 'My temporary residence papers won't allow me to marry. The authorities would want to do a full investigation and that would mean telling the truth.'

'You are German.' It felt dangerous to say the words out loud, even now.

'They would send me back. As an enemy, or as a deserter.'

She stood, her body aching more now, perhaps from cold. She started to slip her clothes on. 'I can't stay here.'

'Please don't go.' He stood up, strangely beautiful in the low light. 'Stay the night. Everyone thinks you are married.'

She twisted off the fake wedding ring. Another lie. 'I need to think, I need time. I don't even know your real name.'

'It is Janssen, just like I said. You called me Piet but my name is Werner.' He took a deep breath, as if it hurt.

She slid her feet into her shoes. *Werner*. That's what she – his wife – had called him.

'I prefer Dutch,' she said. 'The name of my dearest friend.'

He walked to her, naked, and caught her arm. She stared down at the fingers curving over her skin. His touch had always affected her like this, like electricity.

'After our wedding, we spent three weeks together. I never touched her. I tried to be kind, patient. Then I joined the navy.'

'I have to go.'

'Please do not be anger with me. I can't bear it for you to be anger now.' His accent was always strongest when he was upset.

'I'm not *angry*. I need to think.'

'Then think here, with me. Know that I love you. Always.'

It was a strange little speech. 'I loved you,' she said, into the shadowed room, 'from the first time I saw you. There's never been anyone else for me.'

'Good,' he growled. 'I know I shouldn't be, but I am glad. Turn around.'

She did, although her hand had been reaching for the door knob. She wondered how she could have left anyway. She couldn't explain leaving to the hoteliers. They would see her slink away from a man's bedroom, all pretence gone.

He reached for her and held her tight. 'We must think about this night as magical,' he said. 'Maybe this is the only night we will have. Tonight we are just Dutch and Patsy, and we are in a room together, doing whatever we want.'

A strange longing, one that she could now give voice to, consumed her.

'This won't be the only night,' she whispered.

His skin under her hands, his fingers lifting her chin... she gave in to the feeling, and reached up to kiss him.

29

PRESENT DAY, 14 APRIL

Getting the cottage ready for Leo made Ellie look at the place through his eyes. The house looked more decrepit as she renovated. He would hate every crack and stain, the low ceilings, the scuffed doors and the mouse-chewed skirting boards. It didn't smell damp to Ellie any more, but maybe she'd got used to the mustiness.

She'd worked at the lock on the sideboard but, short of splintering the door, she couldn't force it open. There was a locksmith on the big island, but his call-out fee was huge. Whatever was inside, it weighed enough to be bricks. Ellie wondered what could be so important to Patience that it had to be locked away.

Tink had suggested breaking into the cupboard through the back panel, but when they heaved it forward they found it was hardwood and not the bit of plywood he'd been expecting. Even Tink agreed it was worth saving as he ran a hand over it. 'That's solid oak,' was his considered opinion. 'Get the locksmith. It could be something valuable.'

The cottage defied much smartening up, mainly because as she scrubbed, paint and wallpaper flaked off, sometimes with chunks of plaster. But the dresser was clean, and a good scrub had lightened it up. All the china had been put back and things like string and stamps had been put in drawers. Books were on shelves and magazines had been stacked in the shed.

She was just sweeping out more dried grass from the kitchen floor when she realised she hadn't heard the mouse this morning. The day before, she'd found a small hole under a cupboard, and had borrowed a humane trap from Corinne. Now the lid was definitely shut. She lifted it out carefully, feeling the small shift of weight as something slid around. She gently lifted the lid and looked in.

It stared back with eyes like jet buttons, each whisker a silver thread reaching across the trap, its body hunched in fear at the back of the tiny box. It quivered when she leaned in.

'Hello, mousy,' she found herself saying, very softly. At least it was only a mouse and not something larger. 'We're just going for a little ride. There will be lots of food for you, and you'll be properly wild.' She grabbed a handful of breakfast cereal and carried it outside in case it was hungry. *I'm starting to think like Patience.* The idea made her smile.

There was a wild corner by the side of the shed and she sprinkled food all around. A quick check to make sure Bertie wasn't watching, and she set the open trap on the grass. Ellie waited for the animal to emerge into freedom.

The mouse put its head forward and peered around. Ellie stepped back as it inched out, twitching. It moved fast in sharp, angled runs as if dodging sniper fire. It shot towards Ellie, then past her along the shadow of the kitchen wall. As Ellie watched, it squeezed its body into a broken air vent and disappeared back into the house.

Ellie had given up on cleaning and walked down to the quay. Her daily walk had become a sociable affair, with many people saying hello. Ahead of the school holidays, many of the cottages and accommodation were rented out. The new art gallery on the quay was alive with people going in and out, but they were keeping the curious outside until the opening. She bought a sandwich from the shop's newly opened expanded deli department and sat on a bench to wait for the inter-island ferry.

Leo seemed to have enjoyed the helicopter flight, commenting with frequent texts that he was now on the boat. The clear day had blued the water, reflecting the sky overhead, each island ringed with turquoise shallows.

Wow! It's so pretty, you can see all the little houses from up here!
The town is gorgeous, got a lift from heliport in a taxi. Just waiting for the ferry.

Enjoy the trip.

Just leaving. OMG there are seals in the harbour.

Hope it's not too rough. Don't sit at the back.

Why not?
OK, moved up the front. Soaking wet but saw SO MANY birds. Will be ten minutes.

She walked down to the slipway as the boat started its complicated approach between sandbanks, past a bit of a wreck, around buoys and moorings. Many new boats had filled up the shallow harbour over the last week, and the quay had a new park for little dinghies to row out to the boats.

She waved, and Leo stood up to wave back. She involuntarily smiled when she saw him, feeling the excitement of the reunion. His bleached hair was sharply cropped, he was wearing reflective sunglasses and she had forgotten how tall he was.

Ellie was ready to help him off, but Birdie handed her the first of three cases.

'What on earth did you bring with you?' she asked. 'I said pack *light*.'

'That *is* light,' he said, hugging her the second his feet were on the ground. He dropped a quick kiss on her lips, familiar, comforting. 'I missed you.' He released her and ran his hand over her head. 'Your hair is longer.'

She laughed. 'I haven't had a haircut for ages. I don't think there's a hairdresser on the island.'

'I like it.' He grabbed two of the bags, and she took the last one. 'Show me this pub, then. Should I have brought sanitiser and bug spray?'

'It's still the UK,' she said, smiling up at him. She *had* missed him. She hugged him again, bags and all. Even the ferryman was smiling at them.

'Thank you, Birdie,' she said, steering Leo towards the Island Queen. 'Let's get you checked in and we can see the cottage. I booked us a table at the pub tonight. You'll love it. Did you have lunch?'

'I had a cheese roll while I was waiting for the boat,' he said, making a face. 'With pickle, white bread, some sort of margarine. So retro.'

Ellie pushed open the door to the pub and walked in ahead of him. She was acutely aware of the old-fashioned feel. She rang the bell at the end of the bar and Bran poked his head out of the kitchen door.

'Hi,' he said, unsmiling. 'You must be Leo. Elowen's told us so much about you. She's booked you a sea-view room.' He didn't look at Ellie.

Leo's smile faded a little and he shook Bran's offered hand. 'Great,' he said. '*Ellie* told me.'

Bran smiled. 'Oh, I'm sorry. We all have island names here. I'm Branok Shore, but I go by Bran. It's a different world from London.'

'It certainly is,' Leo said, but didn't elaborate as Bran led the way upstairs. He seemed to approve of the room: neutral carpets, white linens on a huge, half-tester bed, a small sofa overlooking the view.

Ellie stood by the window, taking in deep breaths of fresh air from the open sash window. 'I'm so glad you came this weekend,' she said over her shoulder to Leo, who was getting a tour of the bathroom. 'The weather was stormy last week. The forecast for Easter is good.'

'Thank you, uh, Bran,' Leo said, with a polite smile. 'We'll just settle in.'

'Of course. Enjoy your stay.' Bran left and closed the door very quietly behind him.

Leo walked over to Ellie and put his arms around her waist. 'I thought he would never leave. He even showed me how the shower worked. I mean, we do have showers in London.'

'He's just doing his job. Do you want to unpack or go straight to the cottage?'

He leaned down for a kiss, then another, but something felt different. She smiled but stepped away. 'I was hoping we could lock the door and stay here for a while,' Leo said, narrowing his eyes.

Ellie was unnerved by the sudden charge of sexual energy coming from him. She felt uncomfortable, embarrassed at Bran being downstairs.

'It's just...' she said, dropping her voice. 'It's not very private. And I have to check on the sheep. They are just up behind the cottage.'

He looked a little put out, but was in a good enough mood to change his clothes into jeans and T-shirt, with a suede jacket. Ellie was concerned that his white trainers would get dirty on the rutted path, but she couldn't imagine him in wellies.

She took his hand along the quay to walk up the hill, people smiling and obviously curious but no one stopped them. He seemed interested in the craft shop, bookshop and the deli, wondered aloud what was happening at the art gallery, and was a perfect companion. Every now and then he stopped to look down the hill at the view framed by the houses on each side of the road.

'How does anyone get around?' he asked. 'It's beautiful, though.'

'There is a small tractor on the north side of the island, and Tink has a quad bike,' she said. 'He makes a bit on the side ferrying people's luggage to their holiday cottages, but he's taken his girlfriend away tonight. You'll like them.'

'It seems strange that you've made so many friends so quickly.' He stepped cautiously into one of the ruts in the lane, which had at least dried out. 'I don't even know our neighbours at the flat.'

'They all knew me when I was a child,' she explained. 'Tink and I have been friends since we were kids. Patience was his great-aunt.'

'As long as he doesn't expect a share of the money,' Leo said, laughing. 'You'd think the council would fix this road. How would you get an ambulance or fire engine up here?'

'The fire engine is a trailer filled with water, either dragged by the tractor or the quad bike,' she said. 'I've signed up to help. The ambulance is a boat or a helicopter.'

'Well, it's not like we're going to live here. I suppose it's OK for a holiday, though. It's pretty up here.' He stopped outside the first holiday let. 'See, it scrubbed up nicely.'

'Wrong one,' she said, apologetically. 'But you can see how they turn out, once they're renovated.'

They stood in front of Kittiwake Cottage. Tink had done his best to tidy up the brambles and coarse grass at the front, and the bluebells were out along the wall.

Leo didn't give much away as he stared at the house, looking at the roof and windows, the cracks in the front wall. Ellie started to see it as she had the first day.

'Well, maybe it would be easier to knock it down and rebuild it,' he said. 'Did she leave you any money for renovations?'

'No,' she said. 'There wasn't much money, just a couple of thousand. But I get the house and garden.'

Leo walked forwards and pushed the door open. 'You should lock it,' he said, but his voice was flat as he stared down the hallway. 'Oh, Ellie, it's horrible. Poor you, having to stay here.'

'It grows on you.'

She felt defensive as she showed him the living room. He avoided touching anything. Upstairs, he just gravitated to each window and shuddered at the lack of bathroom. Ellie left the cosy kitchen and dining room until last, but Leo didn't want to sit down.

'Do you mind if we see the garden?' he asked instead.

She opened the door and carried two chairs outside into the sunshine. She went back in to make tea, making sure he got the cleanest and most modern mug.

'I don't take milk any more,' he said, looking into the cup. 'I'm on a dairy-free, low-caffeine, gluten-free diet. It's helped my sinuses.'

'Oh. Good.'

'I suppose one won't hurt,' he said, smiling, but he didn't drink it. 'The shed's a good size. Is there anything in there?'

'Not much. There's a pile of boxes of books and papers. There was an old motorbike but it was left to a man in the town.'

'You don't have to deliver the bequests,' he said sternly. 'Your father told you to hold off on them until you've challenged the will.'

'This is what Patience wanted,' she said, taken aback. 'I can't argue with her wishes. These were her friends.'

'But who knows how much that bike was worth?' he said. 'Didn't you say it was an old one? It might be vintage. It could be worth thousands, enough to start the work here.'

Leo didn't understand, she comforted herself. When he met everyone he would get it.

'It could be nice out here,' he said, looking around the plot up to the stone wall. 'At least it's quiet. I thought you said the sheep woke you up?'

Oh my God, the sheep. The constant bleating of the lambs and the answering rumble of the ewes had stopped. Ellie had been given a basic tutorial on sheep care from Tink, which had consisted of 'don't let them kill themselves'.

Ellie raced across the silent garden and jumped up to see over the wall. No amount of pulling herself up on the crumbling stonework revealed a single sheep. She ran back through the house, up the stairs and to the back bedroom window. Nothing. The gate was still shut, at least, but she couldn't even hear them. At least there wasn't a motorway they could wander onto...

The picture of the clifftop came into her mind with a force that made her stagger.

'Oh, no,' she stammered, turning to go back down. 'They're gone.'

Leo was standing in the hall, looking up at her with a frown. 'Why are you so upset? They will probably come home by themselves.'

'It's not like that,' she said. 'Tink said they are his main income at the moment, so he doesn't have to go fishing with his grandad.' She kicked off her trainers and stepped into the wellies in the porch.

'Ellie!' Leo literally stamped. 'You can't just run off! I've only just got here.'

'I have to. Walk back down to the pub and wait for me. It's a small island but the cliffs...'

She heard something then, the distant sound of a lamb crying out in distress. She bolted towards the field gate, clambered over it and jogged across the grass.

Fresh hoofprints in the mud and strands of wool showed the path they must have taken through the hedge into the next field. When she crouched down she could see an open gate at the top, towards the cliff path. She crawled through, getting covered in mud and worse. The sheep appeared to have ploughed right through the polytunnel and knocked over tall plants. Her phone beeped.

Leo had messaged her: *Getting help.*

She felt bad. She'd imagined he was having a tantrum when he was actually going to find someone.

By following the track the flock had created, she found a gate hanging open and a piece of string on the ground. She followed the trail through a gap between two stone walls to a low bank beyond. They had gone through a triangular field, mostly brambles and old nettles. She swore as she stumbled after them. She was approaching the steepest ridge along the top field. Beyond was a drop of maybe sixty feet, the highest point of the cliffs. Her heart was hammering painfully as she imagined the corpses of Tink's ewes and lambs at the bottom, washed away by the tide. *Are sheep that stupid?*

She almost slipped out of the oversized wellies as she ploughed through brambles, arms held high, to a gap where the animals' feet had churned a puddle a foot deep. She slid sideways between two posts. She turned, staring down the slope, and could just pick out a trail between two hedges of the most prickly shrubs she had ever seen, and some of the spikes had strands of wool on them.

She heard the lamb calling somewhere below her. By crouching down, she could see how they had got through. Grumbling, she dropped down onto her haunches and crawled between the trunks. There was a path parallel to the top of the field, getting steeper and more slippery, and she recognised it as leading to the common by the school. Her phone rang as she clambered over another stone wall.

'What?' she managed to gasp. A least she got a signal so high up.

'We've found the sheep,' Bran said. 'I think we've got them contained in the graveyard. Where are you?'

'On my way,' she wheezed, wondering if her childhood asthma had returned.

She slid towards the stone gatepost, a wooden gate hanging off its hinges. She could hear them now, over the rasping of her own breathing and the hissing of the wind. Hopefully there would be all twenty-four ewes and thirty-eight lambs, wandering between the tombstones.

'I can see you. Don't spook them,' she gasped to Bran, who she spotted in the churchyard entrance.

'Shut the gate so they can't go back,' he answered.

'How on earth do we get them back to Tink's field?' she said, skirting the edge of the graveyard. The flock had ploughed through the allotments by the cemetery but at least hadn't stopped to eat everything. They were enjoying the long grass on the older graves.

She hung up as she saw Leo blocking the way to the gate onto the quay. As she walked towards him, she became aware of how she looked and, worse, smelled. Leo laughed, but put a hand up when he got close.

'Stay back,' he warned.

Bran waved his phone at her as he walked over.

'I've called for reinforcements,' he said. 'This has happened before. We normally just chase them back along the quay and up to the lane. Which field did Tink leave them in?'

'The one behind the cottage,' Ellie said, leaning her hands on her knees to catch her breath. 'I thought they had gone over the cliff.' When she looked up, she saw a group of people walking up to the gate. Most were smiling. 'Does everyone know?' she asked.

'Half the town,' Bran said cheerfully. 'Look on the bright side. Most people wanted a look at your boyfriend anyway.'

'Am I the news item of the week?' Leo said, not looking displeased as Bran walked away. 'He's a bit bossy, isn't he?'

'He runs the pub, it's like the town council,' she said.

It took twenty-odd people to funnel the sheep between the church and the pub without them nosing their way into open doorways. People joined in, and several children chased stragglers away from the edge of the quay, until Ellie's face was hot with embarrassment. By the time they reached the corner of Warren Lane, the whole flock was walking as a group, and pottered happily up the cobbles, occasionally stopping to nibble a window box or planter outside a cottage door. They turned the wrong way at the top of the lane, but Leo and a couple of the children flapped their hands at them until they turned left. They trotted along, gathering pace, almost catching up with Ellie. She had gone ahead, ready to direct them into the field.

She heard a woman's voice. 'What's going on?'

Ellie turned to see Jayne, the schoolteacher, walking her golden retriever. Before she could say anything, Callie walked forward and gave a puzzled bark. The sheep stopped walking and bunched up.

Far too late, Ellie remembered she had left the door to the cottage open. They turned as one unit and pranced straight through the gate. She chased after them, seeing the last of their wagging tails turning into the porch. One fat lamb even scampered halfway up the stairs before it lost its nerve. Ellie shouted at them, uselessly. They walked straight through the back door to the garden, and followed the side of the house around back to the lane.

All Ellie could do was chase the stragglers out the back door, where they had nowhere to go but towards the turning into the field. People were falling over themselves with laughter; even Leo was grinning at the chaos and mess. Bran had already opened the five-bar gate to stop them going past the opening. They wandered into the field and inspected the water trough, pushing each other out the way to get a drink.

'That's where they got out!' Ellie shouted a warning, and a couple of locals stood across the gap.

She looked around the field and saw several large plastic barrels, which could be carried over to temporarily plug the gap. As she struggled with one, she could hear people chattering and laughing, looking over the hedge. Ellie had never much liked being the centre of attention, but now she just wanted to disappear. It was only possible to count the ewes, so she had to take on trust that all the lambs would follow their mothers. They were all there.

'Thank you for your help,' she called to the group of dispersing locals.

'I'm not going back in that house until you've disinfected it,' Leo said, folding his arms. He looked her up and down swiftly. 'And yourself.'

He started back down the hill and Bran leaned on the gate. 'Do you want a shower at the pub?'

Ellie walked through and secured the gate carefully. None of the sheep seemed to be able to get through the wedged barrels. 'Thanks, but I normally go to the campsite. I can put a load of washing on there, too.'

He matched his steps to hers as they walked back to the cottage. 'I hope you enjoy Leo's visit.'

'We haven't got off to the best start,' she said, looking into the door, staring at the river of mud on the old carpets and tufts of wool caught on the doorframes. 'He wants me to get builders in to rip it all back to the stone.'

'Even locals have sold their houses to developers. It's a sort of pension fund for them.' He started to walk away. 'The islanders won't like it but, once you're back in London, you won't mind.'

30 DECEMBER 1958

I'm pregnant.

Half a dozen things clicked into place in Patience's mind. For four years Patience and Dutch had stayed in Oxford every school holiday, visiting Susie in her new hospital by day and sharing a room as Mr and Mrs Ellis by night. Susie was happier if not better, and regular contact helped her remember Patience.

Each day they were there, Patience and Dutch walked with Susie around the grounds, even taking her into the local town for a cake or some sweets. Each night, they would return to the nearby hotel. One week of respectable holiday, visiting family. Dutch covered up his absences from work carefully. But the few days and nights they had together were magical.

Despite all of Dutch's precautions, nature had succeeded. Patience leaned uneasily over the lavatory, wondering if the sickness was going to return. Her medical dictionary had rather drily suggested a biscuit or toast could reduce nausea. She pulled her dressing gown around herself and walked back into the house. It was cold. She put a sliver of stale bread in the electric toaster and looked back through her diaries. There. The very week she had chosen to go away because she wouldn't be bothered by her 'little visitor' – that must have been the time. She had bled a little a few weeks ago as if she was going to have her monthly, but it had faded away. Now she was due another but it hadn't happened. She sat calmly, and popped the bread up before it burned. She felt tired and sick, but not frightened. She took a nibble of the toast, which helped.

It's in me, wriggling like a tadpole.

She looked at the parlour clock from her childhood, which Dad had given to her, and realised she had an hour or more before she had to get to the school. She threw on some trousers and a warm jumper, and slipped into her boots.

The school was up a track off Long Lane, and adjoined the 'village green', a piece of rough grass gifted to the village by a long-dead Ellis. The cottage was tucked up behind it, giving her a lot of privacy. She could trek up to the lane and walk to the northernmost point, Lighthouse Rock, the base of a long blown-down tower. There she allowed the wind to fill her lungs and flap her trouser legs while she looked past the edge of the islands.

It was a long view; she could see right to the horizon. Despite the cold, the sun was out, the clouds creating a patch-work of shadows on the sea. The deepest areas were Prussian blue, straight out of a paint set; the shallowest were turquoise, and the seabed created every shade in between. The sunniest parts were sparkling with reflections, the cloud-shaded parts sombre and opaque. As she stood, dolphins arced out of the sea immediately below the bluff. The tide spun around the outcrop of rock, carving a deep channel, and fish concentrated there. The dolphins leapt out of the water again and again, the sun making them look as if they were cast from steel. She allowed her fingers to smooth her flat belly through the thick gansey.

She turned and walked back along the cliff path. She had a couple of months before she started to show. It helped that she was so tall – only a few inches shorter than Dutch, and he dwarfed the men of her family.

'Something will happen,' she thought, staring back over the pink eastern sky. There had to be a way through. She started to smile.

'I'm keeping the baby!' she shouted to the screaming gulls.

31

PRESENT DAY, 14 APRIL

Ellie had showered at the campsite and done a hot wash with her clothes. Freshly changed, she walked down to the pub. She chose the narrower Fore Street to avoid the trail of mud the sheep had carried up Warren Lane. When she walked into the bar, Bran's father was alone. He was in a chair with a good view over the whole pub.

'I heard you had an adventure,' he said, his voice booming out across the low, dark room.

'I expect everyone's heard about it by now,' Ellie said. She couldn't see anyone else, there was always a lull around four every afternoon. 'At least the sheep didn't fall over the cliff.'

'They're stupid but they aren't lemmings,' Joe Shore said. 'Do you fancy a drink? I could do with the company.'

'OK.' Ellie was a bit intimidated by the man. When Max came into the bar, Joe ordered two beers, but Ellie downgraded hers to a soft drink.

'Not much of a drinker, eh?' The man looked at her as if she'd admitted to being secretly twelve.

'I'm not.' She was at a loss as to what to talk about, but Joe had plenty to say.

'That Leo, he's a nice guy. You want to hang on to him.'

'I'll try.' Ellie smiled as Max delivered their drinks.

'Like my Branok, overqualified to run a pub. You educate people, you raise their expectations. But work on the islands is whatever you can do. Hand-to-mouth employment.'

Ellie sipped her drink. 'Bran does a great job,' she said, but Joe had a lot more to say.

He ran through the unfairness of the government, and the inability of the council to understand the needs of these remote Atlantic outposts. Ellie let the words wash over her. Clearly the old man was angry but she could also see how ill he was. His skin was loose on his cheeks and neck, his left hand was shaky even when he was hitting the table for emphasis and the right one was clenched in his lap. She realised he had stopped speaking and was staring at her.

'I had a stroke, you know.'

'Bran told me,' Ellie said, her words gentle.

'Patience got out clean,' Joe said, and lifted his beer to take a gulp. It shook in his hand and a little spilled. 'Died in her sleep. I was stuck in Plymouth for two months, and now I need help standing up.' His jaw worked like he was chewing something unpleasant. 'Bran wants me to have carers, but there aren't any on the island. I'd have to move.'

'I heard you were selling up.'

'Some developers are coming to see it. I priced it high. I didn't want timewasters.' He snorted. 'They'll probably to turn it into a "destination". But where are the local people going to have a pint in the winter? That's what I want to know. Serving fancy food imported from God knows where. Twelve-quid starters by some Michelin-starred chef.'

The old bar could certainly do with a bit of modernising, but Ellie didn't want to say that to Joe, who was struggling to wipe a trail of spittle from the drooping corner of his mouth.

'I'm dying, you know,' Joe said conversationally, his voice

raspy with effort. 'The stroke was a symptom of prostate cancer, advanced.'

'Oh.' Ellie glanced over at the bar, where Max was polishing glasses. 'I'm sorry.'

'It's spread now. I had a bit of treatment but it didn't take. And I hated the side effects. So I came home.' He leaned back and waved to Max, pointing at his empty glass. 'Bran knows, but he thinks it's in remission.'

Ellie didn't comment. Bran had already told her.

Instead, she said, 'He was really successful in London, people tell me.'

'He's very talented. Don't tell him I said that. Don't tell him anything.' He reached for the new pint. 'I saw his work once, in a gallery in Whitechapel. There were some big names alongside my boy.'

Ellie nodded.

Joe sipped his drink, his hand shaking. He set the glass down slightly over the edge of the table. 'I'm going to have to let the pub go,' he said finally.

'Is there anywhere else for people to meet?' Ellie leaned forward to nudge the beer back.

'We used to have four pubs on the island,' Joe said, glancing back towards the bar. 'Mrs Maintree's, the Mermaid's Purse and The White Whale were the other ones, right up to the sixties. They're all gone now. Well, the Purse is being divided into flats, run by some holiday company. The Whale was demolished after a fire, and Mrs Maintree's is a house now.' He turned to look at Ellie. 'We had a population of four hundred people back then, and eight fishing boats. All the islands had fishing ports with enough stock out there for everyone. They did filleting, salting and canning down at Elk's sheds. This was all after the war. Before we ran out of sardines and fishing quotas killed us.'

Ellie could hear the nostalgia in Joe's voice. She looked

around. Old framed photographs competed with boat paraphernalia; the place was like a museum.

'How long have you had the pub?'

'I inherited it from my father. *His* dad went down on the *Island Queen* in 1940. I was a trawlerman from sixteen. When my parents retired, I took over the pub. Bran was born here,' he said. 'I had hoped to leave my half of the pub to him, but he doesn't want it.' He shrugged. 'He'll have a good pot of money when I've gone.'

Ellie finished her drink. 'I ought to find Leo. He's just getting changed.'

'Wait, one moment.' Joe looked down at his drink for a minute as if he was wrestling with something. 'I need you to do something for me. I can pay.'

'No, that's OK. I'll help if I can.' Ellie sat back.

'You're some sort of accountant, aren't you?'

'I'm a forensic accountant. I look for evidence that a client is being defrauded.'

Joe beat his good fist on his knee. 'I need someone who can meet these developers, to work out what they are offering,' he said finally. 'I want to try and keep the pub open for the islanders.'

'I could listen to them, find out what their plans are?' Ellie could see him relaxing slowly.

'You could show them round when they view the place, hear what they are saying. I can't manage the stairs. I can barely walk to the kitchen.' He nodded. 'So, I'll pay you. You'll be working for me, confidentially.'

Ellie nodded. 'I can do that. When?'

'They're coming next Friday and they're staying overnight. They want to see the whole island.'

Ellie looked up as she saw movement out of the corner of her eye. Leo was standing by the bar. 'I'll be happy to help, but Bran isn't going to like it.'

'Not a word to my son, OK? Promise?'

'Yes, sir,' Ellie found herself saying. 'Thanks for the drink.'

Leo came over with Bran. 'I'm ready for you to show me the island,' Leo said, smiling at Ellie. 'Bran's recommended the coastal path and Seal Cove.'

'You'll see the island at its best.' Bran's voice was still cool. 'And we'll have a special dinner for you both this evening.'

Ellie felt uncomfortable, like a traitor for helping Bran's dad. Leo reached for her hand.

Branok and his team had created a feast for them. Even Leo was impressed.

They started with butternut squash and coconut soup, which was full of lemongrass and spices. It was followed by seared bream bought off the quay from Clem's boat, with lemon and herb butter, and finished with a local apple pudding with clotted cream. They shared a bottle of wine and, by the end of it, Leo was happier than he'd seemed in months.

'I missed you,' he said. 'Stay with me tonight.' He leaned forward and she caught her breath.

'I can't stay all night,' she said, swallowing the last of her wine. 'I'll sneak out when you're asleep.'

'Are you really going to sleep in all that mess? And it's going to be cold tonight.'

'It's OK upstairs,' she said. 'I'll get the muddy carpets up. I can put them in the shed now the bike is gone.'

'I looked that old motorbike up on the internet,' he said. 'They sell for thousands, you know. Are you sure she intended you to give it away? I mean, one could argue it came with the house.'

'I'm quite sure. And, honestly, it was pretty old and knackered.'

Which wasn't completely true. The old engine had seized

and there was a fair bit of rust underneath, but it was salvage-able. Ellie had helped Tink load it onto the trailer to take it down to Elk. He had laid his hands on it as if communing with the dead Patience.

'Thank you,' he'd breathed. When they turned to leave, Elk had stopped Ellie. 'If you want money for it, I'm happy to pay.'

'She wanted you to have it.'

'Well, remember what I said.' Elk's face had been serious. 'Patience helped me when I was at a very low point.'

The memory made Ellie smile as she left the table and headed for the stairs at the back of the pub. With the food and the wine, she suddenly didn't care what Bran or anyone else thought about her climbing those stairs with her boyfriend and making love for the first time in weeks.

32

It wouldn't be easy to do, Patience decided. If she hid the pregnancy, she had to be off the island for the shortest time so no one believed she was the mother. Susannah would have to be the reason. Her condition had made her more fragile, and she could be ill for months with a simple cough. Patience would have to create a web of lies and half-truths to get away with it.

The hardest thing would be risking her beloved job, because she would be showing by the end of term. She had arranged to meet the head of the board of governors in private. She wriggled into her smallest and most uncomfortable girdle, and luckily the nausea in the first few weeks had slimmed down her face and she didn't look pregnant yet. With luck, the board would find it impossible to replace her in time and she could be rehired in the autumn. It was always difficult to recruit on such a small wage and with the limited accommodation. She scraped back every tendril of hair. Only Dutch got to see her hair unbound, rippling down her naked back. She blushed at the idea. This wasn't the day for that kind of thought.

Clem, now twenty years old and working on one of the inshore fishing boats, gave her a lift over to the big island. He'd placed a bit of oilskin over the bench seat, where they had landed several crates of lobsters earlier in the day.

'Don't want you stinking of fish for your meeting,' he said, grinning. 'How are you, Patsy? You look a bit peaky.'

'Not used to the boat any more,' she said, settling her good leather bag on her lap, over her tummy. Over the baby. 'How's Dad?'

'He's OK. Missus is a bit fussier than Mam, I'll say that. It's brush your hair and wash your hands *before* you sit on the lavvy.'

She smiled at that. 'She's made the house nice.'

'If you mean full, you're right. She brought everything from her old house over. Some of Mam's stuff is in the shed. Dad would let you have a look through it if you like. Some of our old toys and stuff. I thought Susie might fancy a few bits.'

She relaxed. 'How are your wedding plans going?'

'Oh, you know. Beth wants it to be all flowers and taffeta, but her dad can't afford all that, and neither can I.' He steered expertly alongside Kettle Rock. The blades of sharp rock stood just under the surface, and Patience could see green tendrils of deeper water rushing by. 'How about you? Has anyone caught your fancy yet?'

She shook her head. 'Most of the men in my life are family or under twelve. Except for the odd train ride to see Susie, I don't meet any strangers.'

'I always thought you and Dutch would end up together,' he said, pulling hard on the outboard.

'Well, he got the closest.' She smiled, her heart lurching into her throat. 'But I couldn't give up my job, and he's got his own life in Cornwall.'

'I see him sometimes. We've had a few pints and he talks fondly of you.' He glanced at her. 'You're not pretty like Susie but you're not bad, and you're not *that* old.'

She dipped her hand in the water rushing by and splashed him. 'You were always the pretty one,' she said, laughing.

He brushed a few drops off his blond beard. He was almost as fair as his sisters. 'So, what's this meeting about?'

Her smile faded. She didn't want to lie any more but it wasn't just her secret to keep. 'I'm going to take extra leave, so I can spend some time with Susie. She's not doing very well.'

He clenched his jaw. 'I ought to go and visit.'

'She wouldn't recognise you, now,' she said gently. 'She thinks of you as a little boy. She hardly knows who I am, even though I see her every holiday. The asylum in Oxford is too far to go every month.'

'But you'll be able to help?'

She shrugged. 'Maybe not. But I've saved a bit of money, and I could do with a break. There's an assistant teacher on St Brannock's. I hope she'll be able to step in if I leave plenty of prepared lessons. It's only the summer term coming up. They mostly play cricket on the green and go to the beach.'

'Well, good luck to you,' he said. 'Just make sure you're there to watch me walk down the aisle, as soon as Beth agrees a date.'

'I'll be back,' she said. 'I need to be home for the new term in September anyway.' *If they will take me back.* She caught her breath at the thought of the dangerous game she was playing.

33

PRESENT DAY, 15 APRIL

Ellie crept into the cottage at two in the morning, determined not to break the requirement of living in the house for a year. Opening the door released a strong smell of sheep, manure and mud, but it wasn't too bad upstairs.

The romantic reunion with Leo hadn't gone so well. He was demanding and found fault with everything, especially anything Bran had done. They had fallen into bed and made love out of habit more than anything else. Afterwards, she lay awake, watching reflections of the moon rippling across the ceiling before sliding out of bed and into her clothes. Maybe he was tired; he'd had a long journey and she hadn't given him much attention. Another part of her wondered whether she put Leo first all the time.

When she woke, she got washed and dressed in old clothes, ready to tackle the mess the sheep had made. Getting the carpets up was heavy work, but she rolled them up and dragged them into the hall. The one in the living room had been green, with faded beige swirls. The hall and stair carpets popped off from a thousand tacks and had originally been patterned red. The rug in the dining room on the bare boards had mostly been protected from the sheep by the table and chairs. She sneakily liked it, although it was somewhere between old-fashioned and antique.

The front door opened, and she shouted through, 'Morning, Maggi!'

'Two letters and a package,' Maggi said, coming in. 'My, you have been busy! Those floorboards look good in the hall.'

'Be careful,' she said, pushing her hair out of her eyes. 'There are nails everywhere.' She looked at Maggi's mass of white hair, twisted up on her head into some kind of bun. 'Is there a hairdresser on the island?'

'Well, there's Amber,' she said, holding out her post but hanging on to the parcel. 'She comes over sometimes. She's very affordable. As you can see, I don't need a lot of cutting and perming.' She tossed her head back like a shampoo advertisement. 'But she gives me a trim now and then.' She held out the package. 'This is for you,' she said, her voice dropping. 'I could tell it's important.'

Ellie stared at her. 'What's wrong?'

'I couldn't help noticing you're getting a lot of these letters. This is from a solicitor – it says so on the back. If you were in trouble, you would tell us, wouldn't you?'

She was touched. 'Maggi, it's fine. It's something my dad wants me to do, that's all.' She opened the padded envelope to reveal a whole folder of legal documents, presumably from her father's solicitor. 'My father is trying to help but he doesn't need to. I just need to stay here for a year, and then I'll inherit the cottage.'

'That's what Patience wanted.' Maggi stared up at her for a few seconds. 'You have Ysa's eyes, did anyone ever tell you that?'

An hour later, as she scrubbed the boards in the hallway, two people appeared, silhouetted in the doorway.

'Good morning,' Leo said, holding out a paper bag that smelled like bacon. 'I brought you a breakfast roll.'

Corinne was with him, smiling. 'The hall looks better already,' she said, peering in as Ellie took the bag. 'We heard about the sheep. Tink's fixed the hole. And I met Leo on the quay.'

'Are the sheep OK?' Ellie asked.

'They're fine. A bit frisky after their adventure but none of them are hurt.'

'Good. That's a relief.' Ellie smiled at Leo. 'Come in, I'll put the kettle on,' she said, looking into the bag. The cook had squeezed a fried egg, bacon and a slice of black pudding into a bap, and added a squirt of ketchup. 'Bran knows my favourite breakfast already.'

'I didn't know you liked black pudding,' Leo said, trying to avoid contact with the walls by holding his hands up. 'This place smells like a farm.'

'It will be better without the carpet,' she said, folding the paper down so she could take a first bite. It was lukewarm, but delicious. 'I'll leave all the windows open. Have you had breakfast?' she mumbled through a mouthful of food.

Leo rolled his eyes. 'I had gluten-free granola and orange juice. I'll make the tea.'

Corinne was examining the stack of old carpets. 'Can we have these?' she asked. 'These are proper wool on hessian.'

Leo looked amused. 'What do you need old carpets for? The sheep shed?'

Corinne laughed. 'You really are a townie, aren't you? We lay it down on the growing beds to kill the weeds.'

Ellie finished her sandwich while Leo filled the kettle, grimacing at the rattling sound of the cold tap.

'Honestly, Ellie,' he said. 'You can't stay here all year. What will happen in the winter?'

'I'll have the heating sorted by then,' she said, the niggle at the back of her head tickling. 'There must be gas on the island.'

Corinne laughed her deep chuckle. 'You are kidding? No, you'll be electric all the way and even that's not reliable if we have storms. You could stick solar panels on the roof to help. We have a wood burner but chopped logs have to be imported as well, along with fuel oil or tank gas. We scavenge on the beach for driftwood.'

Leo filled three cups. 'I can't believe you camped in a truck all winter.'

'Until the water froze,' Corinne said, taking one. 'Then we went to stay with Clem and Sarah for a few weeks before the lambing started. The winters here are very mild, normally, but you still need some heating. The wind is relentless.'

'Patience had some logs,' Ellie said. 'I've been using them but I'll run out soon.'

'You need to buy from the collective,' Corinne said. 'Some islanders get together to hire the freight ship and get tonnes of wood and fuel oil delivered to the quay. Then we all run around stashing it away for the winter. The shop gets a few bags a week delivered but it's not enough for everyone.'

Ellie watched Leo sit on a dining chair, elbows against his sides. 'I really don't like the mess,' he said, looking into the cup. He put it down. 'What are we going to do today?'

'I thought we would catch a boat to the opposite island, St Petroc's, and see all the sights,' she said. 'And have lunch in the garden there.'

'Yes, but...' he said, a little upturn of his lips that was almost a smile. 'Then what?'

'I don't know.' She genuinely didn't. 'Maybe we could explore some of the other islands. I haven't had time to be a tourist, not properly, but more of the boats are running now.'

Corinne finished her tea. 'Bran's got a whole load of

brochures at the pub. There are some great places to visit. There are gardens, historical houses, art galleries and shops all over the islands. Good places to eat, too. St Piran's has a great fish place and West Island has a crab shack on the beach that's very popular.'

'I've packed a few walking clothes,' Leo said. He leaned over the packet of papers on the table, nudged it with his hand as Ellie followed Corinne out.

'Can we just come and get the old carpet?'

'Any time, help yourself.'

Ellie shut the door behind her, then went back to the dining room. Leo had prodded the top papers off and turned his head to read.

'You only had to ask,' she said.

'I didn't want to pry, but it's what your father said he was working on. Getting us the house without the stupid conditions.'

If you don't want to pry, don't read my mail. She pressed her lips tighter to avoid saying anything.

'Why don't you go back and get changed at the pub? I'll have a wash and get dressed, walk down to meet you. High tide's about eleven.'

'Bran said he could do us a packed lunch,' he said, standing and drifting towards the hall. 'We could have a picnic, my treat.'

When he was gone, Ellie sat at the table and started looking over the documents. The terse handwritten letter was almost torn in places, where her father had angrily scratched into the paper. *If you can't see sense—*

Ellie forced the whole lot back into the envelope and threw it on top of the bin.

34

Patience had registered for medical care under Susannah's name. She couldn't pretend she was married, and now she was showing. She got second-class care from the beginning. She was five months gone by the time she moved to Oxford, into a boarding house for unmarried women. She continued to visit Susannah, although some of the staff were cool towards her. Susie hardly noticed, and since the regular visits improved her behaviour, no one suggested they stopped.

When the pains started, she was told to walk the half-mile down to the hospital. The labour was worse than a storm, and Patience felt she was going to be wrenched in half. The nurses were brisk but unhelpful, and when the doctor ordered some medication for her it never arrived. Stuck in her bed of pain, she had never felt more helpless. Instead, she tried to stifle the cries, and think of the baby.

The midwife had strong opinions on unmarried women. 'There are plenty of good people ready to adopt babies,' she said briskly, walking over to the window and adjusting the blind. 'Although you've left it a bit late.'

'I'm keeping my baby,' Patience said, before she was caught up again.

'Well, we'll see,' the woman said, leaning over her to press an ear trumpet against Patience's contracting belly. 'He seems to be doing well in there. I'll come in later and examine you again. It won't be too long now.'

'The doctor said—' Patience gasped.

'Well, the doctors don't know everything. It will all be over by tea time, mark my words.'

Patience looked up at the clock, but it was stuck on ten to eleven. She twisted in the sheets, trying to make it better, easier, but any movement set the off pain again. She sobbed into the covers, hiding her face. *Dutch.*

Less than an hour later, she could hear the clack-clack of shoes outside her room. When the midwife pushed open the door, Patience was curled up on the bed, barely able to speak.

'I'll deal with her, nurse. The wages of sin, they say.' She examined Patience deftly but the process set off a huge pain. 'Well, it seems I was right,' the woman said, pressing a buzzer. 'Let's get this little mite out.'

The next few contractions were huge, like winter rollers coming from America across the Atlantic, lifting Patience up and then drowning her in exhaustion. Two women supported her legs, and ordered her to push. With her last energy, Patience put everything into it.

'Push the pain away,' a younger woman said, leaning over her. 'You can do it.'

Her kind smile anchored Patience for a moment, and when the wave lifted her, she pushed. A burning pain made her cry out.

'Well done!' the kind nurse said. 'Just pant, now. Your baby is coming...'

.   .   .

A few minutes later, Patience lay exhausted, the baby in her arms. Six pounds one ounce, they said. A baby girl, alive and well. The attitude of the midwife had softened, seeing them together.

'It's a miracle, every time,' she said, nodding. 'You remember to do what's best for your daughter. You're a mother now.'

My daughter. I am a mother. Patience examined the tiny fingers with transparent nails, curled around one of her own. *Ysella.* She barely looked up when a woman in a tweed suit and a satchel walked in.

'I understand you are not married, Miss Ellis? Most unfortunate, but I am here to help you do the right thing for your child. I represent an adoption agency that has childless couples ready to give a baby a wonderful life.'

'I am taking her home to my family,' Patience said, looking back down at the baby. She had a cap of pale hair, like Susannah. 'They will love her.'

'Many women have tried, but it's natural for there to be some awkwardness. Some stigma for the child. People can be cruel.' The woman sat on a chair by the bed. 'It's better for Baby if she is adopted from birth. Better for you, too. I shall leave you some helpful leaflets. Our social worker will call in tomorrow, to answer any questions you may have.'

'I won't change my mind,' Patience said.

'I understand you are a teacher. How will you make a living and support her, when you lose your job?'

'Please go. I have nothing to say to you.' Patience hardly noticed her leaving. The baby opened her eyes and looked up, her gaze wavering until it locked on her mother's. 'Oh, my goodness,' Patience whispered. 'What a lot of nonsense. I will *never* let you go.' But the plan would have to be perfectly executed, and the hardest thing would be ending any relationship with Dutch.

No one must ever guess.

35

PRESENT DAY, 19 APRIL

Ellie and Leo spent days exploring the islands, finding coves and beaches and the spectacular garden on St Petroc's.

They walked around Morwen every evening, and Ellie was sure she'd now identified every house on the island. They took lessons at the sailing school, during which Leo had to be rescued by the safety boat. They went canoeing off St Piran's and encountered seals in the harbour, and Ellie fell in love with a litter of kittens on West Island. As the week had gone on, they had seen more ladders, white-spattered painters and people carrying power tools in and out of the new art gallery. Judith, the director, and Poppy, the owner, were mysterious about the art inside.

'You'll have to come to the opening tonight,' Judith said, chasing them away from the whited-out windows. 'It's not what you might expect. Living in London, you probably go to lots of galleries.'

'I do,' said Leo, glancing at Ellie. 'She's not so keen.'

'I don't have as much time, usually,' she said. 'I work a lot of hours.'

Judith leaned on the railings which protected part of the quayside. 'Have you been able to work from here?'

'I have a phone and broadband being installed next month. But I've been able to analyse accounts offline most days.'

'Oh, that's right,' she said, looking from one to the other with blue eyes that seemed to see everything. 'You can't leave the island.'

'I can't stay away from the house,' she admitted. 'As far as I know, that means spending each night there.'

'She could challenge the will,' Leo said, staring out to sea. 'I know it's lovely here now, but it won't be so great in the winter.'

'Oh, that's the best time!' Judith said. 'We get rid of the tourists, and get on with our lives. Artists paint, writers write, everyone enjoys the peace and quiet.'

'Do you stay here all winter?' Ellie asked.

'Well, not *all* winter. It's the best time for me to work and make some money. I'm a gallerist and agent. I help my artists display their work in the UK and Italy.'

She was curious. 'Have you shown any of Bran's work?'

'No. And yes. He won't let me exhibit any of his unsold work, most of it's in storage. But I have a piece I bought off him years ago, and I like to show it when I can.' Judith checked her watch. 'Well, I have to go. There isn't a straight wall in the gallery and some of the pictures will need moving. See you for the opening? Starts at seven and there will be wine and nibbles.'

'Definitely,' Ellie said.

Once Judith had gone, Leo made a little face. 'It's probably all seascapes for the tourists.'

'Not if she's an artists' agent.' Part of her was curious to see Bran's work. 'Come on, or we'll miss the boat to the big island. I want to show you this amazing place Tink told me about.'

Leo laughed. 'You've started doing it now. Using all the nicknames for the islands.'

'No one ever calls it anything else,' she said, grinning at him.

Leo was funny. Even when they didn't agree, he was warm and funny and loved her. But his arguments about stripping out and rebuilding the cottage were starting to wear Ellie down, especially when they sounded so reasonable.

That evening, Ellie got ready at the pub. Leo had packed a smart pair of trousers, a pressed shirt and nice tie. The weather was dry but cold as evening fell, but they only had to walk along the quay to the new gallery.

The word 'Seaglass' was freshly painted over the window, and people were standing round both inside and outside holding glasses of wine and talking. As they slowly progressed around the space, Ellie was amazed at the variety and quality of the art. There were gorgeous seascapes in surprising colours that seemed to heave when you saw them at an angle; abstracts with a hint of secret landscapes in their colours; portraits of local people and strangers, in etchings and on glass.

On a central pedestal was a metre-high abstract sculpture in glorious sea and sky colours. Ellie knew instantly it was Bran's, although there were some other ceramics around. It was spiralled around itself like a tornado, as if the sea and sky had been torn up and twisted.

She reached a hand out to touch it, then didn't dare. There were his finger impressions in the clay; she could see where Bran had formed it with his palms, where his brush had applied the glazes. Everything coalesced in her head. This was the Bran she wanted to know, that she had seen in glimpses. He kept so much hidden, tides of anger and frustration rolling in and out, his fierce protectiveness of the islanders, his passionate and raging love for his father. Here was a radiant glimpse of another Bran.

Bran.

She put her hand up to her face to conceal her emotions for

a moment, backtracking fast. Bran wasn't good-looking like Leo, he was prone to being snippy and cool, and he didn't even seem to like Ellie half the time. As she stood there, she wondered if her feelings were admiration, an artistic crush. She glanced across at Leo, also staring at the sculpture. She had wanted the same life that Leo did – he was a match for her. But under that, it felt like the waters of a shallow beach. There was turquoise brine sparkling over pale sand, and nothing else.

'That is lovely. Is there a price?' Leo was talking to Judith, but glanced at Ellie. His face changed a little and she wondered if he guessed what she was thinking.

'No, it's mine. I bought it when it was cheap, straight off Bran's graduation show. It's great, isn't it?'

Poppy joined them. 'Why can't he do more big pieces like this? Judith could get him a show.'

'It would be easy, it's great stuff,' Judith added.

Poppy nodded. 'He just needs a kiln and somewhere to work.'

'Bloody big kiln,' said Branok, right by Ellie's ear, making her jump. 'If you guys can come up with a house and studio for, say, under three hundred grand, I might give it a go. London is easier for work in so many ways.'

'And London was your home,' Leo interrupted. 'You lived there before.'

'I don't think I'm at home anywhere at the moment,' Bran said slowly. 'But I know how to be an artist in the city.' He looked over his own piece with a critical frown. 'I've grown past this stuff, though.'

'I think it's amazing,' Ellie said self-consciously, her heart beating a little bit faster.

'It's getting the gallery off to a great start,' Poppy added. 'It would be lovely to have a few more pieces.'

'I won't even be here soon,' Bran said. 'I think Dad's finally considering selling the pub. There's a viewing.'

'Is it the Americans?' Poppy said. 'I hear they want to convert the Island Queen into a restaurant.'

'I don't know if they are American. They're looking at several places, though, so they might not want our old wreck of a pub.'

Ellie wondered if her thoughts were somehow readable on her face as she turned away from Bran and smiled at Leo. 'Shall we go?'

'We've only just got here,' he said. 'Are you OK? You look a bit red in the face.'

'I'm a bit hot,' she said. 'I'll go outside for a moment.'

Ellie threaded her way through the crowded gallery out onto the street. She was confused. There was a feeling of closeness with Bran, maybe because he held memories of her mother and her childhood. Ellie needed to shake the feeling off.

She stared over the black water, the streetlights along the quay creating moving reflections in the water. The tide was swirling in, the few boats anchored in the Sound pulling against their buoys. *I've never felt more at home anywhere.* Leo wouldn't understand; he was so rooted in London.

A childhood moment unfolded like a letter from the past. She remembered running down the hill in canvas shoes to get a pint of milk from the shop. People smiled and greeted her, and finally she burst out onto the quay, bright in morning light, as the fishing boats were unloading their silvery catch. She was completely happy, at ease with the place, knowing she was going back to Mummy and Nana. *Nana.*

She could see Patience's broad shoulders now, her pale eyelashes and hair and freckled face, the flowery dresses she wore most of the year. She could feel her arms around Ellie; she seemed huge. She usually wore an apron – it smelled of baking and dog. Dog! She had almost forgotten Nana had a three-legged collie that had washed up half-drowned on the shore.

She remembered cooking with her, eating more mixture than cake as they sat in the garden.

'Watch out for the ants,' she used to say. There was a red ants' nest by the back wall, but she was too tender-hearted to kill them. Ellie sat on one once and had an itchy welt for days. She'd cried into the apron but Nana soon gave her something to do.

'Get some milk from the shop, Elowen. We'll have hot chocolate with our cakes.' And they did.

'Are you OK?' Leo's voice came from her left shoulder and she was dragged back into the present.

She wiped her eyes. 'Sorry. It's the wind.'

'The exhibition's better than I thought. Did you see the seascapes? Totally unexpected colours, lovely. I'd put any of them on our walls.'

Ellie moved a few yards down the quayside. Her chest was full of tension, like she was jam-packed with emotions from the last few weeks. 'Leo—'

He put a hand up to stop her. 'Don't say anything. I know you're going through something with this bloody house. I get that... well, I sort of do. It's your mum, isn't it?'

She nodded. *It's everything.*

'It's given me time to think, too. I've loved seeing you, spending time together. We haven't had a proper holiday for ages. But we've got a lot of changes coming.'

'Maybe I do need the whole year,' she said. 'I'm starting to find out so much about my childhood, not just about Patience and Ysella.'

Leo winced. 'That still seems like a long time to me,' he said, with a nervous laugh. 'I do love you, Ellie. I want to be really sure that we have a whole life planned out before we buy a house together.'

'So you understand why I don't want to challenge the terms of the will?'

'God, no!' He laughed aloud at the thought. 'Your dad knows what he's doing. I could probably argue against the conditions in the will myself.'

She tried to smile at him, but couldn't. Her father had swept her mother and all her belongings away by the day of her funeral, just leaving a couple of framed photographs on the mantelpiece.

'He's doing his best,' Leo said, slipping his arm around her shoulders and squeezing. 'He loves you.'

'Does he, though?' Ellie wondered. 'I'm a massive disappointment all the time. I'm too emotional, unfocused; you must have heard him say that a thousand times.'

'He's just not very expressive. But he wants to help with the will and I think you should at least read the documents. It would be awful if there was some loophole that meant you lost the cottage after spending months here.' He looked out over the water. 'Who knows if someone else is already trying to break the will? One of her close relatives.'

'She adopted my mum. You can't get much closer than that. I'm practically a granddaughter.'

'But was she ever *formally* adopted? Surely it's on her birth certificate?'

She thought back through the few documents she had found. 'I don't know. There might be some more documents. I haven't been able to unlock the sideboard yet.'

'Break it open,' he said. 'And speak to your father. He just wants what's best for you, and he probably has more of your mother's papers.'

It occurred to Ellie that Morwen was a fortress against her father. In those terrible days after her mother died, remembered in sharp fragments, her father said over and over that he would never go back to the island.

36

19 AUGUST 1959

Two months later, Patience Ellis stood tall at the railway station. She had acquired more confidence in her posture, strapped into a breast binder and her strictest girdle. She could hardly bend. There were a few tiny lines around her eyes now, and her hair had been cropped short under a little hat. She raised a hand to attract a porter and he came at a run. She shifted the baby further up her shoulder, nestled under a fold of her coat.

'Take my bags onto *Islander II*, please,' she said. 'Except the carpet bag.' She had two bottles of milk formula in there, tucked amongst the spare nappies and clothes, and a toilet bag for changes. *Please God, don't let Dutch be on duty. He hasn't seen the baby yet – he'll give us away.*

'Miss Ellis!'

Mrs Wyndham, mother of Bert and Annie, was approaching fast. The expression on the woman's face cycled through everything from pleasure to consternation to actual outrage as she registered what Patience was holding out of the wind.

'Good afternoon, Mrs Wyndham,' Patience said, and rather

maliciously asked after the children and Mr Wyndham. She could see the older woman was bursting to ask why Patience Ellis had left her post at the school and was now carrying a baby.

'What a young baby to be travelling,' Mrs Wyndham said, her composure returning. 'Is the mother with you?'

'I'm afraid not,' Patience said, weighing up the options. Mrs Wyndham was somewhat inclined to embellish gossip, which might serve Patience's purpose. 'Her mother, a cousin on my mother's side, is unable to look after her at the moment. She is very unwell.'

'That's very noble of you, taking on an infant. Especially as you are an unmarried teacher.' She tittered. 'One wouldn't want someone to jump to conclusions.'

Patience stared her down. 'I don't know what you mean,' she said, her voice cool. She looked down at the baby's head. 'I know my mother would have offered the poor child a home, and her situation is no fault of her own.' She let the coat fall, and Ysella's little face was just visible under her knitted hat. The magic worked, and Mrs Wyndham immediately started cooing.

'Oh, what a lamb,' she said. 'And so tiny.'

'Her mother is very ill,' Patience improvised. 'In hospital. The baby was premature.'

Mrs Wyndham nodded wisely. 'Tuberculosis, I suppose? It's a terrible problem but the treatments are getting better every year.'

'Excuse me,' Patience said. 'I must follow my luggage.'

She gathered every bit of dignity and poise she could manage, lifted the case and walked tall to the gangway. Another officer, thankfully, was helping passengers on. She found a corner seat in the saloon, and opened the carpet bag her mother had brought to the island when she married. She opened it and laid the sleeping baby snugly on the padded contents. By moving the bag out of the sun, she could be sure she was free from draughts and protected from the jolting of the ship as it left port.

Ysella, already the most precious thing in the world, half smiled in her sleep. Patience sat where she could see every expression on the baby's face, and prepared to face more questions.

And Dutch, the most painful thought of all.

37

PRESENT DAY, 22 APRIL

Something fundamental had shifted between Leo and Ellie the moment she had seen Bran's sculpture. It was as if she had seen deep into the artist's soul and been drawn in.

The warmth was still there with Leo, but there was a distance during the last days of his stay. They didn't make love; they were more affectionate instead. When Leo was waiting for the ferry to take him back to the heliport, Ellie longed for the awkward goodbyes to be over.

'There it is now,' Leo said, shielding his eyes from the morning sun as the boat approached.

'It's been lovely to see you,' she said. When he leaned forward to kiss her, she moved back involuntarily. His kiss grazed her cheek.

'Call me tonight,' she said, stepping back.

'I will.'

It was a relief to wave him off, and she stayed until the boat chugged into the Sound.

. . .

Ellie had promised to be at the Island Queen by eleven thirty, to help show the prospective buyers around the pub, although Leo's leaving had left her melancholy.

Branok was standing at the end of the bar when she walked in.

'Dad's said you'll show them around. I'm supposed to stay out the way,' he said, without preamble. 'Even though you haven't seen half the pub.'

'This isn't my idea,' she said, holding his gaze. 'Joe seemed pretty upset about it. I couldn't say no.'

'Well, I'm not going anywhere,' he said. 'This is *my* bar and I've got prep to do for this evening.'

'I'm on your side. I understand you want to sell the pub and go back to London. This is your chance.'

He stared at her. 'I'm glad you know what I want,' he said, snapping the words off one by one. 'Because I don't. Has Leo gone?'

'He has.' Ellie couldn't think of anything else to say.

Five minutes later, Ellie was still pacing nervously, wondering how she could show them the pub without ever having been to the top floor, when three people entered the main door – an attractive blonde woman chattering to a couple in their thirties. She stepped forward.

'Ah, you must be Ellie Roberts? I'm Clare from Garrison Estates.' She shook her hand quickly, smiling at her. 'This is Mr and Mrs Hunter, Sadie and Ben.'

She shook hands with each of them. Sadie was slim and dark haired, and was looking around intensely. Ben was assured, smiling, taking in the bar and the snug around the fire. Suddenly, Ellie could see all the scuffed paintwork, the hideous black paint on the beams, and the busy and worn carpet.

'Where would you like to start?' she asked, stepping back so they could see better.

Sadie walked past her to the row of tables at the front of the pub, flanking the door. It had an elevated view as the whole pub looked over the green-grey Sound, with white-topped waves rocking the private water taxi they had just arrived in.

'This view is fantastic,' she said. Ellie couldn't place her faint accent, but her dark eyes seemed to take in everything.

'It's even better from upstairs,' Ellie said.

'Let's start with the kitchens,' Ben suggested, and Clare smiled at Ellie.

'Um, through here,' she managed.

As the Hunters walked through, Clare gave her an encouraging smile. 'Don't worry,' she said. 'They know exactly what they're looking for.'

An hour later, Ellie was exhausted. Bran had been severe and unwelcoming in the kitchen, although he had answered all their questions. Once they got beyond the ground floor, Ellie didn't have any more information. The first-floor letting rooms were great but even she could see the corridors were scuffed and the paintwork scratched, the bathrooms old-fashioned. The second floor was full of odd storerooms and staff quarters. It was more run-down and shabbier than the lower floors, and the Hunters seemed to notice every crack in the walls, every rotten window frame. She had been asked to leave the dark corridor to a door marked 'office' to last, and the estate agent pushed the door open to reveal a snug room. It had a large desk in front of the window and Joe Shore was sitting behind it. Ellie wondered how he'd got upstairs.

'Ah, Mr and Mrs Hunter,' he said, genially. 'Hello, Clare. Nice to see you again. I expect you have a few questions for me? I put some chairs out.'

Joe made a good case for keeping the pub as a pub, and Ellie chipped in when she could. The pub was literally the beating heart of the town, especially in the evening when the café was shut. Even Joe had to concede that the pub needed refurbishment, and that it would take at least a whole winter, if not a full year.

'We do have a plan,' Ben said, looking at Sadie. 'But it cannot leave this room. We would only be able to afford to buy the pub if our plans are kept completely secret. Otherwise, we risk someone interfering with our other purchases. Can we trust you to keep this confidential?'

'I'm an accountant,' Ellie said. 'I know how to keep things quiet.'

'Anything to help the island,' Joe said, leaning forward.

Clare mimed zipping up her lips. 'Absolutely.'

And then, with the help of pen and paper, Sadie and Ben outlined out their proposal for the island.

Joe leaned back in his office chair, looking completely exhausted. 'I'm shattered. But they'll do a good job, if their plans work out.'

The Hunters, looking relaxed, had gone with Clare to find Bran and check in. They were planning to stay overnight and do more research on the Atlantic Islands. Ellie sat staring at the desk and the pile of notes that Joe had made.

'You take the papers. I don't have any privacy from Bran,' Joe said. 'You can sit in when I talk to the solicitor, the structural engineer and the brewery. I'll pay for your time.' He stared across at her. 'I need to make sure it's all tied up in case I don't last the year.'

Ellie picked up the notes. 'What do we tell Bran?'

Joe stood with difficulty, his hands shaking as he braced himself on the desk. 'Absolutely nothing. Now, you need to help me get downstairs.'

Ellie wasn't strong enough to do much more than help him to the other side of the room and prop him on a chair.

'I'll get Max,' she said. 'Or one of the men from the kitchen.'

In the end, the only one available was Bran, who was used to his father's mobility problems and carried the wheelchair up two flights of stairs for him.

'That's no bloody use,' the old man snapped. 'How is that going to get me down?'

'Well, you stubborn old man, you shouldn't have come all the way up, should you? Either you walk down or I'll have to get a couple more people to carry you.'

Joe managed to walk one step at a time, with Ellie supporting the trembling arm that wasn't clinging to the banister. It wasn't just weakness; when she looked at Joe's face, she could see the agony there. When she glanced at Bran, she could see the pain in his face, too, dark eyes down, his voice brisk.

'Come on then, next step, that's it. Ellie, run up and get the chair, will you?'

Once they had manoeuvred Joe back into the wheelchair, he looked exhausted. Bran turned to Ellie.

'Look, since you and my dad are now best friends, you can take him back to the tug. The tide's going down, so get him across the quay and I'll send someone to help.' When Joe opened his mouth, Bran snapped at him. 'Shut up, don't be stubborn, you can hardly stand. Just do as you're told for once.' He put his hand on Ellie's arm and pulled her away. 'He's going to need to pee. There's a clean bottle in the bathroom. Just get him settled in his chair and I'll be over when I get a chance.'

'Clean bottle, right,' she said, as what he was asking sank in. 'Don't worry, I'll work it out.'

His face twisted up. 'I don't know what you talked about. I don't think I even want to know. Just tell me my island is going to be all right?'

She put her hand over his warm fingers for a second, electricity zinging into her wrist until she let go. 'It will be OK. I can't talk about it, though. Ask your dad.'

'He won't tell me.' His eyes searched Ellie's face, and he nodded. 'I'll have to wait until everyone else finds out, I suppose.'

The *Porpoise* smelled of diesel, along with a hint of rust and paint. Ellie thought it was the most exciting smell for a home she'd ever experienced, and the slight movement of the tug gave her a weightless feeling. Joe was more mobile in his own environment, with things to hold onto all over the boat. He sank into his chair and waved at a narrow door.

'The bathroom. Get the bottle.'

Ellie put it beside Joe's chair, where he was already dozing. He woke, looked at her and sighed.

'I may not see this sale through. My cancer seems to be getting worse now. The doc's coming tomorrow, to have a look at me.'

'Good.' Ellie patted the back of his chair. 'Maybe they can help with the pain.'

Joe snorted. 'Pain? I don't care about pain. No, I'm more worried about what will happen to Bran when I die.'

'Bran? He always seems so practical, so together.'

Joe rolled his head to one side. 'Put that extra lamp on, by the telescope, will you? He's hasn't got over his mother dying, not really.' In the low light, he looked grey, and much older. 'I don't say it much, but he's all I have in the world.'

Something in Ellie was kicked into action. 'How can I help?'

'Help me sell the pub. It's going to be a millstone around his neck otherwise. Give him a fresh chance with his pottery. You should see him work. It's like he's in a trance.'

'I'll do what I can. I really loved the sculpture he had in the gallery.'

'Promise me you'll look after my boy,' Joe said, his voice more slurred.

'I will,' Ellie said, as she turned to leave.

If he'll let me.

38

Patience's father was sitting outside the Island Queen pub with a couple of his cronies, smoking a pipe in a cloud of yellow smoke and grimacing.

She smiled at him. 'Did you drop your baccy off the quay again, Dad?'

He jumped. 'Patsy, what a surprise!' He hugged her, leaned back to look at her. 'I thought you were coming back next month. How's Susie?'

'No better. I did everything I could,' she said. 'I really need to talk to you.'

'All right, my maid. Do you want to go home and talk there?'

She shook her head quickly, smiling to his friends, and watched him dump out his useless pipeful. She waited until they had walked past the church before turning up into the graveyard. Mam's grave was close by the hedge, recently tended. He sat on the raised box grave of her great-grandparents next to it.

'They won't mind,' he said. 'Come on then, out with it. Is it your sister?'

Patience sat down on the grass between the graves, the movement pulling on her corset and her painful, bound breasts.

'No. It's not Susie.'

He put his empty pipe between his teeth and waited for a few moments. 'I suppose we could sit here all evening and miss our tea,' he said finally.

She bent her head, her voice failing her for once. It seemed like half the words out of her mouth recently had been elaborate lies.

'I got pregnant,' she said baldly, not able to look at him. 'And I gave people Susie's name to have the baby.'

The silence stretched out, punctuated only by the odd sucking noise from the empty pipe. 'Bloody hell,' he finally said. 'A baby. How did you manage all that?'

'I registered the birth using Susannah's birth certificate.'

'In Oxford? That's why you insisted on going away.' He frowned. 'You didn't trust us to help you?'

She closed her eyes for a moment to force the tears back. 'You couldn't do what I needed. I rented a room just around the corner from the asylum. I spent time with Susie, but she doesn't know me. They call it premature senility. I just stayed there and got fatter.'

He thought for a long time, his brow wrinkled like it did when he was working out fish catches. 'Your landlord didn't like that, I bet. Single woman and all that.'

'It was a boarding house for unmarried mothers.'

More sucking, more rattling of the pipe stem against his teeth. 'The baby?' He straightened up. 'You didn't give it away?'

'Her. I called her Ysella,' Patience said. 'Great-grandma's name. No, Dad, I didn't give her away.'

He nodded, then frowned. 'So where is she, then? Is she all right?'

She managed a crooked smile but tears were gathering in her eyes as she shook her head. 'She's fine. Six pounds, one ounce. I never considered giving her away, which is the problem. She's back with Missus, at the Drang.'

'Bloody hell,' he said again.

'You're going to have to stop saying that.' Patience took a deep breath, rummaging in her pocket for a hankie to wipe her eyes. 'We're going to tell the islands that she's the baby of a cousin of Mam's, who couldn't bring her up.'

'No one will believe that,' he said, sucking furiously on the empty pipe, then pointed it at her. 'They'll guess it's a lie. You'll be the scandal of the islands. You'll have to give up your job, the cottage, everything. I doubt if you can even stay on Morwen.'

'They *will* believe it's a lie. Which is why we're going to let a second rumour spread that she's Susie's.'

'So, we're going ruin your innocent sister's reputation?'

Patience looked at him. 'She won't mind.'

He looked at her with dark eyes. The colour of a stormy sea, Mam had always said, too beautiful to be a man's eyes.

'Martha would have done that,' he said, glancing at the headstone. 'Her first thought would have been for that helpless baby. It won't be good for Ysella, though, people thinking she's an idiot's child.'

'Oh, Dad, don't call Susie an idiot. People will soon see Ysella is herself, and forget the rumours. We just won't confirm them, we'll stick to the story. One of Mam's distant cousin's girls.'

'How will you keep your job? They advertised it, you know.'

She wrapped her arms around herself. 'Let me deal with that,' she said.

She let the silence stretch out again.

'I'm not going to ask you who the father is,' he said. 'You'll tell me in your own good time.' He stood up, stretched the kinks out of his back. 'I suppose he can't marry you?'

'No. He can't.'

'Married, is he?' He reached a hand down to help her up.

'Well, let's go and meet this first grandchild of mine. We're going to be the talk of the town until *she* marries.'

Patience tucked her hand into his arm.

As they set off through the churchyard he said, almost chattily, 'I always thought it would be Dutch. One day, you'd have teaching out of your system and get married, have a few of your own.'

'No. Dutch and I don't see each other any more,' she said. 'And I'm not getting married to anyone.'

He stopped at the gate. 'We'll find a way through.'

'She's the best baby,' she managed to say before the emotion choked her again.

'I should think so,' he said. 'She's got my grandmother's name and your brains.'

'Not enough brains not to get pregnant,' Patience said, a little laugh making it through the tears.

'We're all stupid with love,' he said, puffing out his chest. 'Just think. My granddaughter.'

'No, Dad. Mam's cousin's child.'

'Adopted granddaughter, then,' he said, and smiled around his empty pipe.

39

PRESENT DAY, 15 MAY

After Leo went home, Ellie began to tackle the difficult jobs. The floorboards were old and some had holes, so Ellie painted woodworm treatment on them all. This made the smell, and probably the toxic elements, unbearable so she went to bed downstairs with all the doors and windows ajar. Having the back door open meant she was listening to the sheep all night, the wind whispering through the hedges and the rustle of wild creatures outside.

She woke early, stretched some of the knots out of her back and walked in her bare feet onto the swept tiles by the outside loo. She'd taken to throwing scraps onto the outhouse roof, and a bunch of small brown birds were squabbling over the last crumbs. A herring gull cried its eldritch wail, then cackled like a pantomime witch.

She boiled a kettle, had a lukewarm wash – God, she missed showers – and made a mug of tea. There always seemed to be nails sticking up that had lost their heads, so she put her shoes on to walk down the hall to the front room and stared out to sea.

Leo's letter had arrived the day before, and was folded up very small in her jeans pocket. She took it out and read it again.

My dearest Ellie,

You have been my best friend for three years. I have loved our life together, waking up in your bed, cooking together, travelling on our adventures. I know I'll never meet anyone as kind or generous as you have been. But these last months have made me selfish, and wonder if I need more.

I can see life on the island really appeals to you. You seem more relaxed there, but that takes you in a different direction than where I thought we were headed. Maybe we have both been too comfortable and settled. Maybe we have forgotten we are still young.

I'm so sorry, but for me it would be better if we end it now, before we are more committed to each other. I'm crying as I write this, because I really love you, but I don't miss you in the way that I expected to. So I'll say goodbye, and move out of the flat before you come back.

Be happy, Ellie (or should I say, Elowen?), and I hope that you find your heart and happiness on your enchanted island.

Leo

She couldn't decide whether she was devastated or relieved, but she felt shaky and sick just reading it. She folded it back into a cube of paper and resisted reading it again.

It was the perfect day to work on the house, but she knew there were still questions to be answered about her mother. She grabbed a box of papers from the bottom of the wardrobe in the front bedroom and made her way down to the café. Lucy was on her own in the Quay Kitchen, just setting up.

'Hi, Ellie,' she said, a shade less smiley than usual. 'Latte, breakfast sandwich?'

In the three years Ellie had been eating at the café local to her work, no one had ever remembered her preferences.

'Yes, please. Is it OK if I just sit in the corner and sort through some stuff?'

She was just setting stacks of papers out on the table when the coffee arrived. Lucy spilled a few drops on the table and seemed unnecessarily bothered by it, polishing it with a corner of her apron.

'Is everything OK?'

'Yes.' Lucy hesitated and turned as if to walk away. She turned back. 'Can I ask your opinion about something?'

'Of course.' Ellie put down the article she was holding.

'You've just got to the island. Why would you *choose* to live here?'

Ellie thought about it. The question tugged at some strings lodged deep in her childhood self.

'I don't know, except I feel at home here. I've never felt like this, it's a magical place, really.'

'I came here on holiday,' Lucy said. 'I was busy, I was happily married and everything was fine. When we grew apart from each other, I came here again to think about my options. The café was up for sale, so...' She shrugged. 'Now I'm not so sure.'

'But you love it here. The café, the people, the staff.'

'I met someone. Marcus is in the police, now he's been offered a job in Plymouth. It's a promotion. We could move in together.'

Ellie sat back, smelling the delicious combination of bacon and coffee.

'But this is your whole world,' she said, thinking about her life back in London. It seemed grey and distant now, without Leo.

'And he stays over. We see each other when he's off shift. But I want more, and so does he.' Lucy shrugged. 'I can't bear the thought of losing him. You must feel like that about Leo. How do you decide where to live when you want different things?'

The tug into her past hurt now, a sharpness in her chest. 'Actually, Leo and I... We split up. He wrote me a letter.'

Lucy sat down. 'I am sorry. You seemed to get on so well.'

'We do. We did.' She rummaged in her pocket and squeezed the folded note. 'There's something about the island. He thought I was different here, I suppose.'

Lucy nodded. 'It's a tricky one.' She stood up as someone walked in. 'I'd be heartbroken to give up Marcus,' she said, 'but I'd be someone different if I left the island.'

Lucy's dilemma had highlighted her own, Ellie thought, as she sorted through the box with her mind racing. Was she heartbroken? Leo was part of a life that seemed far away already.

A gardening brochure joined the pile at the edge of the table, then an old letter from some friend in Tunbridge Wells. A list of gig races and results was carefully wrapped in a plastic wallet. She lifted it into a better light, and her mother's name jumped out at her.

Ysella Roberts, cox, came first in the inter-island women's race, May bank holiday 1992. It was the year before Ellie was born. A line of jubilant young women waved triumphantly, Ysella in the middle with flyaway blonde curls, grinning at the camera. This is why Patience hadn't thrown it away. She pressed her palm to the picture as a wave of grief overwhelmed her, making the table swim and distort before her eyes.

'Hi, Lucy,' a familiar voice cut through the chatter in the room.

With a jolt, Ellie realised Bran was standing by the counter, turning to look at her. She put the article down, her hands shaking. They hadn't spoken since she showed the Hunters around the pub. After a long hesitation, he walked over.

'Is this anything to do with the pub?' He looked over the table, at the piles she was making.

'No. I'm sorting out some of Patience's papers,' she said, realising a tear had tracked down her face. She wiped it off. 'While having breakfast.'

He turned his head to see the clipping, and Ellie pushed it towards him.

'That's my mum,' Bran said, a smile breaking out as he pointed to a woman on the end. 'Winners of the inter-island gig race. They haven't won that in my memory, although we did come third three years ago.' He sat down and lifted the clipping so he could see it better. 'That's Ysella, too. Kerensa – she moved away. Bella, she runs the post office on the big island, now. Wow, look at the date. My mum looks trim. She only had me a few months before.' He placed it carefully on the table. 'If you're throwing anything out, Charlie Ellis would probably like this stuff for the local history project on St Brannock's.'

'I'll ask him. How's Joe?'

Bran's stares always made her think he saw everything she was trying to keep hidden, so she looked away.

'Dad's worse,' he finally said. 'He can't keep it from me now. He's taking morphine just to sleep but I hear him groaning in the night.'

'He said the doctor was coming to see him.'

'He's put in a catheter, and Dad's got antibiotics to take as well.'

Ellie looked up again. 'I'm so sorry. I realised how bad he was the other night.'

'He's dying.' He sounded hard, until his voice roughened. 'So I really do need to know what's going on.'

'If he dies, even if he has to go into hospital, I will be able to explain it all to you.' Ellie shook her head. 'But he's not dead yet, and I promised I would keep his business confidential.'

'At least tell me the island will still have a pub,' he said, standing up.

'Your dad's working towards that.'

Bran sighed and looked over at Lucy behind the counter. 'I'm just picking up the birthday cake for Max, Luce.'

'It's ready for you,' Lucy called, her gaze jumping from Bran to Ellie.

After Bran left, carrying the boxed cake, Ellie returned to the papers. There were packets of old photographs, many of them of Mum with her as a baby. There were newspaper articles of Ysella in London, on the arm of a handsome, smiling man she could hardly recognise as her father. An empty packet marked 'worm tablets – half in food' was presumably for the dog. Hoppity. The name popped into her head and she smiled involuntarily at the memory of the border collie.

Everywhere, Patience's strong handwriting flowed over papers. Shopping lists, addresses of friends, notes, recipes. Nativity plays, school concerts, all with a handful of children. An old train ticket from Penzance to Paddington, so maybe she had visited Ysella. A distant memory intruded of an older lady playing the piano at their London home, lifting Ellie onto her lap, showing her which keys to press. Fairy cakes with drippy icing she helped her pour on, with sugar strands sprinkled over. That was Nana, some inside voice whispered. She remembered carrying them out into the garden, Mum sitting in a wicker chair in the shade with one of her bright scarves on her head. Cancer. *How could I have forgotten this?*

The last of the papers were trivial, and she carefully restored them to the bag. The sandwich hadn't just gone cold, it had congealed, and she didn't fancy it now. As Ellie stood up to leave the now busy café, Lucy came over, looking concerned.

'I can't make my decision quickly, and I don't think you

should, either. Oh, and...' She turned and said something to the staff in the kitchen. Amy came out with a paper bag, flat on her hand.

'What's this?'

'Just a piece of cake,' Amy said. 'It's on its date so we all had a piece and kept one for you. You looked like you needed it.'

Ellie smiled, a bubble of laughter almost making its way out. It was so strange that a kindness – just a slice of yesterday's cake – could lift her spirits so quickly. This was a strange and magical community, and she was finding more of it in herself. Leo was right – she was a poor fit for him now. The island had changed her.

40

21 JULY 1963

Patience could sit in the schoolroom and recognise four-year-old Ysella on the beach just from her almost-white hair. Like her mother and, thank goodness, her late aunt Susannah, she had been blessed with the fairest of hair and china-blue eyes.

Ysa stopped to bend over a shell or some seaweed, to show Clem and his wife, Beth, each holding a hand of their little boy, Billy. Another William Ellis, to replace the brother Clem had shared a bed with.

Since she had brought Ysella home, the family had rallied around her. The children of George and Martha had all inherited a share of Kittiwake Cottage from their paternal grandmother. The house was in poor repair, and with Susie, Joseph and William all dead, Patience had offered to buy out Clem, and Frederick had made over his share to her and the baby.

Dad and Missus had proved loving grandparents, and Patience was certain her stepmother knew the truth. Maybe Dad had told her, maybe she had guessed, but she had offered to mind the baby from the very start without comment or judgement. Ysella adored them both. Getting up at night to a baby and working all day was tough, but Patience got through it and was relieved when the baby finally slept through the night in the battered cot Patience and her siblings had slept in. Dad had fixed it up and painted it pink, and Missus had made little sheets and blankets.

Patience tidied the stack of exercise books and slipped into her beach shoes.

Four years on, baby Billy had Ysa's pink cot. She walked down the lane to the exposed beach.

'There you are,' Clem said, shading his eyes. 'Ysa's found an empty crab shell.'

'Look, Mummy,' Ysa said, squinting up at her.

Patience crouched down. 'That's where the crab needed to grow,' she said, running her finger around the edge. 'It unbuttoned its old shell and walked out, all soft and vulnerable. Now it's going to hide and grow, while its new shell gets hard and safe.'

Clem laughed at her. 'Always the teacher, Patsy?'

She smiled. 'Always.'

'I bumped into Dutch the other day,' Clem said. 'He's given up the ferries and is fishing with the Lannick brothers on *Sea Breeze*.'

Patience tried to put an indifferent smile on her face. 'That's good. Dad always said he was a good trawlerman.'

'It sounded like he was thinking about moving back here.'

She had asked him not to return. The one change that had been necessary, despite his many efforts to persuade her otherwise, was that she had cut all ties with Dutch. Susie's death had been a blessing, but Patience still felt guilty for how she had used her sister as an excuse to see Dutch. *Ysella is the best of us both. Nothing must challenge that.* Cutting those ties had been painful, but most of the time she was happy. Now Ysa was at school with the other children and Patience saw her all day. She never tired of the mobile little face, her curiosity, her loving nature.

'That's nice,' she said vaguely. 'What else have you got there, Ysa?'

'Strings!' The child held up a long strand of what the locals called sea string.

'Its proper name is thongweed,' Patience said. '*Himanthalia elongata*,' she added to herself.

'You should write a book about the nature on the beach,' Beth said. 'You know so much.'

Patience smiled. 'If I have the time, I might.'

But her thoughts were on Clem's news. If it was true, Dutch would be on the island, in the town, every day. It was an intoxicating and terrifying idea. She had arranged to see him a few times with the baby in the first year, but the visits were unsatisfying. Dutch was thrilled with Ysa, but wanted to shout her parentage from the rooftops, while Patience was terrified someone would find out. She had ended their relationship and told him, for the baby's sake, to stay away. She occasionally sent him photographs of Ysella, and she usually added little anecdotes, but begged him not to write back. The only contact she now permitted was an anonymous parcel on Ysella's birthday, and an occasional note for Patience with money he insisted on sending.

Clem looked at her, his face a little lopsided. 'You always liked Dutch. I thought you'd be pleased to see him.'

'It was a long time ago,' she said. 'I might not recognise him now.'

'He hasn't changed much.' He looked at her carefully. 'You haven't either. I suppose Ysa keeps you young.'

She laughed at that. 'You just can't see the grey hairs.'

She kept her hair short now. It was easier to handle and the days of letting Dutch undo her plaits were long gone. She'd taken to practical trousers on her days off, too. The fashion for slacks and sandals suited her and she was reed thin from all the running about after eleven children and Ysa.

They walked along to the slipway and up onto the quay. This early in the summer the new café was just open, and they headed in for a bun and a cup of tea. The owner had cleared the back garden and put tables out there. Young Billy and Ysa sat on the gravel and picked over the best stones.

'Don't eat them,' Ysa said, delighted at Billy's enthusiasm. 'Here, put them in this flower pot...'

The adults sat and watched the children playing. 'So, you don't mind Dutch moving back here?' Clem asked.

'No. Why should I?'

Clem shrugged. 'He gave me the impression you might mind.'

'It's none of my business what he does,' she said with finality, reaching down to accept an especially shiny pebble from Billy.

41

PRESENT DAY, 18 AUGUST

Ellie was sanding the edges of the hallway when she saw brown feet in gold sandals approaching the open doorway. She sat back, squinting up through bright morning sunlight at the tall silhouette.

'Hi, Corinne. How are things?'

'Terrible,' she said, leaning against the door frame. 'I've just had an enormous row with Tink, followed by an even bigger one with his grandfather.'

Ellie could see her red eyes. 'Do you want some tea?'

She held up a bag. 'I brought coffee. I need it strong and black and quickly.'

Ellie wasn't sure she needed any more caffeine, but walked through to the kitchen to make it. Corinne moodily wandered around, picking things up off the dresser.

'Do you want to talk about it?' Ellie ventured, stirring boiling water into the grounds.

'The men on this island are Victorian,' she snapped. Ellie poured coffee into two mugs while Corinne dragged two dining chairs outside the back door.

Corinne calmed down and leaned back in the sunshine.

'I've been offered a modelling gig,' she said. 'I've worked for this agency before. There aren't many black girls in Cornwall with my height and degree of gorgeousness.'

'That's good, isn't it?' Ellie said. 'I mean, a bit of cash is always helpful.' Seeing her long neck stretched back reminded her how beautiful Corinne was.

'It's for a car showroom. Giant, diesel-guzzling monsters of cars. The sort of car that ought to have been outlawed a decade ago.' She opened her eyes and looked at her. 'I hate them. Is there more coffee?'

Ellie refreshed the pot and carried it back outside. 'Is that what you argued about?'

'No. We argued about the fact that I studied fish farming and sustainable fishing at college and have four years working as a marine professional. They won't even let me help on their poxy little boat. I want to go out on the trawler and get salt in my hair.' She stared into her cup. 'Fishing will die out if the dinosaurs carry on trying to recreate the past.'

'What would you do differently?'

'We sell mackerel for about twelve hundred a tonne. Now, guess how much smoked mackerel is?'

Ellie thought about the little packets in supermarkets. 'No idea. Loads more?'

'Exactly. My old tutor smokes mackerel over cedar and alder for a local shop, gets silly money per kilo. Tink can fillet a mackerel in twenty seconds, it just needs frequent checking and turning to smoke it. It's a luxury product. We could vacuum-pack it and flog it all over the islands, even to wholesalers on the mainland. The best thing is, it keeps all year, well after the mackerel season is over.'

That caught Ellie's curiosity. 'So why don't you?'

'Because his grandfather owns the only fishing boat left and *he* prefers to sell it by the boatload for cat food.' She sighed. 'OK, not cat food, but close. And the worst thing is, even with their old-fashioned fishing ideas and unsustainable methods—'

'You'd like to be out there.'

She turned her head. 'God, yes. Apparently, women are useless at sea.' She pulled up the short sleeve of her T-shirt. 'See this? Muscle. I carry sheep and hay bales around all day. And I'm not scared of the ocean.'

'Tink did say he doesn't like deep water.' The green shadows in the water between the islands freaked Ellie out, too.

'And he gets seasick,' she mused, 'whenever the weather's bad, which it often is.' She drained the last of her coffee.

'Why won't they let you help?'

Corinne stood up and took her cup to the kitchen. 'Superstition, mainly,' she said. 'And they want to prove that Tink is a true Ellis and is going to carry on the dying tradition.'

Ellie nodded. 'How are you going to convince Clem?'

'They only talk to me through Tink,' she said. 'I don't *think* it's a racist thing as much as an *old* thing. Clem is over eighty, and he fishes the way his grandfather did. Tink doesn't see it because he loves me.'

'How can you prove that you can work on a boat?'

'I was thinking about applying to become a pilot. The problem is, I'd have to get over to the big island every shift.'

'Apply anyway. There's room to tie up or moor, or whatever it is you do, off the quay, isn't there?'

'Yes,' she said slowly. 'Maybe...' Her voice trailed off. She jumped forward and grabbed her shoulders, kissed her cheek in a wave of perfume and the reek of sheep. 'Thank you, Ellie. You have a way of parachuting in with good ideas.'

'Glad to help,' she said to the empty kitchen as Corinne walked away.

42

Patience saw Dutch stepping off the trawler *Sea Breeze* at high tide, perfectly timing the jump to the quay, rope in hand. He paused for one moment, looking over at her, then tied the boat up with deft strokes. His hair was definitely grey at the temples now, and she realised with a jolt that he must be over forty.

'Welcome back,' she said, without smiling, but inside her heart was pounding like a drum and her palms were sweaty.

'Thank you.' His eyes roamed all over her face, stopping at her hair, her eyes, her chin. 'You look well,' he finally said.

'I am well. Are you?'

He shook his head. 'I can't do this, Patsy. I can't stand here and pretend we're strangers.'

She stared back, seeing the pulse bounding in his throat under the open neck of his shirt. The hands she knew so well. She smiled.

'We're old friends, no one would question that,' she murmured, so only he could hear.

He nodded, once. 'Can I see Ysella?'

'She's in Sunday School in the church hall. I think they're doing Noah's Ark today, and there isn't a cloud in the sky.'

His lips winced into a smile, but there was no humour. 'Is she healthy, is she happy?'

'She's well. Everyone loves her.' She led the way to the prefabricated building off Chapel Hill.

They stood outside, looking in the high window. The children were cutting out animals and colouring them. Ysa had given zebra stripes to a camel in blue crayon.

'Was it worth it?' he said quietly. 'Was it worth ruining Susie's reputation and breaking us up, for your career?'

'Yes,' she said, with certainty. 'She is so happy. She has her grandparents and uncles and cousins around her. She would have lost that, and the island, if we'd run away together. We would always have wondered if your wife or your child were going to bang on the door.'

He nodded. 'But we would have spent every day together.'

She corrected him. 'I would have been living in sin with someone else's husband.'

'You didn't mind sleeping with someone else's husband.' His voice was bitter and hard, and she shushed him.

'I was head over heels in love, I was young. It was different when it was just us. But this is about Ysa, not you or me. If it was just me? Yes, maybe we could have pretended we were married, moved away. Things are changing. But she needs to be here with my family.'

'It is a wonderful family to belong to,' he said, with some pain in his voice, looking back at the children.

'Come back as our dear friend,' she said on impulse. 'Dad will be in the pub tomorrow evening. Bump into him there. I know he'll invite you over for Sunday lunch to see everyone. Where are you staying?'

'I've got a room above the Mermaid's Purse,' he said. Then he looked back at her. 'Does your father know she's yours?'

'He's the only one that knows for sure,' she said. 'He forgave me years ago. I'm not sure he's really forgiven me for blaming it all on Susie, but he adores Ysella.' She stared at him, noticing every change, the extra creases around his eyes.

'And you're happy?'

She smiled at that. 'I love teaching. I read, work in the garden, play with Ysa. I'm thinking of writing a little book about rock pools. I have Dad and Missus, Clem and Beth and now baby Billy. I have Morwen and I see Ysa every day, all day.' She looked down at her clasped fingers. 'I didn't have to give her away.'

'Does George know I am her father?'

She caught her breath. 'No one knows. I try not to think about it.'

He sighed then, and she saw something go out of his eyes. 'So I will be old uncle Dutch, and we will be friends.'

'Good friends. Old friends,' she said, her heart thudding in her chest painfully. Her arms ached to reach out for him. 'This will get easier,' she said, looking over his familiar, beloved features.

He nodded, his face sombre, then he looked back at the children in the Sunday school. 'She looks like you,' he said.

'She looks like *Susie*.'

'Yes,' he said. 'Let her be sweet Susie's.'

43

Ellie watched Bran walk past Kittiwake Cottage. She hadn't spoken to him for weeks. He'd even ignored her in the pub. She grabbed her shoes and headed up the path towards the lookout on the southern tip of the island.

She found Branok balanced on the big boulder, close to the edge of the scrub covering the cliffs. The water surged between the rocks on the shore forty feet or so below.

'Bran!' Ellie couldn't keep the panic out of her voice.

He had his eyes shut. 'What?'

'I just... You're not thinking of jumping, are you?'

'What business is it of yours?' he said sharply. He turned, opened his eyes. Ellie had walked out in untied shoes, and was still holding a tea towel.

'I saw you walk past. You just looked – stormy.' The wind was making her shiver.

'I feel stormy,' he snapped. 'I just wanted to have five minutes alone to say goodbye to the island. I don't have to wait for the pub to sell. I might leave the cantankerous old bastard to look after himself. Only he can't get himself a drink, or dress himself, or remember his tablets without help.'

'Are you really OK?' Ellie crept forward a few feet. He was so close to the edge. 'Please, Bran, come back a bit.'

'I'm about to be homeless, as you well know. I'm exhausted looking after him. I'm cashing in some savings and moving away.' He was standing right on the edge of the rock.

'But he's frail,' she said. 'He's getting worse.'

'So it's my duty, as a good and loyal son, to watch him die? I did that with my mother, it nearly killed me. It cost me my marriage, and his stroke has cost me my career, everything.' He turned back to the sea.

'Bran, please, you're making me nervous.'

'Why?' he said, shuffling his toes right to the edge and closing his eyes. He stretched out his arms. 'Don't tempt me. I'm not in a happy place right now.'

'Bran,' she shouted, 'please!'

He opened his eyes. 'Oh, don't be daft.' He turned away from the edge, took a step towards Ellie. 'What would you care, anyway? How much kickback are you getting from the Hunters? And you'll make a killing on Patience's cottage.'

'I *do* care,' she said, a snap in her voice. 'For your information, I am helping your father for free, and there's no kickback from anyone. Because I do care about the island, and this is the best plan for the pub. You do know the building will fall down if it doesn't get urgent repairs? Some of the roof tiles are held on by tape and cable ties.'

'I know,' he said, his voice rough, 'because I put the cable ties and duct tape up there, for God's sake. I was born in the pub, Ellie. My mother died there, it's my *home*.'

'Come back to the cottage. I'll make you a cup of tea.'

He ran a hand across his eyes. 'I'm just tired, don't take any notice.'

'One cup of tea,' she said. 'Even if you hate me. Your dad isn't going to move out until all the paperwork is done and the money is in your bank accounts.' She turned towards the lane, looking over her shoulder to make sure he was following.

He fell into step with her. He didn't speak until they got the cottage, and he waited on the doorstep while she put the kettle on. When she got back, he was sitting on the low wall looking over the water between the islands. The warm breeze was playing with the tops of the waves, making them look like they were topped with snow.

'I don't really hate you,' he conceded. 'I used to come to think, in Patience's bay window. She always gave me good advice. She didn't pull her punches, though.'

'Come in now, then.' She stepped back to let him walk into the house.

He sat on the deep windowsill. 'This is the best view on this side of the island,' he said softly. 'I always loved it. I used to walk up here with Dutch, and he'd lend me his binoculars so I could watch the ships.'

'Why was Dutch so important to everyone?' A few small birds flew in front of the window, flashing glimpses of red and yellow as they turned. 'Whoa. What were they?'

'Goldfinches,' he said, shielding his eyes against the light. 'He was a lovely man. Big, like a friendly bear. Everyone knew he was rescued after his trawler was sunk in the war. By a U-boat, apparently; he was the only survivor.'

'I heard he was a Dutch fisherman.'

'Just a teenager, really, when the Ellises took him in. He ended the war working for them. That's when Patience met him. I suppose she was just a child then. She was about ten years younger than him.' He rubbed his hands down his arms as if he was cold. 'He knew the waters around here better than anyone.' His forehead creased as he thought of something.

Ellie waited.

'I was competing in a swimming race,' he said. 'It's staged between St Petroc's and Navy Rock every summer, as the tide stands at low tide. It was my first time, and I was one of the youngest. I managed to get to the beach, I had a great swim, came second in the under-sixteens. We celebrated with flasks of hot chocolate, then we were supposed to walk back to St Petroc's along the causeway. I was mucking about, left it too late.'

Ellie nodded. 'What happened?'

Bran pointed out of the window at the corner of the small, uninhabited rock at the north end of the opposite island, the pebble ridge that was only visible at low tide tearing up the surface of the water.

'The tide was like a fire hose,' he whispered. 'The strength of the water as it spills over the causeway, even if it's just six inches deep – it's tremendous. And the further I walked, the stronger it got. It reached my knees and just swept me straight over the north side.' He looked up at her. 'One minute it was bright sunshine, then it was dark green and I was face down in the sand under six feet of water. As the sea pours over the causeway it flows so strongly you can't escape it, you're pinned.'

'Oh, Bran.' She was shocked. For a moment she wondered what it would be like if she put her arms around him, just for comfort. He was shaking, as if the memory swept him along as well.

'I could feel myself being dragged back beside the causeway. It's deeper there, the water is freezing. I tried to swim, but the cold somehow sucked the energy out of my muscles. I knew I was going to drown.' He took a deep breath, looked down.

'You must have been terrified.'

He considered it. 'I'm scared now thinking about it, but at the time, something weird happened. It was all quiet, all calm down there. I was resigned. I must have rolled over – I could see the surface over my head. It's the last thing I remember, silver bubbles floating up.' He looked up at the ceiling.

'What happened? How did you survive?'

He turned to look at her. 'Dutch happened. He leapt into the safety boat as soon as I slipped. He rowed to where he knew the water would take me, where it would pin me in the under-tow. Then he jumped in.' He laughed. 'He wasn't a brilliant swimmer, but he managed to grab one of my arms, and dragged me up with him. Apparently, he cracked his head on the under-side of the boat, then he managed to shove me over the stern. By then, people were heading out to help us.' He looked at his hands. 'One of my friends' fathers managed to get into the boat and help me. I remember coughing and throwing up. When I got to shore, Patience wrapped me in blankets and hugged me. Dutch had to be towed in, too. He'd swallowed a lot of water.' He shook her head. 'God, I haven't talked about this in years. You're a good listener.'

'So, Dutch saved your life.'

'I was taken by helicopter straight to Plymouth, just to be on the safe side,' he said. 'Which was good because I had secondary drowning. Dutch got a chest infection – he could have died, too. They took him to the big island to recover. My dad organised a big party on the quay when we were both home.' He looked back out to sea. 'Dutch knew he'd only have one chance. He calculated exactly where a skinny kid would be swept by the water in one and a half minutes, and he was right there to catch me.' He looked back at Ellie, his eyes shining. 'He became my honorary grandad right then. I would have done anything for him.'

'I'm not surprised.' She smiled at Bran. 'I'm glad he was there to save you.'

'So, I spent a lot of evenings up here, with Dutch and Patience, looking out to sea, or identifying birds.' He stood and took a step towards the door. 'I'd better get back.'

'Wait.' Ellie went to the sideboard and rummaged through one of the larger drawers. There, at the back, was a battered leather case. 'I think... Yes. I think Dutch and Patience would have wanted you to have these.' She held out the antique binoculars in their box.

He put his hands over his face for a moment. 'God, you kill me, Elowen. I don't know whether to laugh or cry.'

Ellie smiled at him, but he didn't take the box.

'You keep them here, as long as I can pop by and look out of the window. At least until you sell the cottage.'

Ellie was silent for a long moment.

'Deal,' she said. 'Any time.'

44

Life for Patience settled into a new normal. Dutch was working from the island and she saw him regularly, but stayed distant. On his first Sunday lunch at her father's house, she took Ysa and was able to introduce her to Dutch without incident. She helped cook, joined in the washing up, then walked down to the beach with the adults and children. She avoided speaking to Dutch beyond politeness.

Dutch became 'Uncle Dutch', to all the children. If he was more protective of Ysella, it seemed it was just because she was a girl among several boys her own age at the school. Patience feigned indifference but, for the first time in her career as a teacher, she felt lonely.

Walking over the headland or visiting the other islands was a help. Dad and Missus loved looking after Ysa, and as Patience had been paid a small sum by a natural history publisher to write her book, she was taking a camera to rock pools and beaches for her research. Again and again, she imagined fruitless plans to get away with Dutch, to resume their doomed love. But it came back to Ysa. People would notice Patience was away at the same time as Dutch, and there was no way she could take

Ysella and expect her to not talk about it. She was just old enough to be curious about her mother and father, and Patience couldn't answer those questions.

'He's a kind man that your mother really loved. He's gone far away.' It was her standard story.

'We could write him a letter,' Ysa had said, bouncing at the kitchen table. And she did: a few lopsided words and a picture of her friend's dog, because that must interest him.

One Sunday, Dad and Missus had Ysa, and Patience visited the rock pools on West Island. She spent the day taking pictures and making notes. As the tide was halfway in, she packed up her camera and sandwich box and walked to the boat landing. The open ferry was manned by various fishermen, pilots and lifeboatmen during the last half-term of the year, everyone grateful for the last holidaymakers.

It was still a shock to see Dutch leap deftly onto the slipway. The boat was heavily loaded with a huge package leaning to one side, making the boat lopsided.

'Just you today?' he said.

'I think so. I haven't seen anyone else,' she said, her breath suddenly coming faster. She looked around. 'Maybe we should wait a few minutes?'

'I'm already late,' he said. He held out a brown hand for her. 'You can balance up the boat for me.'

She stared at the proffered fingers, knowing she couldn't touch his warm skin, even now after so many years. He stared back at her, his eyes dark and impossible to look away from.

'Just friends,' he said.

His skin felt exactly as it had, back in her brother's bedroom in the attic. It shot a bolt of lightning through her, firing up dormant nerve endings.

'Dutch,' she said, clinging to his hand.

'In with you,' he said, pulling her onto the boat and letting go.

She sat on the open boat as far away from Dutch as possible, pressed her knees together and tucked her feet under the seat. 'So, I'm just ballast?' she said, trying to smile.

'For this monster, yes. It probably weighs more than you.'

Curiosity got the better of her. 'What is it?'

'You'll see in a few minutes. I'll need help getting it ashore.' He rounded the headland, the pale water like glass. Tiny fish scattered at their approach, darting along the surface in splashes and bubbles.

He didn't go straight to the quay but slowed his approach to the slipway instead. He jumped out, the water up to his thighs, and hauled the boat up until it grounded.

'Come to me,' he said, holding out a hand. 'I'll lift you.'

'I would rather get wet,' she said primly, taking off her sandals. She stepped into a foot of glassy water, still warm after the summer, and picked her way over shells and stones to the tideline.

Within a minute, two men had arrived to help Dutch. Gryffyn Shore, whose family had taken over the Island Queen pub, was the first to comment. 'It's a big one,' he said, tipping his cap back on his forehead. 'Afternoon, Miss Patience.'

Bill Bligh jumped aboard the boat. 'It's here, then. You got fuel?'

'Of course.' Dutch ran his hand over the parcel. 'She's old, but in good shape.'

The men lifted the parcel – wrapped in layers of tarpaulin and rope – up the slipway, leaving Patience to secure the boat to one of the rings in the wall. By the time she got up to the quay, the object had been revealed.

It was a motorbike, a second-hand one. The men were stroking it like a horse, dusting off the leather seat and the chrome.

'It's a Vincent,' Dutch said, polishing the handles with a cloth. '1934 Comet. It's been restored after a crash.'

'But you live on an island with no roads,' she said, shocked by the absurdity of it.

'It will go on the ferry. I can take it on the mainland, go on driving holidays.'

She folded her arms. 'I think you're being ridiculous.'

He grinned at her and fitted a helmet on his head. 'Perhaps I should give you a demonstration.'

There was laughter from the young men, quickly dispelled by a look from Patience. After a last pat of the bike, they wandered back to their work.

'I am trying to be sensible,' she hissed at him.

'You're too young to be sensible. And it is half-term.' He handed her a similar helmet.

He put a leg over the machine. The long seat would have room for her, although goodness knows where her skirt would end up. She primly seated herself side-saddle, gripping her dress between her knees.

'Very well,' she said, fitting the helmet over her hair.

She had to put her hands on his shoulders as he started the motorbike in a haze of exhaust.

'Started first time!' he shouted back to her, as she realised people were lining the quay.

'Just to the end of the—' she said, the words lost in her helmet as the bike lurched forward and she almost fell off. She put an arm around Dutch as the bike thrummed along the quay, turned into Warren Lane and up, up to the top and the path around the island. It was exhilarating, clinging to Dutch, feeling him breathe and move. She needed the other hand to rescue her skirt from ending up in the engine. The view flashed past. It was the freedom she had felt in his arms, throwing caution away.

He slowed as he reached the old lighthouse foundation at

the northern end of the island, where she used to watch dolphins. There weren't any today, but he circled the bike at the end of the path and kicked its stand down. He dismounted, and lifted Patience off. Without asking, he pulled their helmets off, and kissed her. After a few moments of resistance, she put her arms around him, lost in the familiar feeling of falling.

'This is what I am talking about,' he said. 'If we are seen together now, no one will care. No one will guess.'

She shook her head. 'But we still can't get married, and the council are old-fashioned. They wouldn't accept a married lady teacher anyway, let alone one having an affair.'

'We can be friends. No one would begrudge us that. Just a middle-aged bachelor and a spinster, walking out together.' He touched her hair, shorter than his now. 'You look different. Especially when you wear your glasses. You look... what is the word? Prim. Correct.'

'We can never go away again, like we used to.'

He put a finger on her lips. 'I know we can't. Not while Ysella is a child. But you know what I miss? Watching you read, having a meal together, sitting beside you. Our bodies touching, somewhere.'

Patience stared into his crooked features. 'You are a friend of the family,' she said abruptly. 'As long as you take Clem for rides, too, they are less likely to suspect.'

He patted the bike. 'It's old, it won't run all the time.' He grinned at her. 'I was hoping I could work on it in your shed. Then people will say "He's just tinkering with that old bike. Poor Miss Ellis, stuck with her dad's friend making a mess of her garden."'

'I'll think about it.' She patted his chest. 'Kiss me again, then you can take me home.'

45

Ellie started organising the contents of the cottage more purposefully, putting aside rubbish for a bonfire. Masses of old magazines and paperbacks that had been rejected by the charity shop were added to the pile to burn. She had already got rid of the newer of the two sofas but she couldn't quite let go of the old one. She knew Patience had died on it, and maybe one day she would eventually burn it, like a Viking funeral, and scrap the springs and nails it was constructed from. As she lifted the jug of pens off the locked sideboard, she tipped the contents out on the coffee table. A couple of rubber bands, half a dozen pens and a few coins fell out. At the bottom was a dark key, the length of her little finger.

And I nearly smashed up the sideboard to open it. When she slid the key into the mechanism of the cupboard lock, it worked immediately. The cupboard smelled like wood and dust, and very old paper. A wooden box slipped into her hands, heavily carved with the name 'Janssen' on the top. Ellie sat on the sofa and lifted the lid.

My darling girl, the top letter began, and she promptly put it down. This was a private letter, too personal to read, and not in Patience's hand. Although, as her heir, she might be the only person left who could read it. She picked it up again.

If you are reading this letter then I am dead, and you are free to do one more thing for me. I know we never talked about this, not since we were young, but now you need to look for my son. I believe he was brought up in America. Hopefully, he is married with children of his own. How I wish we could know them! But it was not to be. All I know about him is that his name is Michael Janssen, and his mother's name is Erma. I did wrong by her but I was young and stupid to get her pregnant. You know I never loved her. After I was declared lost at sea, she married again and had two more children.

When I said 'Deutsche' to your father and he told the crew I was Dutch, I thought at any point that if he realised I was German, he might throw me overboard to join the rest of my crew. Of course, he knew from the start. But your father was the kindest of men, and he and your mother kept my secret. I never asked them why they did it, especially after his service in the first war.

But now I can tell the whole truth. I was born Werner Janssen, a German citizen of Wilhelmshaven, and from a fishing family like your own. If we have not yet told the truth to Ysella, please do and let her judge me as she must. You, I know, will give me only love, even when I am in my grave. I will wait for you, my darling girl.

Love always,

Dutch

Ellie found tears running down her face, and carefully folded the letter back up along its original creases. This was the secret they had kept all these years.

The rest of the box was full of papers that had belonged to Dutch. Pictures, many of Patience and Ysella, and some of herself as a baby. There were nautical charts and records, payslips and pension letters, and finally a certificate of naturalisation for 'Pieter' Janssen, born in Groningen on the first of January 1923. A birthday picture showed him on the beach with a cake, blowing out candles. Finally, a folded card, much handled and creased over time. It had a picture drawn in crayon, with a few words:

To Daddy, we love you, my frend is a dog. Love Ysa Ellis.

That evening, Ellie had settled down to watch a box set on her new TV when the landline rang. She answered the phone on the second ring.

'There's a fire at the pub.' Tink's voice was clipped, hard. It cut straight through the box set. 'In the roof.'

Bran. All of the instructional videos and training downloaded into her brain in a terrifying whoosh.

'What do you need me to do?' she stammered.

'Meet me outside. Get your full kit on. We'll head straight there. Ed and Lolly are already on their way.'

Ellie's new fire brigade equipment was ready to step into in the back bedroom. She pulled her heavy boots on and clattered down the stairs. All that running up the hill carrying hoses, and climbing ladders in full gear, had made her fitter. Tink roared up on the quad bike a minute later and Ellie climbed up behind him.

'I got a call from Bran,' Tink shouted, as he gunned the bike along Long Lane, nearly unseating Ellie as he turned down Chapel Hill. 'They've got water coming in the roof. It's set off an electrical fire. No casualties reported.'

'What about the pump?' Ellie clung on as Tink took the corner onto the quay hard. 'Will we need seawater?'

'There's plenty of water but we'll need a powder extinguisher first if the electric is live.'

Ellie could see the water was just starting to go down from high tide. She stared up at the building, and could see a faint orange glow at one end of the roof, outlining a few slates. Two sets of breathing equipment were outside on the pub wall. Ellie got off the bike and grabbed hers. Max met them at the pub door, holding a fire extinguisher.

'Lolly said to tell you, Ed's incident commander. They're up in the roof. We're OK,' the barman said, although his face was soot-smudged. There were no lights in the pub, and Ellie switched her helmet torch on.

'The problem is, the roof joists are like tinder,' Tink said, 'then the rain and wind blew water onto exposed wires.'

Max pointed to the ladder at the bottom of a large hatch. 'Lolly told us to keep the power off. Help yourselves.'

'Follow me,' Tink said, grabbing the extinguisher at the bottom of the ladder and examined the designation. 'Powder,' he said, over his shoulder to Ellie. 'Put your respirator on.' He slipped his visor down and started up the ladder.

As Ellie climbed onto the floorboards in the loft, she realised something her training hadn't adequately prepared her for. The smoke, in an enclosed area, was a rolling wall of darkness, and she couldn't see Ed or Lolly. The low roof had concentrated the heat and, even with her suit on, she could feel it. An orange glow broke through the gloom.

'Watch your step,' she shouted to Tink, as she saw the joists. 'Missing floorboards.'

'Got it,' Tink said, tapping his helmet just in front of Ellie. *Ah, radio.* Ellie switched it on, and immediately heard Ed's instructions to Lolly.

'That's it, maid. You got that spare, Tink?'

Tink shoved it at Ellie. 'Ellie's got it,' he said.

Ellie slid around him, towards the heat. Now she could see two lights, bouncing around the smoke, eerie figures bending to avoid the beams. They seemed to be taking a few slates off the roof. Ed emerged from the smoke to take the extinguisher.

'Good,' he said, and aimed it at the floor of the attic.

The last of the glow went out and Ellie was blinded – she remembered too late to turn away. Even wiping her visor only gave her limited visibility.

'Elowen,' Ed said, 'we'll lift these boards.' Ed passed the smouldering wood to Lolly, who threw the charred timbers out of the hole in the roof.

Ellie could see streaks as the rain pattered down her visor, washing away the powder. Visibility was a lot better now as the high winds whisked the smoke away. She could see right out over the side of the pub towards the edge of the quay. The trawler and crab boats were swaying in the waves. Something about their movement made her look again, then at the tug.

Joe's boat wasn't gently swaying; it was heaving up and down and looked to be further away from the side. She could see Bran standing on the quay, screaming into the wind towards the boat. She unclipped her helmet, wrenched it off. As *Porpoise's* nose swung into the tide, Bran ran down the length of the quay, straight for the tug.

'Bran!' Ellie shouted, waving at him. 'Bran! *No!*'

Tink took off his helmet and stared along Ellie's pointing arm.

'Go!' he shouted to her.

But Ellie was frozen. The gangway to the boat fell with a crash and a spray of white water, making Bran duck down.

Then he took a few steps back. He leapt at the boat, grabbing the rail with one arm. He slipped, then caught it again and pulled himself aboard.

Ellie didn't wait to see what happened next. She raced across the attic and clambered down the ladder.

46

Patience sat with Ysella's A level exam results in her hand.

Ysa had made three applications for teacher training colleges. It had been hard for Patience not to hope she wouldn't get the grades, that she would stay on the island forever. She tucked the letter into her cardigan pocket and started along the footpath around to the back of the island. Ysa was teaching sailing to tourists, and she was so pretty and confident that boys of all ages were queueing up to learn.

'Mam!' Ysella waved to her from the safety boat.

Patience waved back and held up the envelope. Ysella spoke to the other person on the boat, then effortlessly dived into the turquoise water. She swam like a fish; Patience had no fears for her, but she could have at least taken her frock off. The effect on the young men on the beach was considerable, and Patience couldn't help but smile at Ysa's easy confidence. She waded up the beach.

'Open it, Mam. I'm soaking wet!'

Patience handed her a towel, left on the shore by one of the sailing school trainees. 'You must do it.'

'OK, I'm ready.' Ysa took the paper and ripped open the

envelope. 'Upside down... Oh, Mam! Two As and a B. I can go to Winchester!'

Hampshire. So many miles and hours away by boat and train.

'What was the B in?' Patience wondered out loud. But Ysa was so excited she couldn't help but smile.

When Patience pushed the door open, the tears were already gathering in her eyes, tightening her chest.

'*Liebling.*' Dutch put his arms around her. 'She did well?'

'Two As and a B. Her first choice is Winchester.' Her eyes filled with tears.

'You are proud. And she will still be coming home to her mother.'

She pressed her face into his chest and let the tension go. 'But I don't want her to go.'

'I don't either. But look what we have made, you and I! A perfect woman, ready to be a great teacher.' He pulled her shoulders away from him. 'Look up.'

'No,' she said, irrationally, knowing she was drowning in tears.

'I have handkerchief.' That made her smile, and she glanced up and grabbed for it. Turning to the window, she dried her face, letting the sobs turn into tiny hiccoughs.

'I don't want her to leave,' she said. 'That's irrational and selfish, but I want to see her every day.'

'But how will she find her love, her husband? Where will our grandchildren come from?'

That was a nice thought.

'She could marry a nice island boy,' Patience said, knowing what the answer would be.

'When have you ever thought a local boy good enough for Ysella?' he said, laughing. 'Come, kiss me.'

'Dutch, we're right in front of the window,' she said, fending him off. 'I hope Ysa remembers to tell Missus. She hates being the last to hear anything.'

Her stepmother had been hit hard by Dad's death, and had diminished into a querulous old lady.

Dutch pulled her into the kitchen, backing her up to the sink. 'Now kiss me,' he said, and to shut him up, she did.

'Enough of that.' She pushed him away. 'I need to talk to Ysa about what she wants to do and...' she took a deep breath, 'what she needs me to do. She'll need accommodation, books and food and travel money. I have savings but I don't know how she will manage on a student grant. They are pretty skimpy.'

'I will help,' he said softly. 'And you will let me. Because she is my child.'

'She's so happy now, I don't want to burden her with our secrets. I can't take your money – she might find out.'

'My savings will go into your savings. She won't question.'

'But she's still going away,' she said, her eyes filling up again.

'And she will come home every holiday. Maybe she will find a job on the islands. You know how hard it is to find teachers.'

She let him hold her, then, until she had swallowed her fears.

47

PRESENT DAY, 3 SEPTEMBER

Half the island seemed to have assembled outside the pub. A dozen people were clamouring to tell Ellie that Joe's tug *Porpoise* was loose. Corinne grabbed her by the elbow and pulled her out of the fray.

'The trawler could give the tug a tow,' she shouted over the wind and the voices. 'Where's Tink?'

'I'm here,' Tink said, behind Ellie. 'I can't take the *Gannet*. Lolly, Marcus and I are taking the sailing school's rescue boat out. Maybe we can get them off the tug.' Marcus, Lucy's policeman boyfriend, was putting a life jacket on.

Corinne turned to Tink, her voice sharp. 'The inflatable can't tow that weight. We need to get control of her. I'm taking the trawler.'

'You can't manage her on your own!' Tink shouted back. 'You've never driven her.'

'I've piloted a frigate, you idiot!'

'In training, as a midshipman. It's not the same.'

Clem, looking more like ninety than eighty, was puffing hard as he trotted up behind them. 'I can take the trawler out. Tink can help.'

Tink was already running down the quay, towards the pilot gig shed. Corinne turned to Clem. 'He's going with the safety boat. I'm all you have.'

'And me,' interrupted Ellie. 'I'm another pair of hands.'

'I'll take Elowen as ballast,' Clem said. 'Let's see what the Royal Navy can do.'

By the time the old man got to the rocking, bucking ship, a wave surged up between the hull and the quay in a wall of spray, hitting Ellie in the face. Clem timed the step from the ladder to the boat perfectly, leaning back to give a hand to the women.

'Get a life jacket on,' he growled. 'We don't want any extra casualties. Who's on the tug?'

'I think Joe, and I definitely saw Bran.' Ellie pulled herself into the limited shelter of the wheelhouse where Corinne was waiting, already in a life jacket and a harness. She shoved Ellie into an old, stinking jacket and held one out to Clem. He started the engine.

'Never worn one, maid,' he said, over the howl of the wind across the open doorway. 'If the sea wants me, she can have me. Cast off.'

Corinne covered the boat like an expert, unhitching and stowing ropes. Ellie watched as the engines sputtered out smoke, caught in floodlights someone had put on the quay.

'Untie that stern line,' Clem bellowed.

Ellie managed to unhitch the wet rope, heaved it up and left it in a loose coil. Going back to the wheelhouse, she could see the difficulty Clem was having keeping his feet as the boat lurched into the waves and crosswinds.

Ellie could hardly see the tug, drifting past the end of the quay. She leaned out to see more clearly and could see lights on in the cabin.

'She's going to be swept into the Sound!'

'And straight for Kettle Rock,' Corinne shouted back.

'The tide's still too high,' Clem called. He slipped on the wet floor, grabbing at the window frame to keep his feet. 'We're too slow to catch her.'

'Let me try,' Corinne said. 'We can steer into the Sound, catch the tide race and pass her before she gets there. If we can get to her before she hits deep water, we might be able to strand her on Puffin Bank.'

'We'll ground the trawler,' the old man shouted back, looking outraged. 'Or get swept past her straight towards the rock. We won't have steerage in the race.'

'We'll save two lives,' she snapped back. 'We have to try. Let me have the wheel.'

Clem stepped aside, leaned into a cubby area and sat on a bench, bracing himself against the door frame.

'Just don't sink us,' he said.

The ship hit the next wave at an angle as Corinne steered sharply, and Ellie's feet left the deck. The trawler scythed through the next wave, water pouring over the front and flooding across the deck out of holes along the edge.

'Can you see the tug?' Ellie shouted, and Corinne nodded, wiping wet hair out of her eyes.

'It's a bit to starboard,' she said. 'But I can't see anyone and it's rolling all over the place.'

'She's dragging on the bottom by the slipway,' Clem interjected. 'The sand builds up there in summer. Might slow her down.'

'Get out there,' Corinne said to Ellie. 'Get yourself clipped on and see if you can get their attention. Clem, lights?'

He pointed to a bank of switches overhead, and Corinne activated a floodlight that illuminated the deck and the rolled-up nets. Ellie unclipped her line, and attached herself to a rail on the outside of the wheelhouse. The next wave knocked her onto her knees, and she was glad of her fire officer's gear against the wind and spray. She climbed back to her feet and looked over at *Porpoise*.

She could see a figure in the cabin, just head and shoulders showing, disappearing as the waves rolled him cruelly.

Bran. It must be like being in a washing machine.

'We'll swing around the sandbank and get ahead of them!' Corinne shouted out of the doorway.

The tug started to move. Tide, waves and wind were all acting on her, spinning her around. The engines started to growl as the stink of smoke reached Ellie. She could see the gap narrowing as Corinne guided *Gannet* alongside *Porpoise*, and passed into deeper water. The light swept over the saloon, picking up Bran's pale face. The inflatable safety boat had already reached *Gannet*, and was close. Tink, Marcus and Lolly were being thrown around in their seats. Waves were breaking over them as they reached the lee of the trawler.

'You need to get down to the gunwale,' Clem's voice reached her. 'The side down there, to starboard. You'll need to catch the rope from the safety boat.'

Unfastening the line from her harness felt dangerous, especially going down into the belly of the ship with all its machinery and nets. She unclipped with cold hands and clung to the handrail of the metal steps, struggling to keep her footing.

Some instinct warned her that the ship becoming still meant a wave was coming. She didn't have time to secure her lifeline as a wall of water blocked out the view of the tug. She wrapped both arms around the handrail as it hit; it was like being smacked by a barn door made of ice. The world went dark for a moment; the cold made her take a tiny gasp of salt water before it drained away, dragging her across the deck as she dangled by one arm. The ship went calm again as she crawled to her feet and clipped on. She had barely coughed up the last of the brine before the next wave hit, but she could feel the trawler turning.

She caught sight of the sea boiling alongside the ship. It was black, surging and coiling around lines of white spray, picked up by the lights. It looked like it was reaching for her, and for a moment she was frozen with fear, clinging with both hands. If the next wave swept her overboard, the only use for the lifeline would be to make it easier to retrieve her battered, drowned body. She glanced up to see the tug drifting faster now, leaning a little, the lights off.

Bran.

The next wave soaked her with spray, and she could see where Corinne was aiming the trawler. The safety boat's lights were focused on the tug, highlighting Bran standing on the deck, a tall figure in yellow waterproofs. He leaned over a wire barrier, trying to catch something. Now Ellie could see the stockier figure of Tink, throwing a thin line up to Bran. It fell down, and Tink started reeling it back in. Snatches of voices drifted over him, garbled with the sound of the straining engine. Tink shouting, Bran yelling back.

Bran dipped almost over the rail but when he straightened up, he showed Tink the rope in his hand. Bran ducked down and crawled to the front of the tug.

Corinne was at the top of the steps. 'Bran will pull up the towline and secure it. Then Tink will throw a line to you,' she yelled. 'You need to catch it and then we'll pull the bigger rope from *Porpoise* aboard and secure it. Clem's got the wheel. Clip yourself onto the rail.'

The figure driving the inflatable turned back into the heavy water between the larger boats. A wave lifted it, crashing down, the figures sprawling with the shockwave. *Tink and the others could die. Lolly has kids.* It made catching the rope even more important as the rib pulled up alongside.

'Ellie!' She could see Tink's face gleaming in the light from the trawler. 'Ready, two, three—'

Ellie reached over and the wet rope slapped her in the face

as she grabbed it. As the boat moved, it was almost wrenched out of her grip, stinging as it slipped, but a knot towards the end caught in her palm. She hauled it in, hand over hand, and Corinne was behind her, grabbing it, too.

'It's going to get heavier,' she shouted in her ear.

Ellie didn't understand until she saw the size of the rope being pulled off the tug. Corinne pulled up coils of the light rope to loop it around some sort of bollard. A minute later it gave way to a wet, heavy rope, much harder to grip. When they had about thirty metres, Ellie was hot and out of breath. Corinne started securing loops of it at the stern of the boat.

'Stand away!' Corinne's voice floated down to her over the roar of the storm and the growl of the engine. She stepped back as the slack started to be taken up. The inflatable veered from between the bigger ships and curved back into the wild water.

'Will they be OK?' she shouted up to Corinne.

'I bloody hope so. That's the father of my child,' Corinne replied, her teeth shining in the lights.

'What?' Ellie could see her face streaming with the rain.

'I just found out! He doesn't know yet. Don't tell him!' She staggered and clung to the rail to get her balance.

Ellie leaned back over the side to squint at the tug. Bran was standing at the front of the boat, to the side of the heavy rope stretched between the two vessels. He waved, and after a moment, she waved back.

'You OK?' he seemed to say, snatches of his voice reaching her.

'OK,' she said, giving him a thumbs up.

The engine sounded like it was straining as it pulled the rope, water spraying off it as it straightened. The trawler started creaking, the deck juddering under Ellie's feet. She wondered whether the old ship was up to the job – the tug looked squat and heavy.

'I'm going to help Clem,' Corinne shouted in his ear. 'Watch Bran!'

He was staggering as the tug started to turn, the sea now making him jump with every wave. The tug was definitely turning now – Ellie could see sand churned up behind the trawler as it hauled the heavier vessel around. She couldn't see the rescue boat for a minute, then it shot alongside the tug, lights scanning *Porpoise*'s upper deck. The cabin looked empty, the black windows gleaming with rain.

'Tink is taking soundings,' Corinne shouted. 'They're going to lead us to the right place and we'll haul the tug there. I think it's going to work. Can you see Bran?'

Ellie turned. 'He's just by the door,' she called back.

'When the tug grounds it might roll around. He'll be safer in the cabin, it's reinforced.'

Ellie peered into the dark, the lights flashing over *Porpoise*, dead in the water. There was a shock, a grinding noise and the trawler rocked. It flung Ellie hard against the rail, giving her a terrifying glimpse of the water rushing up to soak her. The vessel seemed to judder again, as if it was scraping over the sand.

'Hold on!' Corinne's words reached her on the wind, thin and broken, and the engine screamed in protest as the ship jerked and turned, rocking the deck violently from side to side. As the trawler surged to starboard, the lights swept over the tug. Ellie could see Bran, in his yellow waterproof, outside the cabin.

As the slack was taken up, Corinne tried again to haul the rolling houseboat.

'Hold on!' Clem shouted, his voice cracked with effort.

The sea boiled yellow with sand, and the engine noise changed to a low rumble. *Gannet* surged forward, then was snatched back by the rope between the vessels. The trawler pushed forward into the waves smashing over the bow, half submerging the front of the ship. The tug, dragged along behind, looked dangerously unstable. Ellie could imagine Bran crushed under the ship as it capsized.

'Bran!' she screamed. She was shaking with cold and adrenaline now, her stomach cramping.

The trawler's engines groaned and heaved, filling the air with exhaust. The tug seemed to turn on its axis a few degrees, a few more, and stopped. Its stern was now half into the waves, whole walls of black water curling onto it until it looked like it would fill up and sink. The trawler's engines were turned down a gear, and Corinne tapped Ellie's shoulder as she vomited over the side, shaking with relief.

'It's OK,' Corinne said. 'The tug is grounded. The tide should leave it high and dry. We'll hold it and wait until the water goes down.' She looked over to the stranded boat, shielding her eyes. 'Where's Bran?'

Ellie looked around. Something caught her eye, something pale clinging to the outside of the guard rail of the tug. Bran's arm, his body in the water, his waterproof billowing with trapped air. He must have been washed over the low rail by a wave breaking over the tug. Then he was gone, and his waterproof disappeared beneath the water.

Ellie jumped.

48

Patience answered the recently installed phone on the second ring. It was Clem.

'I went to see Missus,' he said, stammering like he had as a child. 'I was going to make breakfast, and... I think she's dead.' He didn't sound forty-five. 'Patsy, I don't know what to do.'

He had recently lost Beth, his wife, after she had a fatal blood clot. He had transferred a lot of his time to Missus.

'I'll come down,' Patience said. 'Just leave everything.' She turned to Ysa, visiting from her teaching job on the big island. 'Call Dutch, and tell him to come to Missus's house for me.'

'Can I help?'

'No, I'll go. Just clean up here, I'll sort it out.'

She pulled on her wellies from the porch and slipped into a warm coat. Poor Missus; she had been ill since Dad died. She wasn't even that old, although she would never say the exact date. As she marched down the hill, she hoped Clem was wrong.

But he was right. Missus had been dead a while, her body cold and stiffening. Clem wanted to close her eyes but couldn't do it, so Patience covered her in a clean sheet and called for help. The doctor wouldn't be on the island for a couple of hours.

'Well,' Patience said, pressing a cup of tea into Clem's hand. 'There's no rush. When he gets here, I'll call her boys. They'll want to come back for the funeral. And Billy will be home soon to keep you company.' Patience could see him nodding his head. 'I've told them to meet you at your house. Once you feel better, you can walk home. I put two sugars in, drink up.'

Missus had been a large part of Clem's childhood. 'I don't want to leave you here,' he mumbled.

'I don't mind,' Patience said. 'She was kind to me while she was alive. What's she going to do now she's passed away?'

'She'll leave the cottage to her boys,' he said, and sipped his tea.

'Dad always said you could have it, but we can't blame Hilda if she leaves it between you all,' Patience said. A shadow over the window was tall enough to be Billy but turned out to be Dutch, who walked straight in.

'Ysa called me from the school. What's wrong?' he asked, glancing at the sheet over Missus's chair.

'We're all right,' she said. 'But Hilda's gone. You could help Clem home, if you like. He's a bit shaken up.'

'Of course,' Dutch said, sitting at the table. 'I'm sorry, Clem. She was a kind lady. And her pies will go down in local history.'

That made Clem smile, and he finished his tea. 'Scones like rocks, though,' he said wryly. 'They were stale before they hit the plate.'

The three of them laughed, which echoed around the still house until it felt unseemly.

'Go,' Patience said. 'I'll do the phone calls. I've got her address book. And we know she wants to be cremated and her ashes buried with Dad.'

'In Mam's grave,' Clem said, an echo of his old grin coming out. 'The three of them can sort it out, wherever they end up.'

When the men had gone, Patience walked around the house, up to the room where she and her siblings had slept. It was just an anonymous guestroom now, but for a moment everything was very clear. The indentation Clem had put in the doorframe trying to build a fort, the little hollows where Patience and Susie's bed frame had once worn away the plaster, crayon peeping through layers of paint after Susie had drawn on the wall. Susie, Mam, Dad, Missus, William and Joseph, all dead.

She hoped the house wouldn't be split between Hilda's children, because that would be another loss for the family.

49

As Ellie jumped off the trawler to save Bran, the cold water made her gasp.

A mouthful of salt water shot down her throat. She held her breath, feeling her hair lift in the water. It was black as ink, and the light from the trawler had disappeared. She wasn't sure if she was upside down, but her life jacket was tugging in one direction, which must be up. She kicked hard, breaching out of the water like a dolphin. On the surface she could see nothing but the next wave, and the one after that, touched with a little light. The blaze of the beam from the safety boat blinded her. For one moment she was lifted by a wave and saw a yellow waterproof a few feet away. She swam, tugged back by the life-line, missing Bran's coat by inches. She screamed. The yellow scrap drifted away, gathering speed.

It was only then that she saw something, a different texture in the next wave, something breaking up the surface. She reached out and grabbed short, thick hair. As she rolled the heavy weight towards her, she saw Bran's face, bleached white as he came to the surface. Ellie clutched him in her arms as she realised the life jacket wasn't enough for both of them. Holding

Bran's face in the air pushed her under water. She could feel
her harness tighten as someone dragged her closer, bashing her
against the side of the trawler. She saw stars for a moment, but
clung to Bran. They wouldn't be able to pull him up, she
realised – he was a dead weight. She managed to gasp half a
breath of air before Bran's weight pushed her back under. The
safety boat slid closer, then someone in fluorescent clothing
leaned forward. Marcus. She could see his mouth open,
shouting directions, but Ellie's ears were full of water.

Marcus reached for Bran. When Ellie came up for air again,
Tink was heaving Bran up, too, his face set and determined.
Another wave pushed Ellie down. Then the weight in her arms
was lessened, and she bobbed back up. Marcus and Tink were
hauling Bran over the side by anything they could reach – a
foot, his jeans, an arm. He slid into the boat as the inflatable was
smashed against the trawler, thudding Ellie's head against the
hull. The world faded to a quiet place where Bran was rescued
and Ellie stopped worrying. Her arms and legs didn't seem to
work, just drifted like seaweed in the current and spun in the
waves.

When strong hands grabbed her around the collar of her
uniform and lifted, her muscles were weak. The life jacket
tipped her head up as she was pulled backwards; voices shouted
commands she tried to obey. She was dragged and dumped into
the bottom of the boat. The engine accelerated the inflatable
away from the danger between the two ships. Bran. *Bran.*

Ellie could hear Lolly shouting, and when she lifted her
heavy head she could see Marcus pushing on Bran's chest. Had
she been too slow? Was he already dead? The agony of seeing
him lifeless put some last energy into her limbs and she sat up,
caught by surprise by an internal wave of vomited seawater. She
coughed, caught her breath and stared at Marcus and Lolly.
They had driven the boat into the lee of the quay and had
ripped Bran's clothes open.

Tink shouted, 'Hold on!'

The boat scraped over the sand at the bottom of the quay, and many hands seemed to catch it, pulling it to the safety of the slipway. Ellie had no time to react, and she was thrown backwards. The world spun as she realised how leaden her chest felt, how every breath was rasping in her ears.

Bran was carried over the side and up the slipway, the way pallbearers would lift a coffin. People were huddled around him as he lay on blankets. Iona, the retired nurse, was there in an oversized coat; Marcus, too. She could hear the 'whop whop whop' of a helicopter overhead. Lolly and Tink came back to the safety boat and started to pull Ellie upright. She couldn't move. In the end, several hands bundled her over the side and carried her up the concrete slope.

She could hear someone shout 'Clear!' and she knew they were trying to save Bran. The defibrillator from the pub, she thought, as she slumped onto the slipway. They shouted something from far away, then an oxygen mask was pulled over her face, pinging against one of her ears. She fumbled to pull it away.

'Keep it on,' someone growled. Tink. 'We're just going to carry you up to the pub.'

'Bran.' Her voice rasped. It didn't sound like hers.

'They're going to take him by air ambulance. They're doing everything they can. He has a heartbeat.'

Relief made her sag back onto something. 'Corinne?' she suddenly remembered, as she was lifted along the quay, lights flashing in her eyes.

'She's still out there, helping the lifeboat transfer Joe.' Tink's words were clipped. 'Come on, Elowen, focus on yourself. Your oxygen's low, you're not breathing properly. Deep breaths, now.'

Ellie tried, but it started a storm of coughing. A surge of shivers started in her legs and around her jaw, then spread through her body. She shuddered against the straps holding her on a stretcher.

'C-cold,' she managed to say before the sounds and light slipped away again.

The next face to lean over her was Iona.

'We're going to warm you up. You're freezing.' Her voice was sensible, but Ellie could see tension in her face.

Iona pressed a pad of cloth to her forehead, making it sting. When it came away it was bloody. She recognised the porch of the pub as she was carried through, the stretcher bumping against the door jamb.

'Take her to Bran's room,' Tink said.

They laid her down on the bed and Bran's aftershave and laundry soap permeated her shivering. Iona started to undress her, Tink also shedding his uniform down to jeans and T-shirt. 'Come on, maid. Up you get.'

Iona and Tink carried her into the bathroom, where clouds of steam greeted her. They let her slump into the shower tray and Tink got in, standing over her. He started to pull at Ellie's T-shirt.

'Look up,' he muttered. 'Come on, Ellie,' he said to her, pulling at her jeans. 'Help me out here. Get these cold things off.'

The water streaming over Ellie got warmer and warmer.

'I'll do the rest,' Iona said. 'We've got some of Bran's dry clothes. She won't need much. The lifeboat will be here shortly, we'll get her to hospital.'

A woman in a paramedic's uniform leaned over Ellie. Something cold touched her chest again and she realised she was almost naked. The warming stream returned like hot needles. Her face felt scalded, but she didn't care. The sensation in her hands came back abruptly in pins and needles.

'Ow, ow,' she said, under her breath.

'You'll live,' the paramedic said, but she was still frowning. 'But you need to get checked.'

Iona stripped off Ellie's wet underwear and socks as if she was a baby, turned off the water, and wrapped her in two thick towels.

'Sit on the bed, we'll get you dressed,' the paramedic said.

'How is everyone?' She turned to Iona. 'How is Bran?'

Tink was still there, looking through Bran's chest of drawers for clothes.

'I don't know yet.' His voice was deep and when Ellie looked at him, some of the water dripping down his face looked like tears. He was also wrapped in towels, and sniffed loudly. 'The trawler's still out there, pushing the tug onto the sandbank. I've got to go and see if Corinne is OK. I just need some clothes.'

Bran. Ellie tried to sit up.

'Stay still,' Iona said, dressing her in oversized T-shirt, jumper and sweatpants that all smelled like Bran.

Ellie could hear the wind buffeting the windows. They waited for a few minutes, her chest feeling more leaden and burning inside.

'We're ready for you,' the paramedic said. 'They've picked the last casualty off the tug already by lifeboat, and the male casualty is flying straight to the mainland by helicopter. Now it's just you.' Her hands were moving, lights shining in her eyes, something clamped on her finger. A stethoscope pressed to her chest again. 'Swallowed a bit of seawater, huh?'

'Where's Corinne, Max?' Iona asked over the paramedic.

'She's fine,' the barman said. 'They're going to anchor in the Sound and wait it out. Corinne's on the radio with Tink, they're having a bit of a moment.' He smiled, an unfamiliar expression on his face. 'Did you hear? She's pregnant.'

'She said,' Ellie said, the words coming out like a croak. She was so, so tired, and her muscles didn't work.

'And don't worry about Branok,' Max said. 'He's being looked after by the best.'

Ellie could only nod, her words stifled. She felt a combination of sick and suffocated, and her head was spinning. An oxygen mask was put on her face, she was wrapped in blankets and slid onto a sort of chair. The paramedics and Iona encased her in what felt like a plastic bag.

'It's not raining much, just very blowy,' Iona said.

'I thought Bran...' She couldn't finish.

'He's strong,' Iona said, her voice full of emotion. 'He came round fast and was conscious when he left for Plymouth. You'll be going to hospital on St Brannock's. We'll come and get you once you're on the mend.'

The room was full of people, in uniform, in waterproofs. She was aware of being lowered, terrifyingly, onto a ship; then she was being strapped onto a trolley in the back of an ambulance, but she remembered nothing in between. Each time the thought intruded: *Is he OK, is he alive?* The swaying of the vehicle lulled her to sleep; it continued long after she was laid in a warm bed in a dimly lit ward. She opened her eyes to realise there was a drip in her arm, a bandage over her forehead and pillows raising her up. She felt sleep creeping up on her...

Bran.

50

12 APRIL 1987

Ysella walked down the aisle holding Patience's hand. Clem would have been honoured to take her, but Patience knew if Dutch couldn't do it, she had to do it herself. Her girl, her baby, was getting married.

Patience didn't know Malcolm Roberts well, but Ysa did, and she was head over heels in love. She had met him on the beach where he had been trying to launch a rowing boat into the tide and wind. Every time he stepped in, the boat lurched back to land, grounding on the sand under his weight. Ysa had laughed at him, rolled up her jeans and slipped off her sandals to give him a push out. In an impulsive moment, he had asked if this pretty, shining girl wanted to come with him, and she had held out her hands to be pulled up.

When Ysella had walked in late that afternoon, Patience recognised that look. A pang of grief pierced her that her daughter had taken another step away. She was almost twenty-eight; she knew her own mind.

'Oh, Mam, he's so interesting,' she had sighed, leaning back in one of the dining chairs. 'He lives in London and works at a bank. He's been to France and Italy and he's going to America next year.'

'Makes you wonder why he's here,' Patience said. 'Brush the sand off your feet, maid.'

'He's here with friends from college. He went to Oxford, studied economics.'

Patience watched Ysa twirl in the garden, shaking her shoes and clothes free of a dusting of white sand. 'Looks like you went to West Island.'

'We did. We had an ice cream on the beach. The sand over there is dazzling.'

She had certainly been dazzled. 'I expect he will be busy with his friends the rest of the week, then,' Patience said, stirring dinner.

'Oh, they've invited me along, too. Since it is the summer holidays, I said I'd meet them on the big island, show them around.' She stood, holding her summer dress out. The wide skirt had taken a whole evening of hemming. 'I might go into Penzance with them, if you don't need me for anything.'

No, I don't need you for anything, although the day will be very dull here on my own.

Now they were getting married. Telling Dutch that Ysa was being escorted down the aisle by her mother was tricky. He sat in the fourth pew, arms folded, looking uncomfortable in his only suit. He must have had it thirty years and it didn't quite fit any more, and a couple of the buttons had mismatched thread.

Patience would be on her own every day, and Ysa would be teaching in London. Science for primary schools, they called it. Patience couldn't imagine teaching science to children without taking them out into nature, feeling the muscles in a worm fighting to dig into the soil or sampling a flower's fragrance like a bee. But her way of teaching wouldn't work in a school with a concrete playground and thirty children to a class.

Ysa smiled as they reached Malcolm. Seeing the look on his face as he watched Ysa walking in was reassurance enough for Patience.

Ysella kissed her mother and gave her the bouquet, before putting a hand out to her groom. Patience could feel her heart clenching in pain. Ysa had been so much hers for so long...

She stood back, realising tears were streaming down her face. One of the bridesmaids, little Josephine, Missus's grand-daughter, crept her damp fingers into Patience's.

'Don't cry,' she said, looking terrified. For teacher Patience to cry, there must be something wrong.

Patience crouched down in her mint wool suit, the skirt restricting her a little. 'It's quite all right, maid. These are happy tears. Most people cry at weddings.' She straightened the four-year-old's dress, lifted her chin with one finger and said, 'Look at the bride, that's what we should be doing.'

And she did. The wedding went off without a hitch. Ysa laughed and hugged everyone, and Patience greeted all Malcolm's relatives who had been shipped in at enormous expense. By the end of the evening, the reception at the hotel was getting rowdy and Patience was ready for bed. It was then that she felt Dutch's hand on her waist, guiding her outside.

'Did you tell her?' he asked, his accent more exaggerated than usual. 'About her father?'

'No.' Patience sighed, exhausted. 'Please, Dutch, can we talk about this another day? Anyone could overhear us.'

'Does she know who her mother is?'

'Of course she does,' Patience hissed back. 'For God's sake, Dutch, lower your voice. I told her when she was a teenager. But Malcolm thinks she is Susie's child, because that's what it says on her birth certificate. She will tell him the truth when she's ready.'

'You should tell her about her father.'

'What does it matter, now? But if you want the whole island to know we've been—' Patience spread her hands out and lowered her voice. 'We've been living a lie, Dutch, for thirty years. That was the price of keeping her close, being able to watch her grow up.'

'I don't want to live a lie any more.'

Patience realised he was more than a little drunk. 'I'm not going to let you ruin Ysa's wedding,' she said, taking him by the elbow and steering him through the garden towards the gate onto the beach.

'I'm not talking about Ysa,' he said. 'I know that's gone, I accepted that. No, you stupid woman, I mean *you*.' His arm around her waist pulled her hard to him, and he kissed her mouth, half open with astonishment. It was like the old days, but darker, more intense. She grabbed his jacket to push him away, but he somehow ended up kissing her again.

'I love you. I *never* stopped loving you.' He then rambled on in drunken German.

Patience gave him a little shake as Clem walked out of the hotel.

'Dutch has had a bit too much to drink,' she said loudly.

Clem blinked at the two of them. 'Better take him home then, maid,' he said, before walking back towards the hotel.

'Back to the Purse,' she said, grabbing him around the waist and physically guiding him onto the path.

Dutch stopped so fast she staggered. 'No. To your cottage,' he hissed. 'Or I'll tell the island about us.'

She stared at him. 'I've never known you behave badly,' she said to him, shaking him a little. 'You've been a perfect gentleman to me, respecting my decision.'

'I *love* you!' he shouted, and she shushed him. 'Don't shut me up. I kept quiet for Ysella, I watched you take my daughter, my child...' He dissolved into tears, and leaned against her.

She wrapped her arms around him and let him cry. 'All right,' she murmured to him. 'You can come back to the cottage and sleep on the sofa. That's all.'

She could feel his head nodding in agreement. 'Then we speaks,' he said, his voice slurring.

She hitched one of his arms across her shoulders and started walking.

'Then we speaks,' she said, a smile building.

51

Ellie was exhausted after three days in hospital. No one had told her when Bran would be back, although she was relieved he was going to be fine. Iona and Corinne had come to fetch her, sympathising as she threw up again and again on the boat. She felt flat, as if the minutes in the sea had washed something vital right out of her, leaving only fear behind.

Tink gave her a lift up the road, but Ellie didn't want to talk. She walked into Kittiwake Cottage alone to find a handwritten letter from a solicitor. She had missed three nights on the island, and a claim had been lodged against Patience's will in favour of her closest blood relatives.

On the doormat was also a hand-drawn get-well card from the islanders. Her father was suspiciously silent. Her 'heroism' has been reported on the local news but maybe it never went national. *Heroism*. It was stupid instinct. She could have died, and Bran could have drowned anyway, but she knew she would do it again to save him.

. . .

The next day, a letter came from her father, delivered by a subdued and gentle Maggi. She knocked on the door, but didn't invite herself in, just took one of Ellie's hands for a moment as if she had been bereaved.

But everyone's OK, she wanted to say, except she'd somehow lost Bran. She couldn't say how but she knew he would leave the island now. The houseboat was unsalvageable, having been battered by the next tide and smashed on the rocks. Most of Joe's and Bran's belongings were trashed, too.

Ellie now knew that she loved him, a useless, hopeless love. Joe had moved back into the pub for the moment, the roof made temporarily watertight, but the sale was about to be completed and no one thought he could live independently. Tink, on one of his regular visits to make sure Ellie ate and drank, had told her Joe had neighbours from the town looking after him, but that it couldn't last.

Ellie sat on the sofa with care. She had a feeling the mouse had built a nest in the base, and she didn't want to squash her. Mrs Mousy, who had access to a thousand male mice outside, was probably raising a brood of a dozen baby mice right under the cushions.

She shut her eyes. It would be someone else's problem soon. Perhaps she wouldn't cremate the sofa; she would just drag it into the shed and let the mice multiply in comfort forever.

Later, she woke to the sound of knocking on the door. She wanted to shout 'go away,' but the door scraped open.

'Elowen?' Iona, the nurse, had a melodic voice, quite deep for a woman's and easily recognisable. 'I need to talk to you.'

'Come in,' Ellie called, sitting up and trying to straighten her hair. She was in yesterday's T-shirt, pyjama trousers and bare feet. 'They said I should rest.'

'Well, you've been resting,' she said, with firmness in her voice. 'But now Joe needs you. He'll be homeless in a few days when the sale goes through, and you've been dealing with the business side for him.'

She shook her head to wake up her fuddled brain. 'How is Joe? I meant to go and see him.'

'The doctor thinks he may die in the next few days.'

'What?' The more important question floated up again. 'Where's Bran? I mean, how is he?'

'He's coming back to the island this afternoon. Judith and John are picking him up from St Brannock's in a water taxi. I'm worried about how he's going to cope with Joe's decline.'

Ellie felt a mixture of painful excitement at the prospect of seeing Bran, and despair at the unrequited, agonising feelings she had for him.

'What can I do? For Joe, I mean.'

'He's been writing reams of notes since he got back.' Iona sighed. 'He's on a mission. He wants the whole town to come to the pub this evening as he has something to say to us all. Can you help him with that? So that he can relax.'

See the whole town? The idea filled Ellie with dread. Especially if Bran was going to be there. Maybe it was time, especially if it would help him.

'I'll come,' she said, surprising herself. 'What do I need to do?'

Joe's business didn't take long, which was good because he fell asleep in the middle of it. Sat in his favourite wing chair by the fire, in a nest of blankets – Iona also in attendance – he had explained his wishes in detail.

Joe had done so much for the town, for the new owners when they took possession, for the future. But the money would be tied up in probate if he died before the sale went through. Joe was in no state to transfer monies to Bran now.

The pub's computer was still in the office and Ellie knew the password. She plugged the printer in and started work, trying to read her own scribbled notes.

By the time she came back down a couple of hours later, the whole pub was filled with small groups of people talking quietly at tables and at the bar. Joe's cronies were sitting in a half-circle around him, laughing because, somehow, it didn't feel sad. Next to him, on the window seat, was Bran, looking almost as pale as he had when they fished him out of the sea.

Ellie was momentarily elated, unable to stop smiling, wanting to run over. His eyes met hers for a long moment, then he looked away, expressionless. Ellie didn't know what she'd expected or hoped for, but it wasn't *nothing*.

Max tapped her on the shoulder. 'It's an open bar. Do you want anything?'

Ellie almost refused but then thought about the pages creased up in her pocket. 'Actually, can I have a whisky? Single malt and lots of ice.'

Max patted her again. 'I'll bring a sandwich over, too. You look like you need it.'

Ellie worked over the notes, watching Joe as the late afternoon sun moved around the pub, greying the old man's face. He had managed a few words for everyone, shaken a lot of hands, held court in the middle of *his* pub. Bran went off with Corinne for a while, and avoided looking in Ellie's direction. Joe had sunk lower and lower in his chair, and was speaking less. The doctor appeared, a small space was created around him, and a syringe was taken away. That brightened Joe up, and he was able to sit up and look more alert.

Max beckoned to the doctor. 'This is the third casualty, if you want to check her over.'

The doctor smiled. 'If she managed that whole sandwich,

she should be all right. I understand Joe wants you to make some sort of announcement?'

'He does,' she said. 'I don't know when, though.'

'Soon.' The doctor looked over at Joe. 'Very soon. He's exhausted. He's hanging on, but his batteries are running down.'

'OK.' Ellie finished the last of her whisky.

Someone had lit the wood burner when the light faded, and the pub was warm. But not hot enough for Joe by the look of it, who was wrapped in layers of blankets like a mummy. Ellie watched Bran sink onto the floor next to him, his forehead resting against his father's chair, and Joe's hand resting for a moment on his head.

Ellie stood up, catching Joe's eye, and the old man nodded.

'Quieten down, now!' he called in a cracked, thin voice. It cut through the chatter and Max rang the bell to finish the job. The rustle of people shifting in their seats wasn't enough to cover the crackle of logs.

Ellie stood up, cleared her throat and looked at Joe.

'Joe has asked me to explain what's happening with the pub,' she started.

'Get on with it,' Joe cackled, then started coughing.

'When Mr and Mrs Hunter came over to look at the Island Queen, Joe impressed upon them that the pub is *essential* for the island to survive. No new houses have been sold to residents for a decade. Jobs are scarce and the pub is a big employer, as well as somewhere we all meet. But the Island Queen has structural problems, not to mention the fire damage in the roof. Ben and Sadie have come up with a plan that will help the island, as well as develop a profitable business.' She waved towards the back of the room. 'Sadie, do you want to explain what you're doing?'

Sadie Hunter walked to the middle of the room and looked around.

'We have bought the Mermaid's Purse,' she said, with

heightened colour. 'I know some of you thought it was just being upgraded into holiday flats. But our application to reopen it as a pub is going for planning permission and we've been told it should go through. Some jobs will transfer there.'

The pub erupted with excited chatter, questions, people waving their hands. Ben Hunter waved at one of them. 'Yes?'

'Can we play darts there?'

Ben smiled over his shoulder at Sadie. 'We were told by Joe that darts were essential. Skittles might be out, though, as it's a lot smaller than here. Max is going to run it for us.' All heads swivelled to Max. Ellie was astonished he'd managed to keep that from everyone, but then, he was taciturn by nature.

'But what about the Island Queen?' someone at the back called out.

'Well, it needs completely ripping out and rebuilding.' He shrugged. 'But this way we keep both pubs.'

'But will you change the Island Queen into something else?' Bran climbed to his feet. 'Everyone has so much history here,' he said, his voice harsh with emotion.

Sadie looked at Ben. 'It's time to update the pub,' she said simply. 'It's going to be an amazing place to drink local ales, eat great food and support our local producers. Not to mention, the rooms above have amazing views, and it will be a great holiday destination.'

Bran stood, his face working as he digested the news. Ellie winced at the word 'destination'; she knew he hated that term.

'How long before the sale goes through? Before my dying father and I need to leave, before you pull our home down about our ears?'

Ellie stepped forward. 'That's not fair, Bran,' she said, to the stormy face in front of her. 'Joe's planned all of this. He's done everything he can for the island, and so have Sadie and Ben.'

Bran pushed between people to get beyond the bar, into the back hall. Joe nodded his head as if he wanted Ellie to follow.

When she reached the hall, Bran had already slammed shut the door to the ground-floor bedroom Joe had been using. Ellie tapped on the door.

'Bran, please. Just talk to me.'

'No.'

She pressed her hands against the door. 'Listen. You've been saying he needs to modernise all year. This is him repaying you for giving up your life when he had the stroke. You'll have the freedom to go anywhere, and build a new life.'

The long silence that followed made her uncomfortably aware of the hammering of her heart.

'Bran, please.' She could feel emotion crowding her throat, choking her words. 'I'm not leaving until you talk to me.'

'You say he's doing all this for me?' His voice was rough. 'He didn't *ask* me, he *told* me. He blackmailed me into coming back with what my dead mother would want me to do, he said it would only be a few weeks. I hate him. I hate *you*. And now he's going to die.' His voice choked.

Ellie flinched. She wasn't expecting him to feel about her the way she did about him, but it was painful to hear him say he hated her.

'He's dying. Please don't let your anger at me hurt him. Please come back. The doctor said he didn't have long.'

'He wants to die there in the pub,' he said. 'Like an emperor in front of his people. Who he's sold out for a *destination*.' She could hear rasping sobs through the door. Ellie put her fingers on the handle, but didn't try it. She leaned her forehead against the door. Tears welled up.

She turned back and walked to the bar, where people gripped her shoulder and smiled sadly. The group around Joe was quieter now. She stopped in the middle of the pub, knowing Joe's last wishes.

'Joe really wants to hear some local music,' she said, looking at Elk. 'Then he says he'll sleep better tonight.' Joe lifted his head a little at her words and managed a small smile.

Elk stood up, ducking under the beams to walk over to the corner of the pub where a couple of musicians already sat with their instruments.

'Right, any suggestions?'

The attention was turned, finally, away from the dying man, grey-faced in his nest of blankets.

She walked towards a table and a chair was cleared for her. 'Well done,' Judith said, at her shoulder. 'You've done a great job for the town.'

Ellie couldn't answer. She was exhausted, and Bran's crying was still lodged in her head.

Later that evening, Ellie was sitting on a picnic table outside the pub, unable to watch the old man's dying any more. Corinne had tempted Bran back to sit with his father and now he was huddled at his feet, the doctor close by, and Joe had slumped into unconsciousness. The music had quietened a little during the evening, children had been taken home and put to bed.

Ellie jumped as someone – Corinne – put her arm around her. 'You OK?' she asked. 'It's getting late, but most people are staying for the shanties.'

'What time is it?' she asked, leaning into Corinne for a second.

'Ten past eleven. I don't know how much longer Bran can cope.'

'I'm not sure how much longer I can either,' Ellie said.

Corinne was staring at her in the low light from the windows. 'You've got it bad, haven't you?'

She smiled into the darkness. 'Oh, *yes*. But he hardly cares I exist. I'm the one helping to sell the pub.'

Corinne leaned close. 'Selling the pub will be the best thing for him, you wait and see.'

'The sale will still go through. They've already exchanged the paperwork. Bran might have to wait for probate to get his share.'

Corinne's voice was warm, kind. 'I know he says he wants a clean break, but all his friends are here. Lots of people have offered him somewhere to stay.'

The door to the pub opened with a scrape, and Tink walked out into the pool of light. 'We're starting shanties. You know some, don't you?' he said to Corinne.

She fitted into Tink's arm. 'Compulsory curriculum in the Royal Navy.'

Ellie followed the two of them into the porch. The atmosphere in the pub was intense, the music pulsing in the warm air.

Someone had dimmed the lights and Max was going around with matches, lighting candles and lanterns on tables and walls.

Elk ended the last song, the voices fading away. He looked over at the dark corner where Joe slumped, laid back a little as someone had propped up the front legs of the armchair. Bran was hunched up on the window seat.

'We're going to sing Joe's favourite song before we all go,' Elk announced. 'The fisherman's shanty, the story of island trawlers like the *Cormorant*, *Gannet* and the first *Island Queen*.'

There was a murmur of approval, and a lone violin played by Birdie cut through the dense air in the pub. Other instruments joined in as the singers told the story.

Boys cut their teeth on the Morwen Bar,
And sailed for Newfoundland,
Many men drowned in seas afar,
Their bones all rolled to sand.

So ring the harbour bell, me love,
We'll sail in on the tide,
And kiss the girls and choose the one
To be a fisherman's bride.

The song built in intensity, people joined in the chorus, feet tapped then stamped. But all Ellie could think about was Bran, waiting for his dad to die.

The final chorus was a crashing wave of sound, fading to the backwash, dragging sighs out of the listeners. They started clapping, cheering, letting the tension out. Ellie found herself applauding, too, tears streaming down her face as she remembered the hollowness of her mother's death, of the love that Patience had woven into the will.

Elk's powerful voice boomed out. 'Time to go home, leave the man in peace.'

There were hugs and goodbyes as people started collecting coats and moved towards the door. Some stopped to speak to Bran, who had seemed lost in his own world but nodded or said a word of thanks as people filed past. Corinne grabbed Ellie's arm.

'Say goodbye, and we'll walk you home,' she said.

Ellie walked over to Joe, grey-faced and still.

'Is he...?' she blurted out.

The doctor packed his stethoscope away.

'He went before the last song,' the doctor said to Bran.

'I know,' he said, uncurling from the window seat. 'It was just what he wanted.' He held up a hand as Corinne moved forward. 'Not now, I can't. I'm sorry. Just make sure everyone goes home, will you? Max is going to help me.' He looked straight at Ellie, for the first time in hours. 'Tell the Hunters I'll be out by the weekend, ahead of the completion date.'

She shook her head. 'They wouldn't mind if you need more time.'

He couldn't answer, and turned away. Iona put her arm around Bran's shoulders.

Ellie walked to the door, shrugged her coat on. She ached for Bran and could do nothing to help him.

52

Hilda Ellis, known universally as Missus, had left the Ellis cottage to Clem, Fred and Patience. The three surviving Ellis siblings agreed that Patience should keep Kittiwake Cottage and that Clem would have their childhood home in Noah's Drang.

Clem had a new wife, Sarah, who was already 'Nan' to everyone. It was good for him to be able to carry on hosting family get-togethers, especially now his son Billy had a baby girl, Beatrix. Being a grandfather had revitalised his enthusiasm for the sea. With Dutch and several others, he now owned the only deep-water boat on the island. *Gannet* was younger than *Cormorant*, leaner, cheaper and more stable in bad weather.

Patience had allowed Dutch to stay over once or twice a week, telling people the walk down the hill was too much for his old knees. He was almost sixty-eight. She was coming up to retirement age and intended to continue teaching as long as possible. She set up the spare room for him, although he only used it for his clothes. Instead, they laughed about their sagging bodies and extra wrinkles, and made love with as much joy, if less energy, than when they were young.

They wandered down to the town for one of Clem's Sunday lunches, a new tradition Patience was keen to promote. Sarah could be relied upon to produce an amazing meal. Dutch and Patience would always part ways at the top of Warren Lane so they could arrive separately.

Clem opened the door and beamed at her, and immediately looked over her shoulder at Dutch. 'There you are. I could do with some help, mate.'

'Always happy to help, *mate*,' Dutch said. 'What do you want done?'

'Billy's up in the eaves,' Clem said. 'He's getting some old boxes down of Mam and Dad's. We're going to have a look through to see if we need to keep anything.'

Patience walked through to the kitchen, admired baby Trix and helped Sarah peel vegetables. There was a crash overhead and, seeing Sarah's alarm, Patience walked around to the bottom of the stairs.

'What on earth are you doing?' she called up.

'Just bringing a box down.' Clem and Dutch carried down something not much smaller than a coffin.

'What is that?' she asked as the musty, salty smell hit her. 'Phew.'

Clem laid it on the living room floor. 'I think I know what it is.' He glanced at Dutch, who seemed to have stepped back to distance himself.

'It's *the* box,' Dutch said. He looked at Patience, looking a bit dazed. 'I think it's the box I was floating on when I was rescued. Why would your father keep it?'

Clem looked from one to the other. 'Maybe he thought people would guess you were off a German U-boat if they saw it,' he answered.

'You know?' Patience was shocked.

'Of course I know. Half the island worked it out,' Clem said.

'Dad told me years before he died.' He fiddled with the lock. 'It's shut tight, though.'

'I hardly remember anything except that box and an old coat I pulled over myself,' Dutch said, his voice hoarse.

Clem wrestled with the hasp and the lid flew up, releasing a mouldy smell.

'I'm guessing that's the coat,' he said, pulling it out.

Dutch took the heavy overcoat in his hands. 'Not mine,' he said, in a low voice. 'An officer's, maybe. I was just a boy, a new recruit.'

'It saved your life,' Patience said.

Patience told Clem she would keep the box in the shed until Dutch decided what to do with it.

'You'd better take him home with you,' Clem said. 'He's a bit of a mess.'

So she did, steering him to one of the sofas as the sun went down. She worked around him, getting lessons ready for Monday, washing up the breakfast things, ironing the week's washing. Still he stared over the sky as it turned orange, then red, the few clouds gathering purple under them until the light faded completely.

'What are you thinking?' she asked, sitting next to him, taking one of his hands.

'I've been a part of these islands for nearly fifty years,' he said, his voice dry and croaky. 'But I've never felt as much of an outsider as I do today.'

'But you're *not* an outsider. You're part of this family. You fathered an island child who might one day have another island child. You've worked on the ferries, the trawlers, the pilots. You've changed the island just by living and working here.'

He turned to stare at her, and when she saw how upset he looked she hugged him.

'I thought I was going to die,' he said. 'Out there in the cold. I knew I was going to die in the sea. Then your father dragged me out like a landed fish. And I betrayed him with you.'

'No,' she said, squeezing him, whispering right into his ear. 'You made me happy. You looked after me and Susie, you gave him Ysa. You gave back much more than he gave you.'

'But why?' He pulled back to look at her. 'Why did he save me?'

'I don't know,' she said simply. Maybe George, whose own child had drowned in the cruel, dark sea, couldn't watch it happen to another boy. Maybe just because his humanity exceeded his sense of Britishness, as an islander, separate. Maybe it just wasn't his war with Germany, it was the government's. 'But he and Mam did. And now we are here, together.'

'I don't deserve you,' he said, staring at her.

'Well,' she said briskly. 'You've got me. So come to bed.'

53

PRESENT DAY, 28 SEPTEMBER

Three weeks after Joe died, Ellie still hadn't spoken more than a few polite words to Branok. So her heart felt like it somersaulted when she looked up from her desk to see him standing in the living room doorway.

'I thought you'd gone,' she said, around a tightness in her throat that made her voice high.

'I did knock.' He winced a small smile. 'I'm catching the four o'clock boat. The tide's coming in.'

She glanced towards the bay window, its panes embracing the wide view. The sun was sparkling on the water so much it was dazzling, and exposed sand lay in yellow ribbons.

'I thought you weren't talking to me,' she said, looking back at her computer screen.

He walked into the room, and she felt an odd flare of anger.

'Do come in,' she said, with unavoidable sarcasm. 'Make yourself at home.'

Bran didn't reply, just perched on the corner of the old sofa.

'I don't have a home any more,' he said, his face averted, so she hardly heard him. He turned to Ellie. 'I just wanted to say goodbye to Patience, you know? This is where she sent me on my way to university to become an artist.' His face was calm, but his dark eyes were narrowed and shining. 'I thought I would come here and she would tell me to spread my wings again. But you're here and I can't hear her.'

'Sorry,' she said, reflexively. *No, I'm not.* 'Do you need me to tell you to run off, never come back?'

A tear ran silently down his still face.

She stood up, took half a step towards him. 'You know I don't mean that, it's just you haven't come near me since...'

'Since you saved my life?' He half laughed, a sad noise, and looked away to wipe his eyes with the back of his hand. He turned back to the sea. 'It does make things a bit awkward. I suppose I should say thank you.'

'You're welcome,' she said, half-jokingly. 'No trouble, any time.'

'You could have drowned,' he said to the view, his shoulders hunching forward. 'You nearly died.'

'*You* nearly died.' Ellie moved behind him, seeing the same view over his shoulder, close enough to smell the scent of his hair. 'Could you just slow down, not make any snap decisions? Like catching the four o'clock boat.'

He turned a little, looking back at her, his face close. His eyes were brown, with sparks of amber glowing around the edge.

'Why did you do it?' he said, his voice rough.

'Instinct,' was her first reply. Her next thought found the words. 'I-I just couldn't bear the thought of losing you.'

He stared at her for another long moment before dropping his gaze. 'Why? I was hateful to you when you were helping my dad.'

She smiled at the memory. 'You *were* pretty hard on me.' Her hands itched to make some contact. 'It's good enough that you're OK.'

He stood, standing disturbingly close. 'As long as you're all right.'

She reached out then, putting one hand flat on his chest, lightly holding him away. The warmth of his chest spread to her fingers. 'I will be. But I thought you were dead.' She couldn't help the anger that bubbled up. 'And then you wouldn't let me see you, or visit.'

'Joe needed you to be there for him,' he said. 'I was confused and angry and upset. It turns out that I really loved the miserable old git, you know? You can't switch it off.'

'I know.' She could feel the ragged bumping of his heart. 'My dad saw me on the news. He wants me to meet him in Penzance, but I told him no.'

'Will you meet him eventually?'

She was getting a little breathless from the connection between them. 'He took my family away from me. He broke off all communication with Patience just when I needed her.'

He squeezed her hand, then dropped it. 'You do love him,' he said, pulling back. 'Take it from me, you do love him, no matter what he did.'

She nodded, once. 'Maybe. But the more I find out, the worse my anger gets. Especially as it turns out he was right about the cottage.'

'What was he right about?' He sat back down on the arm of the sofa.

'It turns out I have broken the conditions in Patience's will,' she said, rummaging in the sideboard drawer for the letter from the solicitor. 'When I was in the hospital, just those three nights, I wasn't here. Someone challenged the will on that basis. I may lose the cottage to her great-nieces and nephews. I suppose Tink will get a share, at least.'

'That's so petty,' he said, frowning. 'That must be Gemma. I hardly know her. She's Tink's first cousin.'

'My solicitor says if the will is challenged it will go to the nearest blood relatives. I'll inherit, if I can prove my mother was formally adopted. Alternatively, if I can prove I am Susannah's grandchild, I'll share it with the others. But then we still have to sell.'

Bran looked back over the view. 'I'd better get a move on,' he said. 'I've got a last bag to pack.'

The pressure built up in Ellie's chest like a wave. 'Don't go.'

He turned around to look at her. 'Why not?'

Ellie couldn't speak and she realised she was shaking. She half wanted to shout at him, half wanted to kiss him. She shuffled closer, looked at him.

Bran wasn't conventionally handsome; he often looked severe when he wasn't laughing, but now he had a lopsided smile. His hands were clenched together, the knuckles white. He looked like he was hanging on to his composure as hard as he could.

'I don't have anywhere to go,' he said, in a deep voice. 'I know I could stay with friends, but I'm not up to it. I can't cope with all... the...' He swallowed hard. 'Kindness.'

'Then stay here,' she managed to say, her gaze roaming over his face, his lowered eyes. 'I won't be kind.'

She wrapped her arms around him in a hug. After a long moment, he reached around her waist. They leaned into each other.

'You'd better not,' he said, her voice muffled into her hair. He let her go, even pushed her away a little.

'I have a spare room,' she said, afraid to spook him. 'You can hide out. We all need some time. You can help me fight for the cottage if you like.'

'Can I put my stuff in your shed?'

'Of course.'

'OK. But no funny business.'

'Of course.'

'I'll give it a go, if you help me up the hill with my bags and boxes,' he said, as if he was doing her a favour. 'But I just want to say one thing, and then it's done. All right?'

She nodded.

Bran took a deep breath, looked into her eyes. 'I would have jumped in to save you, too,' he said, and turned away towards the door.

54

Ysella was triumphant, the baby in her arms. Small but healthy.

'Oh, Mam,' she said, and Patience could see the tiredness as well as the joy, all feelings enhanced by the situation. 'She's so beautiful.'

Patience bent over to kiss Ysa's damp forehead and then the baby's. All was done and safe. Or not quite safe. Ysa still had cancer surgery to come, once she'd recovered from the birth.

A midwife came in and checked the baby. 'She's lovely. Do you want to put her to the breast?'

Ysa nodded. 'I just don't know how, she's so tiny.'

The midwife helped Ysa support the baby on her chest, and they watched in surprise as the baby pursed her lips and opened her mouth.

'Ow. Wow!' Ysa stared down at her. 'That feels weird.' She laughed up at Patience. 'I wasn't expecting that.'

Patience could feel the answering tug in her own breasts, which had been bound after Ysa's birth. She had wept milk and tears in equal quantities when she had fed Ysella her bottles, when she knew that a patch of milk could have betrayed her.

'Will she have to go to special care?' she asked the midwife.

'We'll need to keep a very close eye on her, so we'll watch her closely overnight. We'll probably supplement her milk with a nasogastric tube. Just until she's feeding well and your milk is in.' She turned to Ysella. 'Little and often in the first few days, so she doesn't get too tired.'

'What about later, when Ysa has chemotherapy?' Patience asked.

'Don't worry about that now,' Ysa said, staring at the baby. Malcolm put his arms around them both, tears leaking from under his glasses. 'It's going to be fine. Isn't she amazing, Mal? She's got your chin.'

'She's got your colouring.' Malcolm sniffed. 'She's so small.'

The midwife scoffed as she gently unlatched the baby and helped Ysa offer the other side. 'She's a good size for four weeks early.'

One of the baby's arms wavered out of the blanket and Malcolm took her hand, the fingers curling around his own.

He laughed through the tears. 'She might be tiny, but she's strong. Wiry.'

'Like her daddy,' Ysa said, the two of them exchanging a glance that made Patience catch her breath.

'I'll take a few pictures for Malcolm's mother and get back,' she said. 'I'll leave you three together.'

'Mam.' Ysa stretched out her free hand. 'Wait a minute. I need to say something.' She waved Patience to the chair next to her. 'I'm going to get through this, you know that. I have to be here for the baby.'

Patience nodded, her voice thick in her throat. 'You do, maid, she needs you. We all do.'

'I'm going to call her Elowen, a proper island name. Claire for Malcolm's mum as a middle name, but Elowen for the island. Then she'll always belong to Morwen, wherever she ends up.'

Malcolm opened his mouth as if to say something, then

closed it. 'I suppose after all your hard work, you ought to choose.' He smiled. 'I'll get used to it. At least it's not Mildred, like my great-grandmother.'

Ysa laughed. 'God, I'm tired. All that work for five and a half pounds of baby.' She brushed her lips over her baby's head. 'Hello, Elowen.'

55

A week after Bran moved in, Ellie was still tiptoeing around him, letting him adjust. He slept a lot and spent a lot of time brooding on long walks around the island on his own. Sometimes he gave her intense looks when they met on the landing or in the kitchen, glances like he was weighing something up. If she tried to start a conversation, he just walked away and shut the bedroom door. She wasn't ready for him to leave, so didn't force it.

She was washing up, wondering for the hundredth time if she could squeeze a dishwasher in somewhere, when someone hammered on the cottage door. It wasn't even shut, and normally people would just shout through the house for her. Whoever it was banged again before she could get there.

'Hang on a moment,' she muttered, pulling the door back. She froze, the man looked older, more tense; his mouth was tight and his compact figure was hunched over.

'Dad.' It was all she had. 'You should have said you were coming.'

'I tried to. You don't seem to read your post.' His words were clipped and hard, his close-cropped hair more white than dark now. He looked thinner, too.

For the first time in weeks a spark of humour was lit. She leaned against the door, aware that her pyjama bottoms and a faded T-shirt was hardly power dressing.

'I don't have to read anything. This is my *home*,' she said.

'Not for much longer,' he snapped out. 'Are you going to let me in?'

That did it. Weeks of frustration and depression started to ease aside.

'You can wait outside,' she said, 'while I get dressed.' She waved at the front garden. 'That wall is fairly solid if you want to sit down.' She shut the door very firmly in his face.

Not for the first time, she wished there was a shower in the house, but she did boil a kettle for some hot water and took it up to the sink in the front bedroom to have a proper wash. Her hair was beyond a quick fix, so she twisted it into a pony-tail and cleaned her teeth. Only then did she bang on Bran's door.

'Time to get up,' she called cheerfully.

'Why?' he growled. 'Who was banging?'

'That,' she said, tension cramping her shoulders, 'was my interfering, bossy father. He's outside, sitting on the wall.'

By the time she had run around the front room and given it a quick tidy, Bran was dressed and she was ready to open the front door.

Her father glowered at her.

'Would you like to come indoors and sit down?' she said politely.

He scowled as he walked through the hall and into the living room. He stopped when he saw Bran, then looked around.

'It's hardly changed,' he said, in almost a whisper, and walked towards the window. 'I remember this room. There used to be a cushion on the window seat.' Only then did he frown. 'It needs replastering. And a new ceiling.'

'I know. I did start renovations but then I got the letter from the local solicitor.'

Ellie walked over to the desk and pulled out the letter. She had cleaned and reframed some of the best pictures and put them along the sideboard. Dad looked at each one in turn, flinching slightly. He walked over and picked up the one with Tink, his sister Trix, Ellie and Bran. They sat in a tiny rowing boat that Ysella had towed around the beach.

'That's you, isn't it?' he said, his finger brushing the glass and turning to Bran. 'I knew I recognised you. You're Joe Shore's son. I'm sorry, I don't remember your name. I'm Malcolm Roberts.'

'I'm Branok Shore,' he answered as Malcolm looked at more pictures.

Ysa in the gig team, or sat between Patience and Dutch on the same sofa with the baby on her lap. Elowen as a child, looking sombre in Ysella's arms as she laughed at someone off camera.

'I never thought I would come here again,' Malcolm said. Then his voice grew harder. 'I never expected to return, but now Ellie has forced my hand. She stands to lose this cottage, which Patience always intended her to have.'

'Look, I'm going to make some tea. Would you like some?' Bran said, walking to the door.

'I won't be staying long.'

Ellie gave her dad the letter and followed Bran into the kitchen. Anger was growing in her chest and thudding in her ears.

'He can't just turn up and start telling me what to do,' she hissed. She slammed the door of the new fridge.

'He's almost as annoyed as you are.' He started to smile. 'I've never seen you like this. It's a bit sexy.'

'You can't just ignore me completely and then say stuff like that,' Ellie hissed. She laid out three mugs, the rabbit-shaped sugar bowl she had always loved, and a blue milk jug on a tray. She filled up the teapot and Bran took the tray into the front room.

Malcolm didn't even look at him. 'I'd like to talk to my daughter in private, if you please,' he snapped.

'I want him to stay.' Ellie looked over at Bran.

Bran knew about the letters, the birthday cards and loving messages that Patience had sent her as a child, that had been denied to her as a bereaved and devastated little girl. With his own grief like an open wound, perhaps he appreciated what Ellie had lost.

'Actually, you would have to bodily drag me out,' Bran said, splashing milk in his mug and sitting on the sofa. 'Other people's dramas are so much easier to deal with. There's a chair behind you, Mr Roberts.' Bran passed a cup to Ellie as she sat next to him on the sofa. 'It's OK,' he said, barely above a whisper. 'I'll referee.'

'There are bigger things at stake than what you want or don't want,' Malcolm said to his daughter.

'Like what?' Ellie's fists were clenched in her lap.

'Like this cottage. I know how it was left; I know you interpreted the will as requiring you to stay here for a year.'

'Which I couldn't do because I was in hospital.' Ellie glanced at Bran. 'We both were.'

'She saved my life, by the way.' He smiled, and Malcolm looked more uncomfortable. 'She hurled herself overboard to rescue me. She was my hero. Heroine. She was amazing.'

'So I heard,' Malcolm said drily, turning to Ellie. 'But the fact remains that *you* decided that staying every night was required. When you didn't achieve that, you left the will open to be challenged.'

Ellie carried on looking at Bran. 'I don't care any more,' she said. 'I mean, I'll be sorry to lose the cottage, but it will go to Patience's family, and maybe some money will come to me.'

Bran's smile widened further, although she could see sadness and tiredness around his eyes.

'On the other hand, I will be loaded now the pub has sold,' he said. 'It will be fine.' He looked deep into her eyes. '*We* would be fine, if you still need a flatmate.'

Ellie could feel her face warm like the sun coming out after a rainy day.

'*We*, huh?'

When she looked back at Malcolm, she could see him speculating, thinking. He shook his head.

'Whatever you two have going on, you should inherit the cottage, free and clear. You are Patience's granddaughter.'

Ellie looked up. 'Maybe, but I can't prove it. There was no adoption.'

'I don't know quite how we are going to prove it,' Malcolm said. 'But Ysella told me the truth when we got married. That Patience gave birth to Ysella under Susannah's name.'

'People did used to wonder if Ysa was Susannah's,' Bran said, slowly. 'Patience always insisted Ysella was the child of a distant relative.'

'Her sister Susannah had been ill. She died the following year,' Malcolm said. 'Patience registered Ysella's birth with her sister's documents.'

'And they came back to the island, with the baby asleep in the carpet bag,' Ellie said slowly. 'Did Mum tell you that?'

Finally, Malcolm smiled. 'She did. Patience just let the island speculate both stories, showed the false certificate to the school board, and let the rumours circulate.'

Bran was curious. 'Did Patience's family know the true story?'

'Patience's mother died when she was at school,' Malcolm said, 'and I don't know if her father ever asked.' He turned to

Ellie. 'You are the rightful heir to this very small estate, just the same, even if the will is overturned. Biological granddaughter trumps cousins, nieces and nephews and even brother, if we can prove you are Patience's direct descendant.'

Ellie felt quite shaky, having it said out loud. Suddenly, she really wanted the cottage. When Bran reached out a hand, she took it.

'She *was* my grandmother, then,' she said, her voice croaking in her throat. She turned to her father. 'That's who you kept me away from. Mum died, I lost my grandmother, I lost the island.'

'Patience always wanted Ysella to come home,' Malcolm said. 'She never liked me, she blamed me for taking her away.'

'But you cut her off!' Ellie said, realising how much agony Patience must have been in, right after Ysa died, unable to fight for her grandchild. 'You cut *me* off!'

'I didn't know what to do,' Malcolm said, shaking his head. 'I was broken after your mother died. Can't you understand? Patience tried to take Ysella away from me. I didn't want to lose you, too.'

That had the sound of truth in it. 'Or share me,' Ellie snapped. 'You're so possessive, aren't you? God, Mum must have hated living in London.'

'She loved London. We loved each other. I didn't understand why she wanted so much time on the island but I let her go—'

Bran wasn't taking that quietly. 'You *let* her go?'

Malcolm stared back at him. 'You don't understand. Ysa was fragile, she was fighting cancer most of our marriage. She chose to leave the island to marry me and live in London, and we made a good life there.'

'We did,' Ellie echoed. 'I remember some happy times. But the best memories were always on the island.' Her eyes narrowed. 'You came here sometimes, too.'

That made Malcolm smile. 'I came as much as I could. We used to rent a little house at the end of the road for the summer. You loved that coastguard place – it had a swing in the garden overlooking the cliff. You used to say it made you feel like you were flying.'

'I remember.' Ellie squeezed Bran's hand, let it go and glanced at the clock. 'The last boat back is in half an hour, Dad. You'd better be on it.'

'I thought I might stay at the pub,' Malcolm said. 'But I see it's closed.' He took a deep breath. 'I know you're angry and I know I made a lot of mistakes when your mother died. Please let me explain. I love you, Ellie, and I don't want to lose you, too.'

Ellie opened her mouth as if to say something, but Bran got in first.

'You can stay with us,' he said. 'It sounds like you two have a lot to talk about. The plumbing's a bit primitive but we can give you a bed, at least.'

Ellie was about to question him, then she shut her mouth with a snap. Bran smiled back at her and a warmth spread in her chest like fire. She might be hurt and angry at her dad, but at least Bran was looking at her with the crooked smile she loved.

She managed to speak. 'Shall we go for dinner and talk about it?'

56

6 FEBRUARY 2003

Ysella was the centre of a circle of love. For once there was no discord between Malcolm and Patience, and they seemed to seamlessly fit around Ysella's needs. For the first time, two reserved, private people had their guard down, and the thing they had in common was Ysa. Patience had finally won an argument against Malcolm and his parents, and Elowen was kept home from school. She was colouring pictures of seabirds for Ysa's room, looked after by a watery-eyed housekeeper and her father, while Patience kept watch over Ysa.

'Mam?' She winced when she moved. 'Do you remember that rock pool book?'

'Of course I do,' Patience said, leaning forward to stroke Ysa's short hair off her face. Her skin was hot and dry, like she had a fever. It was if the last of her life force was working its way out. 'You have a copy in the study downstairs.'

'I remember you doing the third edition,' Ysa said, her eyes creeping open. They were filled with thick tears, her lips were cracked and white, she looked like she was drying up. 'I love that book. Make sure Elowen reads it.'

'She's already read it,' Patience said. 'And she doesn't need a book to go rock pooling, she has me.'

'Dutch used to take me,' Ysa said, closing her eyes again and smiling. 'Can we call him Dad now he's gone?'

Dutch's death was a raw wound, and Patience closed her eyes for a second to let the agony subside. Dutch had had a fatal heart attack outside the pub. He'd already died when she got there. She couldn't conceal her grief, the devastation, especially with Ysa's relapse and referral to palliative care. She took a few days to bury him, then returned to Ysella.

'Of course we can.'

Ysa shook her head. 'I want to see Ellie. I need to tell her I love her before I run out of energy.' She sighed, and was asleep before Patience got to the door.

Malcolm walked in and stopped her with a touch on her arm.

'Better we don't upset the child,' he said, his own voice wobbly.

'It might not be long. It might be her last chance.'

He shook his head. 'We have time.'

The two of them sat either side of the bed and, in a strange synchronicity, took a hand each. A soft groan left Ysa.

Slowly, it dawned on Patience that there were no more movements, no more breaths.

57

PRESENT DAY, 7 OCTOBER

Malcolm unpacked his things in the front bedroom, while Bran and Ellie moved her clothes and toiletries into the back room.

'Where am I going to sleep? The sofa is falling to bits,' she hissed, dragging a brush through her hair.

'You can kip with me,' he whispered back. 'What are we, teenagers? You'll behave yourself, or sleep on the floor.'

'He'll think we're a couple,' she said.

Bran stared at her, which made her face warm up, her brush stall.

'Maybe he will.' He smiled. 'Let him think what he wants. Is it such a bad thing? I'll phone the hotel, see if the boys can squeeze us in for dinner.'

'What if he finds out we're just—' Ellie stalled. Neither of them had worked out what they were, and it had seemed too delicate a subject to discuss while Bran was so unhappy.

'He'll assume you're an idiot,' he answered, putting a fresh pillowcase on. He grinned at her. 'Turning down a fantastic and good-looking man who's been living under your roof for more than a week.'

She rolled her eyes. 'Not *that* good-looking.' She straightened the duvet cover. 'You'd better behave. And no snoring, or *you* are on the sofa.'

'If you talk in your sleep, I'm going to boot you out of bed,' he warned, and they both started to laugh.

Malcolm sat opposite Ellie, staring at her over the top of his glasses. 'Are you all right with this?'

'You were the one who wanted to talk,' she said, still a bit snippy. Bran nudged his knee against her leg, the warmth comforting.

'The crab is the best on the island,' Bran said. 'Now the pub's gone, anyway.'

'I was surprised to see it was sold.' Malcolm looked back at the menu. 'Has your father decided to retire?'

Bran shut his eyes for a moment. 'He died,' he said.

'Oh, I'm sorry.' Malcolm looked at Ellie. 'I thought he had been rescued off the boat, the one that got loose in the storm.'

Ellie nodded. 'He died of cancer,' she said softly. 'The funeral was a few weeks ago. He was only home for a few days after the accident.'

'I'm so sorry.' Malcolm looked mortified. 'Bran, my condolences. He was a very fine man.'

Bran nodded, once. 'He was. Now, I'm bored with crab, so I think I'll have the partridge. This seems like a special occasion. What do you think of the cottage?'

'It's not changed that much. The view is still incredible.'

'The beds creak like old ships,' Bran said, with a smile at Ellie. 'I'm always waiting for the bottom to fall out.'

Malcolm looked embarrassed. 'I'm sorry you've given up your own bed. I could have had the spare room.'

Ellie waved it away. 'The best view on the island,' she said. 'And both of us are still recovering from the storm, so we could probably sleep anywhere.'

'Are you fully recovered?' He looked at Bran and then back to Ellie. 'I phoned the hospital a couple of times, but they wouldn't tell me much.'

'I still cough at night,' Ellie said. 'Bran's very tired, but that could be all the stress of losing Joe, moving out of the pub and recovering from a head injury.'

'I've been warned I may make some impulsive decisions, and may suffer from random emotional outbursts,' he said, through a tight smile. 'Especially when I'm hungry.'

Justin, the hotelier, was hovering nearby with a notepad. 'Hi, Bran.' He smiled at them all. 'What can we get you?'

'Have you got any partridge left?'

'For you, we do. If not, I'll nick it off a plate in the kitchen. How about you, Ellie?'

Ellie and Malcolm ordered the warm crab salad. She was watching Bran closely. 'You do look a bit pale,' she said, *sotto voce*, as Justin left.

'I feel better,' he hissed in reply. 'So, Malcolm, what do you think we should do about the will?'

Malcolm nodded, leaned back in his chair. 'Well, I consulted a solicitor who specialises in inheritance law. If Ellie made Kittiwake Cottage her main address, she would have been within her rights to be in hospital. No, the main problem was that she didn't answer the legal challenge.' He turned to Ellie. 'A great-niece has challenged the will and, so far, you don't seem to have replied. The deadline is coming up. If you do nothing, it looks like you are conceding the inheritance.'

Ellie looked at Bran, and when he stretched his fingers towards her, she put her hand over his.

'The thing is...' She cleared her throat, squeezed Bran's hand and let it go. 'I know the people on the island now. Tink is Clem Ellis's grandson – Daniel Ellis. He's living in an old lorry. Part of the money from selling the cottage could help him create a home out of the barn on their land. The great-nieces both have children. The rents are so high that if they lose their jobs, they could lose their homes.'

'And the house will become a soulless holiday let,' Malcolm said. 'Another nail in the coffin for the local population, who will never be able to buy it back.' He looked at Bran. '"The best view on the island," you said. Are you prepared to give that up?'

Bran glanced over at Ellie. 'I would love to live there. I would buy it, if it came up for sale, even though it will probably cost almost as much as the pub sold for.'

'You would?' Ellie looked up, stared at him.

'*We* could,' he said, smiling, entwining her fingers with his again. 'We could buy Trix, Gemma and Tink out if we have to. Have breakfast every day looking over that view. If you want to.'

It was a strange declaration, she thought, before they had even kissed. But she knew that this was a face she could look at, laugh with, forever.

'I do want,' she murmured back, and they both smiled. He lifted her fingers to his lips. Then Justin was there, holding three plates and giving her a knowing look. They let go.

'Robert is just putting Merryn to bed,' he said, 'but he'll be down to say hello later. One partridge, the last one so we didn't have to rob anyone. Two crabs, brown shrimp butter, sea vegetables. Enjoy.' He squeezed Ellie's shoulder as he passed, and she smiled back up at him.

'Another old friend?' Malcolm asked.

Bran answered. 'Actually, they've only been running the hotel for a few years. It was falling down before the boys took it on, a proper restoration project. We used to run past it when we were kids and tell each other it was haunted. Now I can't imagine the island without them.' He looked back to Ellie. 'Running the pub didn't make my heart sing.'

'What would you like to do?' she shot straight back.

'I never really got ceramics out of my system,' he said. 'It really hurt to throw away everything I had worked for.'

'How much room do you need to work?'

'Well, that's the problem. Most of the larger spaces on the island are already taken. I'd need a space the size of a large garage and probably a decent generator to provide the power to run a big kiln.'

Ellie sat back in her chair and lifted up her hands. 'What about the shed?'

'Maybe,' he said, thinking about it. 'We'd have to rebuild it from scratch. It's only held up by ivy.'

'And the mice,' Ellie said, starting to smile at him.

Malcolm looked from one to the other. 'We'll talk to the lawyers tomorrow. Then you can think about all your options. Now, eat your dinner before it gets cold.'

Ellie stared through the darkness at the shadow of Bran as he climbed into the old bed. The whole thing creaked and she could feel the headboard wobble. It was narrower than her bed, and the dodgy springs tended to make everything roll into the middle.

He thumped his pillow and lay down facing her, his breath smelling of toothpaste. 'I could sleep on the sofa,' he whispered.

'Don't be daft,' she answered, although her skin was tingling and her breath was quicker. 'But you've hardly talked to me for weeks.'

'I know. I'm sorry. I was working some things out.' He ran a finger over her lips. 'I just didn't think this moment would take place in the back bedroom with your dad in the next room.'

She shushed him, but the humour of the situation caught up with her, too. The amusement faded away gently, leaving her staring at his silhouette, trying to make out the features that she knew so well.

'Is it going to happen?' she whispered. 'You and me? I kind of thought—'

His finger pressed against her lips. 'Sh.'

'I need to know,' she mumbled around the finger. She could smell his soap now, and the light cinnamon scent of his skin.

'I can tell you one thing,' he said, wriggling a little closer until their knees touched, the bed clanking and springing. 'It's not going to happen tonight. This bed sounds like a bag of spanners.'

She smiled broadly at that. He moved closer. When he kissed her, it was a surprise, but she soon leaned into it. The world disappeared for a long moment.

'Oh my God.' He pulled away a few inches, his hair tickling her forehead.

'What?'

He pulled her in for a bigger kiss and she could feel him catch his breath. She could feel him smile. She slid one leg between his, wriggling to get closer.

'Wow,' he said. 'Definitely tomorrow. Get your dad on the first boat. When's the tide?'

'Two o'clock,' she said, hugging him back. 'In the afternoon. We can wait.'

He kissed her again and leaned his head against hers. 'OK.' He put a hand on her shoulder to push her a little away. 'Now, turn over. I'm in my most modest pyjamas so don't try anything.'

She fitted into his body perfectly, she thought, hip to hip, her cool feet nestled between his warm ones. He buried his face in her hair and put an arm around her.

'I love you,' he mumbled.

'Me too,' she murmured.

'Go to sleep. Ignore anything going on downstairs,' he said, kissing her where her neck met her shoulder

'What, like the cat?' she giggled.

He pressed himself against her. 'I can have these pyjamas off in ten seconds. Five.'

As she pulled away, the bed clanged and banged again. 'I

said, *tomorrow*.' She felt sleepy now, and she emphasised it with a theatrical yawn.

His voice turned serious. 'You're not just being kind, are you? You do love me?'

'I do.' She heaved a frustrated sigh. 'Which is why I'm not tipping you onto the rug right now.'

'Tomorrow,' he said softly. 'I love you too.'

58

Patience knew she had gone a little mad. Slowed by the wound of losing Ysa and Dutch, she now struggled to do everyday things. The agony of missing Elowen was worse, because she was still somewhere in the world. She'd consulted lawyers and social services, she'd tried to establish that she had a right to see her, help care for her and her clearly deranged father. But as she wasn't legally Ellie's grandmother, she had no right to access, no matter how important she had been in her life.

She walked along the back path of the island, looking out over the sea, to the bottom of the cliffs. Seals basked on the rocky beaches, birds dived into the water after fish, and her heart was a stone in her chest. She couldn't even sit by Ysella's grave. Ysa had been buried in London, when Patience longed to have her home, tucked into the churchyard beside George and Martha.

Her sensible walking shoes carried her along the path, left, right, left, right, while her heart longed to jump to oblivion and silence. Her mind was never still.

Was Elowen all right? Was she crying for her mam and her nana? Her last picture of Ellie, eating an ice lolly that had stained her face green, was propped up on the sewing machine. The prints came back three weeks after the funeral, when Patience had been searching the house for more evidence of Ysa. A shopping list she wrote, an old birthday card used as a bookmark, a few snaps on the camera.

Patience walked down the steps to the sailing school, a sandy cove with boat sheds. She was glad she had retired; she had no concentration for the job, nor softness for the children. The new teacher was a man, Jim Williams, so painfully thin his Adam's apple jumped up and down when he talked. It was distracting; she wondered if the children found it distracting, too. Her feet took her across the sand to the edge of the sea. The tide was creeping in with little fuss, no big waves. She could walk into it and float away...

She sat on the rock at the side of the sailing school, the water just nudging it, and let her feet dangle in the sea. She would ruin her leather walking shoes but she didn't care. Their weight could drag her down like a fishing weight, for the fish to nibble.

A stab of pain, a longing for Dutch, cut through her. The loss was still agony, only months before losing Ysa. After Dutch had collapsed with a heart attack, and Ysa knew the cancer would eventually win, she had simply asked, 'Dutch is my father, isn't he?' Patience had been sitting at the table, and all she could do was nod.

Ysella put the kettle on and came to sit beside her. She had let her head drop on her thin neck, every vertebra showing out of the top of her shirt. 'I would have loved to have known while he was alive. To have told him I knew, for certain.'

'I'm sorry,' Patience whispered. 'It was a necessary lie, forty years ago. Then we got caught up in a net of our own weaving.'

Ysa looked down at her clenched fists. She wasn't wearing her rings; her fingers had shrunk to old lady's hands a couple of months ago. 'You could have told me. I can keep a secret. I never told anyone you were my mother.'

'It's complicated,' Patience said. She thought about it. 'But we should have told you, maid.'

'Why couldn't you get married?' She flattened her hands onto the table with its floral cloth.

'He was already married,' Patience whispered, the secrets pulling at her to lock them back in the past. 'A long time ago. It doesn't matter now. He always loved you.'

'I know.' Ysa looked up, the sky-coloured eyes as piercing as ever. 'Oh, there she is! Ellie, for God's sake, wash your hands.' Ysa sat straighter for the child. Patience noticed she always did for Elowen, as if trying to hold off the effect her illness was having for as long as possible.

The child held up hands stained a lurid red and green. 'Bait,' she said, wrinkling up her nose and waving her hands at Ysa, who shrieked and laughed. 'Fishing worms.'

'Wash!' Patience said, smiling, and ran a little hot water from the kettle into the sink and topped it up with cold. 'Lots of washing up liquid. Did you catch anything?'

'One bass, two pouting. Uncle Clem made us put the pouts back but he's going to cook the bass for dinner.' The girl looked over her shoulder at them both, her smile as wide as Ysa's had ever been. 'And Tink sat on a king ragworm and it bit him on the bottom!' Her joy was infectious, and they all laughed.

'Is he all right now?' Ysa asked.

'He had to use the pliers to get the jaws out, they were in really deep.'

Elowen dried her hands. Her hair had been bleached almost white by a few weeks of summer, and she was covered in freckles. Malcolm didn't seem to have passed much to Ellie beyond his chin and his crooked smile.

'Mm. You smell like the sea,' Ysa said, drawing Ellie off the chair to hug her. 'And fish guts. Go and change, we'll go out for an ice cream before dinner.'

Once Ellie had scampered up the stairs, Ysa turned to Patience.

'I don't blame you for keeping it secret. And I couldn't have loved Dutch more if I'd known.'

Now Dutch and Ysa were dead, and Elowen was ten, a year Ysa would never see. The water was all around the rock, creeping up the side with delicate nibbles, darkening the dry surface. She looked out to sea, squinting into the light, almost blinded.

'Patience?'

She closed her eyes and let the word sink in. It sounded like Dutch, it sounded like Dad. They were together now, with Ysella. She longed to be with them; it was a physical yearning.

'Patience?' It was louder now. She could imagine Dutch waving his big hands, walking along the sand, not white-haired any more, not bent at the shoulders.

'Patience!' The sound cut through her thoughts and made her look. It was Clem, waving and stumbling on the steps down to the cove. 'Come in, you daft maid, you'll get soaked.'

She could see him shaking. His hair was more salt than pepper now, and he was wobbly under the jowls like Dad had been. He was right to the edge of the tide – had it really come up that much? She would have to wade back. Maybe she could save her shoes if she rinsed them well, then saddle-soaped them. Dad did that to his work boots.

'I know it's been hard, but you have to go on,' he said, and she could see what he had been thinking.

Well, he was right, wasn't he? For a moment there I just wanted to drift away.

She paddled back, having to lift her skirt as it was a foot deep.

'It's been bloody hard,' she said to him, watching the tips of his ears go pink. He probably had never heard her swear. 'Bloody unfair.'

'No word from Elowen or Malcolm?'

She reached the edge of the sand and found Clem's arms. He hugged her hard for a moment, then steadied her up the beach.

'Malcolm wants me to cut contact with "the child". He sent my letters back, unopened. Elowen never even saw them.' The tears came, great hot floods of painful spasms.

'That bastard.' Clem put his arm around her and squeezed. 'You cry, Patsy.'

She cried, not because Malcolm was a bastard, but because he was just weak in the face of the tidal wave of Ysella's death. She cried because Dutch and Ysa were gone, and Elowen was lost.

'I've changed my will,' she said, blowing her nose and mopping up her wet face.

'Now Patsy, don't you get all morbid on me. You've got a long way to go yet.'

I know,' she said, shutting her eyes for a moment. 'I know that's not the way. I just wanted to say, legally, that Elowen deserves the cottage, that she is part of this family.'

'Well, then,' Clem said, reaching into his pocket for his pipe, another of Dad's habits he'd picked up as he got older. 'That's fair enough. You brought Ysella up as if she was your own flesh and blood.'

He raised an eyebrow, and smiled around the pipe. In that moment, she knew he had always known, and that he loved her anyway.

59

PRESENT DAY, 2 MARCH

The deadline of Ellie's full year of living in the cottage was approaching, and she'd been with Bran for five months. Living together wasn't always easy. He was prickly and grieving some of the time, but joyous and loving at other times. Although the will hadn't been settled, they felt confident enough to start doing the important changes to the house.

Corinne shouted in the front door. 'You lovebirds home?' She walked down the hall and put her head around the door.

'Just me,' Ellie said. 'Cleaning up.' She glanced up at her. Corinne was tall and the baby bump looked good on her, in a sleek, patterned dress and heeled sandals. 'You look great.'

'I feel great.'

'Did you need something?'

'Not really. I'm just bored and lonely. Tink's out crabbing. Grandad Clem won't let a pregnant woman on the boat.' She smoothed her tummy. 'I might capsize it, I suppose. I feel *enormous*. Where's Bran, anyway?'

'He's working on some pieces in the shed. Seriously, why are you here?'

'To make you coffee and inhale the delicious aroma,' Corinne said, switching the kettle on.

Ellie sensed something different.

'Are you OK?' she said, putting out the cafetière.

She smiled at that. 'I'm supposed to give you a message but I'm so nosy I want to hang around and see what it's about.'

'What's the message?'

'Well, Birdie's got a private charter to the island. Someone who is coming over just to see you. Birdie called Jayne – they are definitely an item by the way – and she told Linda when she was walking Callie on the quay. Linda told Tink and he texted me to give you a heads up.'

Ellie shook off the unnecessary information. 'What did he tell Birdie?'

'He asked about the cottage. Oh, and he was American.'

'OK,' Ellie said, sitting down. Corinne put a mug of coffee in front of her.

'Who do you think it is?'

Ellie looked around the kitchen. She and Bran had managed to put in new base cupboards and got a plumber from the big island to do the sink. They had saved a few of the original wall cupboards, which weren't too rickety or wormy. They had also found Mrs Mousy in a nest of chewed-up paper and dried grass behind some pipes, with eight pink babies. They had caught her and put her in an old fish tank that had been in the shed. After ten minutes of jumping up at the corners and quivering in shock, she had settled back in with her babies. They were furry and playful now, and two old books stopped them getting out, or Bertie getting in.

'Is it to do with work?' Corinne asked, cupping her brew, which smelled like hot fruit.

'It might be. I investigate white-collar crimes,' she said.

'Do you work with organised crime? I could stay, be a witness or bodyguard or something,' Corinne said.

Ellie laughed. 'The people I investigate aren't like that. They're cybercriminals. Tax dodgers, embezzlers.'

'Wow.' She looked down at her drink. 'Ugh. I hate herbal teas.' She put the cup down. 'The cottage is all yours soon, isn't it?'

'Seven days to go. Patience's DNA proved she was my biological grandmother. Guess where we got it from?'

Corinne looked around. 'I don't know, hairbrush, toothbrush?'

'No. She wrote me letters after my mother died, loads of them. Birthday and Christmas cards, presents. My father sent them all back.' The memory of finding them all still caught her breath in her throat.

Corinne smiled. 'She licked the envelopes. Go, Patience.'

'Every single one.' She smiled at the thought. 'I opened them all. She really loved me, you know, and my mum. I just wish I could meet her now, talk to her.'

Corinne wrinkled up her nose at that. 'Even though you are shamelessly stealing Tink's inheritance, we love you.' She put her hand back on her tummy and started rubbing in slow circles.

'Thank you,' Ellie said.

'Do you want to feel the baby kicking?'

Ellie was shy, but she pressed her hand onto the bump. She held her breath for what seemed like a couple of minutes, then she felt it. Tap, tap, and a long slide across her palm.

'Oh, wow.' She couldn't help laughing as she pulled away. 'Do you know if it's a boy or girl yet?'

'Not really, we want to be surprised. But Nan Sarah has about a hundred old wives' tales that say it's a boy. He'll be your second cousin once removed or whatever it is.' She finished her fruit tea and grimaced. 'Pineapple and chamomile. Ugh.' She shuddered. 'Let me just smell yours.' She breathed deeply. 'Ah, there's my brew.' She picked up her cup and rinsed it in the sink. 'I can stay, if you like.'

Ellie laughed. 'You're just being nosy. Get on with you. Grow some food for the island.'

'I will,' she said, grinning. 'I'm just harvesting some purple sprouting and leeks for the shop.'

'Save some for us,' she said, pointing at the new cooker. 'It's Bran's turn to cook tonight.'

Ellie was working at the living room desk when someone knocked on the door. A man close to her own age stood there: tall, broad shouldered, dark haired.

'Hi,' Ellie managed, seeing something familiar about him.

'I'm Peter Janssen,' the man said, not moving. 'I'm looking for Elowen Roberts?'

'You found her.' Ellie couldn't stop staring at him. The curve of his mouth, especially now he was smiling, reminded her of Ysella.

The man stared at her for a few seconds and shook hands. 'I was hoping you could tell me about my grandfather.'

'Dutch?' she said. 'Come in.' Ellie led the way to the living room.

Janssen stopped as he got inside the door and was captivated by the view. 'Look at that,' he breathed.

Bran and Ellie had repaired the windows. Newly sanded and painted they looked great, and the clean glass revealed the sparkles on the water in the Sound. It even looked nearer.

Ellie stood next to him as he walked to the window. 'It's beautiful. Bran, my partner, says it's the best view on the island, but I think the viewpoint up by Lighthouse Rock is even better. On a clear day you can see three more islands.'

'I can see why he settled here.' Janssen looked at him. 'My grandfather was Werner Janssen.'

'He's buried in the churchyard, in the same grave as Patience, my grandmother. But everyone called him Dutch. Come and sit down.'

Bran and Ellie had re-covered the sofa and moved it opposite the restored window. It was better than watching the telly, watching the sea change and the boats power up and down.

'Thank you. I should explain how I know about you and your grandmother.' He sat on the sofa, leaning forward to look out of the window.

Ellie sat in her office chair. 'Go ahead.'

'A few months ago, I got a letter from a solicitor in London. I'd never heard of Patience before. Here, you read it.'

He dug out a folded letter from a jacket pocket. Ellie slid it from its envelope, a single sheet of heavy paper.

Dear Mr Peter Janssen,

I am instructed to inform you that as a relative of Werner Janssen (also known as Piet Janssen or Dutch Janssen), born 16th August 1921 in Wilhelmshaven, Germany, you have been named as a beneficiary in the will of Miss Patience Ellis, Kittiwake Cottage, Morwen Island UK, who died on 23 January this year. Mr Janssen had previously passed his entire estate, in trust, to Miss Ellis, to be administered by her as she pleased and the residue passed at her decease to you. This was delayed at her request to one year after her will was read. You may seek answers to any questions about Mr Werner Janssen by consulting Ms Elowen Roberts at the above address, who is Miss Ellis's granddaughter through her late daughter Ysella Roberts. I can confirm that it was Mr Janssen's belief that you were his grandson through Mrs Erma Janssen of Wilhelmshaven, his wife. Miss Ellis held documents estab-

*lishing his identity, which are held at Kittiwake Cottage, if
they still exist.*

Ellie looked up at him. 'Dutch left everything to Patience? Well,
that makes sense. Was it much?'

'About two hundred thousand English pounds. His life
savings. She never used any of it. And she left you her house?'

'She did. How did the solicitor know who you were, or
where to find you?' Ellie asked.

'I've been searching for any news of the U-boat my grandfather sailed on. He was young, just a teenager, when his boat
went down on 11th November 1940, off these islands. I placed
a few adverts in the local papers back in 2015, and the solicitors
found them.'

'That must be the night the *Island Queen* went down.
Patience's father rescued a half-drowned lad, just in his underwear. Dutch Janssen.'

'My grandfather, I believe. So that's when they met,' Peter
said softly.

'Patience was just a child then. Maybe nine or ten.'

'He was nineteen, but in the few pictures my grandmother
kept he looked more like sixteen, seventeen. He was just old
enough to join up for the submarine service. He'd married my
grandmother a few weeks before; she always said he ran away to
sea to get away from the responsibility. Then, four months later,
he was declared dead. My father thought he was born
posthumously.'

Ellie took down her favourite picture of Dutch and
Patience. Sat together, their shoulders were just touching. Both
were in late middle age, and the way they were smiling
suggested Ysella had taken the picture.

'This was them, together. They never married but everyone

accepted them as closer than friends.' She brought another picture down. 'This was Dutch with my mother. The baby is me.'

Peter stared at the picture, and looked back at her. 'I wish I'd met him.'

'I wish I'd known she was my grandmother. When my mother died, my father cut off communication with Patience and the islands. I found out last year.' Ellie smiled at Peter. 'She left me the cottage with the proviso that I live here for one year. Which reminds me, I have a box of Dutch's papers. I suppose they're yours, now.'

'Actually, they're *ours*. I think we're cousins. The solicitor said as much.' He opened his mouth then hesitated. 'I don't suppose you'd be OK with having a DNA test?'

Ellie looked at him and thought about it. She could see the jawline that was in all the pictures of Dutch, the deep-set eyes.

'My mother never told me who her father was,' she said. 'No one seemed to have suspected Dutch at the time. My mother actually had Patience's sister on her birth certificate and it didn't name a father.'

'But you can see a resemblance.'

Ellie started to smile. 'You do look a bit like Dutch. I'll get you the box.' She bent down to open the sideboard and slid out the heavy wooden case Dutch had left on his death. 'I'm sorry, I did read the letters. They were so beautiful.'

'I think you're his grandchild as much as I am,' Peter said, as Ellie laid it beside him on the settee. 'Wow, this is lovely.'

'It was made by Clem, Patience's brother. He's still alive, he's even still fishing.' Ellie watched as Peter opened the box, revealing the last letter Dutch had left for Patience on the top. 'He always felt he'd let your grandmother down.'

'She was a difficult woman,' Peter said, unfolding the letter. The room fell silent as he read the words, the slow ticking of Patience's newly repaired mantelpiece clock the only sound.

'He held this, these are his pen strokes,' Peter said, his eyes shining with emotion.

'That's how I felt, when I first saw it,' Ellie said, sitting on the coffee table. 'There are lots of pictures, too.'

'I can hardly believe he survived,' Janssen said. 'The German records said the U-boat got caught in fishing nets and collided with the hull of the *Island Queen*. Divers found it, years ago. They said it broke in half. How on earth did anyone get out alive?'

'God knows. But he sat on that sofa, looked out over that view. He essentially lived with Patience at the end of his life. The coat he was rescued under was in a box in her brother's shed. The local museum has confirmed it's a German submariner's coat – it's going on display there.' Ellie smiled as Peter started looking through the pictures. 'Let me get you some tea. Or coffee?'

'Coffee, please.'

Bran walked through to the kitchen while she was filling Patience's old china for the occasion, cups that Dutch might have drunk from.

'Who's the visitor?' He rummaged in a cupboard for a packet of biscuits.

'His name is Peter Janssen, he's Dutch's grandson,' she said. 'Patience's solicitor wrote to him. She apparently kept Dutch's money for him. He was married back in Germany before he joined his submarine. The solicitor said Dutch was Ysella's father.'

Bran hugged her. 'You aren't surprised, are you? So, you're both Dutch's grandchildren.'

'Actually, I'm *very* pleased,' she said, kissing him. 'Go, say hello.'

He grinned at her and disappeared down the hall.

She took a deep breath and followed with a tray of cups. Bran and Peter were looking at an old photograph in an album.

'Oh, look, Ellie! It's you and Tink in the paddling pool at Clem's.'

'Who's that disapproving boy in the shorts?' Ellie asked, putting the cups down.

'That's me. I'm the only one not widdling in the pool. Tink must have been all of eighteen months there.' Bran laughed.

'Who is this Tink?' Peter said, looking from one to the other.

'Tink is Daniel Ellis,' Ellie said. 'Clem was Patience's youngest brother and Tink is his grandson.'

'Do you remember Dutch at all?' Peter said to Ellie.

Ellie shrugged. 'I sometimes think I do. Mostly, just the feeling of being on a lap, falling asleep, or being carried on someone's shoulders as a child. I think he may have taken me swimming at least once. He was just a presence.' She took a biscuit. 'My mother didn't even tell me Patience was my grand-mother, she just called her "Nana Patience".' She thought back. 'I was very young. Mostly I think I remember Dutch's voice, really deep, rumbly.'

'His voice!' Bran jumped up and rummaged through the desk drawer. 'Where's my tablet? Ah, here it is.' He sat next to Peter. 'Come on, Ellie, squeeze in. I know where you can hear Dutch speaking.' He pulled up an old file on local news. 'This is an old film of him talking about the end of the deep-sea fishing industry around the islands. It was a couple of years before he died.'

A commentator spoke over a shot of the quay at high tide.

In this quaint fishing village on Morwen Island, the fishing fleet is being diminished. This week another trawler was sold and another family gave up its traditional living...

The film cut to a tall old man with a shock of white hair. His face was tanned so deeply his wrinkles looked like white webs.

'We all see how much the catch falls every year,' he said, with more of a Cornish accent than a German one. The caption said 'Dutch' Janssen. 'Some days we throw most of the catch back, it's all too small or the wrong species. We hardly see the dolphins around the islands now – there's not enough fish for them.' He stared into the camera. 'Big factory ships are taking our native species. The stocks must be allowed to recover.'

'He was an early environmentalist,' Ellie said, staring at the image as Bran froze it. 'I do remember his voice.' She felt a bit dizzy.

He started the film again, and the shot panned out, across the Sound.

'There are only three working trawlers, now,' Dutch said over the film. 'The smaller boats are catching crabs and lobsters.'

Bran stopped the film at the end. 'I'll send you both the links. I'd forgotten about that. I knew Dutch until he died. We all loved him. Just talk to the locals, we'll tell you all about him.'

Peter sat back and folded his arms. 'Why did they rescue him in the first place? They could have sent him to a prisoner-of-war camp somewhere.'

Bran reached for Ellie's hand. 'If they knew a U-boat had sunk the *Island Queen*, with their neighbours and relatives on, they might have dropped him back overboard. Several Morwen men died that night.'

'But afterwards?' Peter persisted.

'Talk to Clem,' Bran said. 'He told me the whole story. George Ellis was a decent, kind man. His own son had drowned in the early weeks of the war.'

'He couldn't save his own child,' Peter said slowly, 'but he could save this kid.'

Bran nodded. 'And he was desperately ill, half drowned with hypothermia.'

Peter brushed his hands over his eyes and Ellie patted his shoulder.

'I just wish I had known about this in time to meet him,' he said.

'Me too,' Ellie said. 'If I'd only known I had grandparents that loved me. That would have helped me get through the death of my mother.'

'It turned out OK, in the end,' Bran said. 'Thanks to Patience's will.'

Ellie leaned forward for another biscuit. 'So, what happened to your grandmother, back in Germany?'

'She kept the telegram that told her he had died until her death. As she told it, she and Werner had a very brief relationship followed by what sounds like a shotgun wedding.'

Bran sat on the computer chair. 'Poor girl. Pregnant, married and widowed in a few months.'

'But respectable,' Peter said.

'Patience and Dutch did much the same thing, to save Ysella from being adopted or creating a huge scandal,' Ellie said. 'They kept the island guessing for years.'

'I think people worked it out when Dutch came back into Patience's life,' Bran said. 'And Ysella looked like him. You do, too. Maybe they admired Patience for having her cake and eating it. She wasn't the sort of person you challenged; she could be really stern.'

'He really loved her,' Peter said.

'He did,' Ellie said. 'I have letters from Patience to Dutch, too. Some of the cards and letters he kept were from her childhood; she always loved him, even in an innocent, childish way.'

Bran jumped up to get his favourite picture down. 'They never held hands or anything obvious, they just sort of leaned together.'

Ellie nodded. She squeezed next to Bran and showed Peter the picture of Dutch and Patience, their shoulders touching.

She smiled. 'Just like that,' she said, staring into Bran's eyes. 'Like they belonged to each other.'

EPILOGUE

Ellie sat in the sand, Zillah Patience Shore between her legs, sorting shells. Bran sat down beside them, reaching out for Zillah as she screamed 'Daddy!'

'Is that it?' Ellie said. 'Is the gallery happy with the show?'

'All ready to open on the eighteenth,' he said, including Ellie in the group hug. 'Thankfully, apart from the opening, that should be it. I'd forgotten how much last-minute work there was.'

'Is it easier now you're doing paintings as well?'

He half smiled. 'It would be easier if I made little water-colours rather than giant oils. But the ceramics are my first love.' He looked intensely at her. 'Kiss me again.'

Ellie obliged. 'What are you thinking?'

He put out his arms, Zillah scrambling onto his lap.

'Do you think Patience had this in mind, when she made the will the way she did?'

Elowen smiled, gazing out to the scalloped edge of the sea.

'One year on the island, to work out her secrets? And to find you. She knew what she was doing.' She turned to him, put a hand on Zillah's dark curls. 'It was the best gift of all.'

A LETTER FROM REBECCA

Dear Reader,

Thank you for reading *Secrets of the Cottage by the Sea*. I hope you enjoyed meeting Elowen and following her journey towards solving the mystery of the house, and finding love on the island. If you did, you can keep in touch with future island stories by following the link below. Your email will never be shared and you can unsubscribe at any time.

www.bookouture.com/rebecca-alexander

I have spent many years living on islands. I love the feeling that we have to find everything we need within the community, and every trip on the ferry seems like an adventure. I first started the book during lockdown, when a lot of villages felt like islands, when we became closer to our neighbours and were limited by how far we could walk. My coastal village in North Devon started to feel more and more like an island of people being themselves, and the cobbled alleys, narrow streets and tiny cottages all seemed to have their own stories – and secrets.

I'm looking forward to writing more stories based on the islands. Living in a community where everyone knows everyone means secrets have to buried very deep indeed. But secrets have a way of worming themselves back into the light.

If you want to support me and the books, it's always helpful to write a review. This also helps me develop and polish future books! You can contact me directly via my website or Twitter.

Thank you and happy reading,

Rebecca

www.rebecca-alexander.co.uk

 twitter.com/RebAlexander1

ACKNOWLEDGEMENTS

This book wouldn't be in your hands without the brilliant editing of Jess Whitlum-Cooper, who took my rambling lock-down novel and trimmed and tidied it into shape. This is my first venture into writing women's fiction, and she has been a great source of knowledge as well as inspiration. Thank you, Jess, and also the wonderful team at Bookouture, for shaping the novel and making me love my characters even more.

Much gratitude goes to my son Carey Bave, my first reader and energetic editor, who knows all my books. He keeps me writing and asks unexpected questions.

As always, my thanks and love go to my long-suffering husband Russell. He takes me on long drives to talk about plot, on ferries to find secluded islands and generally allows me to ramble about my characters as if they were real people.

And finally, to my friends in Appledore, Devon. It is a beautiful village and just inspires stories of mystery.